RUN FOR THE HILLS

RUN FOR THE HILLS

A NOVEL

KEVIN WILSON

ecco

An Imprint of HarperCollinsPublishers

RUN FOR THE HILLS. Copyright © 2025 by Kevin Wilson. All rights reserved. Printed in the United States of America. No part of this book may be used or reproduced in any manner whatsoever without written permission except in the case of brief quotations embodied in critical articles and reviews. For information, address HarperCollins Publishers, 195 Broadway, New York, NY 10007.

HarperCollins books may be purchased for educational, business, or sales promotional use. For information, please email the Special Markets Department at SPsales@harpercollins.com.

Ecco® and HarperCollins® are trademarks of HarperCollins Publishers.

FIRST EDITION

Designed by Alison Bloomer
Chicken illustration © Artstock/adobe.stock.com

Library of Congress Cataloging-in-Publication Data
Names: Wilson, Kevin, author.
Title: Run for the hills: a novel / Kevin Wilson.
Description: First edition. | New York, NY: Ecco, 2025. |
Identifiers: LCCN 2024031182 (print) | LCCN 2024031183 (ebook) |
ISBN 9780063317512 (hardcover) | ISBN 9780063317536 (ebook)
Subjects: LCGFT: Domestic fiction. | Novels.
Classification: LCC PS3623.I58546 R86 2025 (print) | LCC
PS3623.I58546 (ebook) | DDC 813/.6—dc23/eng/20240712
LC record available at https://lccn.loc.gov/2024031182
LC ebook record available at https://lccn.loc.gov/2024031183

25 26 27 28 29 LBC 5 4 3 2 1

FOR KRISTEN, MY SISTER

RUN
FOR THE
HILLS

PROLOGUE

COALFIELD, TENNESSEE, 1982

Mad stood beside her father, close enough that nothing he did would escape her attention. On the farm, if you wanted to know anything, you had to be watching all the time. She walked with him along the stalks of sorghum as he clipped the grain heads off the crop and dropped the bundles of seeds into the basket she was carrying.

"We'll give those to the chickens," he told her, "and they'll love it."

"Could we eat it?" she asked him. She wanted to eat everything.

"It wouldn't be that great, but, yeah, we could," he said.

She thought about it. "I guess I'll give it to the chickens."

He then stripped the stalks of leaves and clipped the bottoms, until he had an armful of the sorghum stalks. This was new to both of them, but her dad wanted to test it out for the farm. He'd seen some Mennonites in the next county run their sorghum mill, and he liked that it was pretty resistant to drought and didn't need much care and would be a good ground-cover crop. Mad liked corn better, the sound it made as you brushed by the tall stalks, and she loved corn bread, but she knew, or her parents had taught her, that you had to be open to change, because you never knew what the weather would bring, what the earth would allow. It was not something she cared for, relying on anyone else, hoping she got what she wanted.

Back with the chickens, Mad threw the grain heads like grenades toward the birds, and she delighted in the way they hopped away from the impact before running back to inspect the offering. "They like it," she told her father, who nodded.

"Sorghum is good chicken feed," he said.

At the shed, she watched as her father fed the stalks through the secondhand cane press he had recently bought, the stalks flattening out and splintering, dry as a bone on either end, and Mad collected those, too, wondering what her dad would do with them later.

After a while, they had nearly a gallon of juice, which greatly pleased her father and underwhelmed Mad, who was always disappointed that the labor involved, all the waiting and cultivating, never quite added up to be what she hoped. The juice was bright green like celery, and he poured it into a big pot to let it settle before they began to reduce it and make syrup.

"What is it gonna taste like?" she asked him, and he told her that she'd had sorghum syrup before, in the apple cakes an older woman sold at the market, but Mad said she wanted to know what *their* sorghum would taste like.

"Like the sun, kind of?" her dad offered. "I'm not a poet, Mad."

"Sweet?" she asked. "A sweet sunny day?"

"And bitter," he offered. "Sweet and bitter is best, and we'll pour it on biscuits and corn bread."

"But it's going to be a while, isn't it?" she asked, already knowing the answer. Her father nodded. "Longer than you'd like, but shorter than you'd think."

Once the cooking started, it would require constant stirring to get it to the right consistency, so Mad and her father sat on the front porch and she leaned against him. Her mother was in town to pick up some groceries and visit a friend who was sick, so the two of them listened to the sound that swirled around them in the valley. She felt most at peace when all three of them were together, but she did cherish these moments with her father, who was harder for her to fully understand. Her mom was open and kind and had an abundance of joy, but her father seemed to always be thinking, the gears in his brain forever turning, and it fascinated Mad. She wondered how much of what was in his head was dedicated to her, and it was nice when it was just the two of them and she could see him consider her as she was, regard her as someone who deserved his attention. It was fall, the air cooling, and bird calls echoed across the trees through the valley.

"One day," her father suddenly said, "you'll be making syrup with your own kids."

"*You'll* be making syrup with my kids," she told him. "And I'll be in bed and you'll bring me pancakes with sorghum."

"Oh, okay, that works, too," he said. It was quiet between them and then her father said, "I don't know why I said that. Don't feel like you have to do anything for me or think about the future. Just enjoy this, okay, Mad?"

"I am enjoying this," she said. She didn't consider the future that much. She would get older, and her life would change, and she got bored thinking about it. She was more interested in right now, finding the exact moment where things changed or you finally understood that they were important. She liked the present. The past wasn't that far away and the future seemed undefined, so she sat with her father and focused on this moment, the chickens clucking, scratching at the ground, and the steady breathing of her and her father.

"It's time to make the syrup," he finally said, and she followed him back into the kitchen, where they would look at the thermometer, stirring the sorghum, watching as it took on a darker hue, little by little, bubbling and steaming, until it was perfect. Her father would dip a spoon into the syrup and let her taste it, and she could not wait for that moment, when she got to experience the singular thing that she had made. It would be so sweet.

CHAPTER ONE

Strange people often came to the farm, but they tended to be late risers, so Mad knew the first few hours would be easy. Starting at 7:00 a.m. every Saturday, the Running Knob Hollow Farm's roadside stand welcomed their weekly regulars, people who lined up for the kind of food that Mad and her mom, Rachel, grew and gathered and made and sourced. Since they'd been featured in magazines like *Bon Appétit* and *Southern Living*, the organic eggs sold out in less than an hour, as well as the week's offering of produce and fruit. The cheeses, which were her mother's domain, a few varieties that people swore by, would go next. By 10:00, the people who arrived at the farm had to make do with whatever was left, talking themselves into the possibility that, even though they'd hoped to have a dozen eggs and some escarole, maybe they actually wanted half of a lamb. Did they want half a lamb? Mad could usually talk them into it, these people slightly dazed by the sunlight, possibly hungover from the night before. It all happened without having to think much about it, money changing hands, people talking, a little community. But by 11:00, with only an hour before closing? That's when weird things happened.

Mad swept the floor, took stock of what was left, rearranged some garlic bulbs. "I've been very lonely, Carl," she said to herself, one of the last sentences in Willa Cather's *O Pioneers!*, a line that always occurred to her when she was the slightest bit tired or inconvenienced.

O Pioneers! was one of the few works of fiction that her father had liked, preferring the *Old Farmer's Almanac* and Wendell Berry essays, and he read the book to her when she was nine years old, just before he left her and her mother twenty-three years ago, ran out on them, never to return.

Sometimes she thought if she ever met a nice guy named Carl, she'd marry him just so she could say the line to a real person. But there weren't any Carls in this little valley in Tennessee, not many Carls left in the United States, she figured. And, honestly, she wouldn't have married him. She wasn't sure she wanted to marry anyone, but it would be nice to have a handsome farmhand named Carl to whom she could say this line at the end of every day. And then they'd go to their own rooms, alone, independent.

"You're married to the earth," her mother once said, more to herself than to Mad, as if consoling herself that she might never have grandchildren. "Do you think that's right, Madeline? That you're married to the earth?"

"God, Mom," Mad had said, "*no.* There just aren't many cool dudes out here." Mad was thirty-two now, and she realized that her mom at that age was about to have her husband disappear and leave her with a young girl and a farm to run. Mad had avoided being left, she supposed, by not having anyone arrive.

"Well, you don't have to marry anyone to be happy," her mother finally said, "not even the earth."

"Thanks, Mom," she replied. After a second, she asked, "Aren't *you* the one married to the earth?"

"After all that headache and heartbreak with your father, I wouldn't want to get involved with *anyone,* especially not the earth. Plus, you know, the earth is a woman, and I guess it's good just to be friends with her. I'm happy enough with that."

"Well, I'm happy, too," Mad told her.

"Sometimes it doesn't seem like it," her mom had said with a hint of sadness in her voice, and Mad wasn't sure she wanted to belabor the point so she just let it drop.

NOW SHE LOOKED UP TO SEE A CAR DRIVING DOWN THE DIRT ROAD, A PT Cruiser, which was not a car that you saw in this area. It was not, she considered further, a car that made much sense in pretty much any area, the absurd mixture of too-far-in-the-past and too-far-into-the-future, but dirt roads made PT Cruisers seem especially ridiculous, like the slightest bump would send it upside down like a bug.

A man got out of the car, and he was dressed appropriately for a PT Cruiser, khakis and a baby-blue oxford shirt, hiking boots, a pair of flip-up sunglasses. He looked like he was in his forties, tall and pale, not a product of this area, she guessed. He was out of place in so many ways that she started walking toward him as if prepared to offer directions back to . . . the past? The future? A city? Anywhere but this place, she figured.

He was reaching into the passenger side of the car to get a leather satchel, but when he noticed that she was approaching, he abandoned it and straightened his posture, holding up his hands like he was surrendering to her. "Hello," he said, with his teeth showing in what she imagined was a smile. She hoped it was a smile.

"Hi," she offered.

"Nice day?" he asked, like he wondered if, on this farm, the day would be considered nice to people like her.

"Yeah, I think so," she replied. "Nice day."

"Oh, good! I think so, too."

"Are you lost?" she asked.

He smiled, embarrassed. "Yes and no?"

"Oh, okay," Mad said. Afternoon weirdos. Then she realized that maybe it was making him nervous for her to be meeting him at his car, that he hadn't been prepared for conversation. Was it possible that *she* was the weirdo?

"Are you Madeline Hill?" he blurted out.

"Madeline Hill?" she asked, making sure she'd heard him correctly. Only her mother called her Madeline. Everyone else called her Mad, an invention of her father, who loved nicknames. Not Mads, which was worse than Madeline. Mad Hill.

"I'm looking for her."

"That's me, yes," she said.

"And—sorry, I'm nervous." He fumbled for the next word but couldn't quite get it. Mad decided she'd tell her mother that they were closing the stand at ten from now on, that the extra sales weren't worth the awkwardness of moments like this. He was holding this smile for so long, a kind of forced jocularity, that she realized it was maybe a grimace. She was so interested in his face, the strangeness of it, something about it making her want to stare at him even longer, however uncomfortable it was. She did not like to stare at a stranger's *teeth*, but here she was, an afternoon weirdo.

"Did you read about us in a magazine?" she asked, trying for anything that would, she hoped, move the conversation forward toward a resolution that did not involve someone having a nervous breakdown.

"Us?"

"Me and my mom? The farm?"

"Oh . . . yes and no? I mean, later, yes, I did read about you in a magazine."

"You say 'yes and no' a lot. I mean, you've said it twice already."

"Were you born on June 1, 1975?" he asked suddenly, as if he hadn't heard her.

"Yes . . . and no," she said, shocked by the intimacy of the request but unable to stop herself from answering. She had been born, on this very farm, so close to the minute when June 1st turned to June 2nd that her parents just made a decision to say June 1st. But they usually had two celebrations when she was growing up, one on the first and then staying up until midnight to have a second piece of cake. It was disarming to remember those times, and then she realized that she was talking to a stranger, a stranger who knew her name and date of birth.

"Who are you?" she finally asked, and the man, so pale, turned red. He was sweating in the sun, blinking rapidly.

"I'm your brother," he answered. "My name is Reuben Hill."

"My brother?"

"Well . . . yes and—"

"Stop doing that," she said, her voice rising. "I want you to tell me real things, specific things, and if I ask you a question, I want answers that are either yes or no, and not both. Okay?"

"Sorry," he replied.

"So you're my brother?"

"Yes . . . okay, yes."

"What the hell," she offered. "What a bizarre thing. A dude in a PT Cruiser shows up at my farm, and he's my brother."

"Half brother," he offered. "We're half siblings."

"Okay, this is helpful," she said. "This is the information that I need, you understand? Like, some tangible data to make sense of this." She thought for a second. "Dad. Of course, Dad."

"Yes, our dad. Charles Hill."

"Chuck."

"That's what he went by?"

"Yeah, Chuck Hill."

"He was Charles when he was my dad. But I get it. He liked nicknames. I go by Rube, which is what he called me."

"He called me Mad."

"Mad? Like, angry?"

"No . . . and ye— Shit, sorry. Who knows, honestly? He just liked the way it sounded. But, can I tell you this? I haven't seen our dad in over twenty years. He left us."

"I haven't seen him in over thirty," he admitted. "He left us, too." The man, Reuben or Rube or whatever, her brother or half brother or whatever, looked down at the ground. When he looked back up at her, he was crying a little, his eyes red, but still smiling.

"Jesus," Mad replied, "I'm sorry." She didn't go to him, didn't know how to comfort this person. But she *was* sorry. It wasn't hard to say.

"It's kind of made things difficult. I haven't really let go." It was the beginning of March in Tennessee, and though it had been in the forties just three days before, the sun was bright, and wherever Rube was from, he clearly wasn't made for even this slight heat. He was sweating quite a bit, mixing with the tears, and it made it hard for Mad to fully look at him, to get a sense of how they were made of similar material. Half of them should look alike, right? What half? They were both tall, she could see that. But what else? She had a lot of questions.

"Do you want to come to the house?" she asked him. "Sit down? Have some iced tea or something? Have you eaten?"

"I would love to sit down," he admitted. "Oh, I've got a bunch of papers in the car, just in case you think I'm making this up."

"Why in the world would you make this up?" Mad wondered.

"Well, I have some documentation, that's all."

"Come on," she told him.

"Let me get my satchel," he said, and after a few seconds, he was beside her again, standing a little too close, like he thought she might start running into a field and disappear. Mad suddenly thought about her mom, could not imagine how she would react to this. Then she wondered if her mom already knew. Then she wondered why her mom hadn't told her. There was too much wonder in the world, and the day wasn't even halfway over.

This wasn't supposed to be how a family worked. Family was just there when you appeared in the world, waiting for you. Each new addition after that, you had time to prepare, to make a place for them in your heart. The only danger was reduction, the numbers thinning out, people leaving. You weren't supposed to suddenly get a new family at eleven o'clock on a Saturday after you'd sold out of eggs.

All she could do was stand next to this man, older than her, her *brother*, she supposed. *Half brother*, she supposed. But he wasn't her brother yet in any discernible fraction. It would take time. They had a long walk to the house. So she started to walk, leading the way.

"I've never had a brother or a sister," she remarked, looking out across the fields, the sun so bright.

"Me, either," Rube replied. He kept a respectful distance now, walking exactly in the footsteps that she made.

"I'm gonna need some time to get used to it," she admitted.

"Of course. I needed a lot of time," he told her. "I'm still not sure I should have done this. But here I am!" Tonally, he was all over the place, these shifts between exclamation and seriousness. Mad, on the other hand, had one tone. It was a tone of patient acceptance with a simmering undertone of deep reticence.

"Yep. You're here."

"Mad?" he asked. His voice was quieter, and she realized that he had stopped walking, was just staring at her, holding so tightly to his satchel.

"What? What is it?"

"There's more of us," he finally said. "More kids."

"Dad's?"

"Yeah. We have other siblings."

"Oh, shit."

"It's a lot to handle," he admitted. "Maybe I should have told you later. I've been alone, you know? It's been hard to think about this stuff. When I saw you, I just felt like I could tell you. I felt like maybe you and I could figure it out."

"We don't know each other. You don't know me. I could be so awful, you know?"

"I don't think you are," he said.

"What was wrong with our dad? God, what an idiot."

"You haven't wondered where he was?"

"I haven't. He left. He didn't want to stay. He doesn't deserve my thinking of him. And it sounds like he didn't care. He just made more of us."

"Would you want to find him?" he asked.

"Let's just keep walking," she said, because she wasn't sure what she wanted at the moment. "Let's go home and then we can talk. We can get to know each other." She was leading her brother to her home. She was taking him home. She didn't want to talk about her dad. He was gone. He had been gone. But here was Rube, her brother. It was enough. Maybe it would end up being too much, more than she could handle. Maybe it would all get so much worse. How could it not get worse? But for now, walking across the grass, to the only place she'd ever called home, it was enough to have someone walking alongside her.

CHAPTER TWO

Rube had spent the last forty-five seconds wiping his hiking boots on the welcome mat. Mad had opened the door, walked inside, and was about to speak when she realized he hadn't followed her, and now she was just standing there like some dope. She had the urge to inform him that his hiking boots were already pristine and he was actually kind of ruining their welcome mat with all that scuffing, but she thought, Do not ruin your relationship with your half brother in a single day. Do not kill your half brother on the threshold of your own house, because it will be so hard to explain to the police.

She allowed Rube to prepare himself in whatever way he needed to step into this new reality, a world where he had a sister. She had, she reminded herself, home field advantage in this situation. Before this morning, only he had known the truth, but now they shared the information, and he was walking into her home. And if it did turn out to be an elaborate scam, she could beat him half to death inside the comfort of her own living room. She wondered why she was thinking so much of doing violence to this recently discovered sibling. There was all the psychic weight, sure, but it was also just that he was a guest, and she didn't have many of them. Because, she reasoned, they were usually an inconvenience. They showed up and created work for you. They asked you about your feelings, your day. They asked if you maybe had a beer in the fridge. They asked if you could adjust the air-conditioning just, like, two degrees. They asked if you knew the location of any legal papers that might speak to the true identity of the father you had not seen in over twenty years. And you just had to nod and smile, because this was hospitality. He was a guest, she reminded herself. He was more a guest than he was a brother at this stage in their relationship, so she would let him wipe his feet for fifteen more seconds before she made a small noise of irritation.

Her mom wasn't at the house, thank god. They worked the farm mostly on their own, aside from some seasonal help and a few student interns from a community college nearby, but the two of them didn't overlap as much as you'd expect. Mad could go nearly the whole day without seeing her if the two of them were pulled in different directions to do whatever needed doing. Other times, though, when the work was hard, she and her mother were on top of each other so much that Mad thought about setting fire to all the crops and running away and becoming a costumed mascot at some low-level amusement park. This was the range of her escape fantasies, ruining the thing she loved and then punishing herself by doing the most humiliating work she could imagine to atone for it.

Now, with her half brother walking into her home, she wondered if her dad had been the same way. And, if so, would that mean the farm had been a punishment for what he did to Rube and his mom? She sometimes considered that wherever he had gone after he left the farm had been the punishment. But maybe not. It made her head hurt, honestly, trying to imagine the timeline of her father's life and keep her own story firmly placed within a distinct part of his narrative.

"This is a really nice place," Rube told her, and she felt grateful for that. She looked at him a little more closely. He was tall, like her, but thinner, so pale, whereas she was tan and already starting to get lines from the sun. Rube's hair was brown, while hers was blonde. But she could see the resemblance, like their wide noses, just like their dad. Mad had a squarish jaw, which had always made her feel mannish, while Rube's was a little less defined, but they both had that tiny indentation in their chins. That was something she had understood about her father. He was ridiculously attractive, looked like a movie star without the fake sheen of fame, but it was probably his deficient character that mutated the genes with his children, made them sturdy and plain so they wouldn't run off to follow him. She suddenly realized that he had stopped looking around the house and was now awkwardly staring at her, waiting for her to notice that he had stopped talking. And she found that she couldn't speak, couldn't stop staring.

"Rustic," he finally offered, and she was not so jazzed about that adjective, but whatever. He wasn't from around here. He was from . . . where the hell was he from?

"Hey," she then said, a little louder than she'd intended, "where are you from?"

"Oh, yeah," he replied, smiling like he'd forgotten his change at the store, "you have no idea where I came from."

She thought that sounded ominous, but then she remembered that, wherever he had come from, he'd been conveyed by PT Cruiser, and she felt less worried. "No idea," she admitted.

"Boston, Massachusetts," he replied. "Which is also where our dad was from."

"Wait, is that where our dad was from? Like, is that where he started?"

"What did he tell you?"

"He said he grew up in Maine, way out in the country. He said his parents had been chicken farmers, and that's where he'd learned a lot of the stuff he brought to the farm here, but that big processing plants took over and he'd realized he wanted to get back to the land."

"He was not from Maine," Rube said.

"Can I just ask you something?" she replied. "How are you so sure of all this? How do you know he didn't make up a story for you and your family? How do you know that there wasn't a family before yours? How do you know everything you ever knew wasn't a lie?"

"Those are good points, and I have spent a lot of time—and, you know, money—in therapy working through some of those concerns, and I accept that there are elements of our dad's narrative that will never line up, and I'll never fully know the man. Fine. But I have a workable timeline for the man. I have a birth certificate, a copy of it. When he was married to my mom, I guess he hadn't yet fully embraced the idea that he needed to reinvent himself and create new narratives of his life. He was just himself."

"So he wasn't from Maine?"

"He was not," Rube replied. "He was from Boston. His mom ran a dress shop. His dad—I can't find anything on him—wasn't a part of his life."

Okay, her dad grew up without a dad. Maybe this was all she needed. This one piece of information gave her some context, and now Rube could go back to Boston. But he didn't seem like he was going to leave.

"He never left the city of Boston until he left us."

"And came here?" she asked, gesturing to the room, which, if she closed her eyes, she could remember her father within.

"Yeah," he replied. "Near as I can tell."

"He just, like, got on a bus and ended up in Coalfield, Tennessee, a town he'd never been in, and became a farmer? And kind of started talking with a southern accent?"

"Yeah, pretty much."

"He wasn't a farmer?"

"In Boston?" he replied, laughing. "No."

"What was he, then?"

"I mean, lots of stuff. He sold insurance, and he worked in advertising, but he was also a writer."

"Wait, a writer? Of books?"

"Yeah, he wrote five books. Detective novels. Under the name C. A. Hill."

"Are you serious?"

"I'm dead serious. That's actually the name of one of the novels. *Dead Serious*. The third book in the Detective Harry Bucket series." Rube shook his head. "They're all out of print."

"Hard to believe," she replied.

"It's just . . . there aren't any royalties if you were wondering about that."

"I was not," she told him. She wanted him to calm down. If this was a scam, it was so incredible that she'd honestly be fine if she ended up bankrupt and in the hospital, missing a kidney. It might be preferable to what could end up happening.

"Our dad wrote books?" she asked.

"Five books and maybe ten that didn't get published."

Mad could only shake her head. Her father was a man of letters. Or had been.

"I write, too," Rube continued. He said this almost sheepishly.

"For money?" she asked.

"I mean, for my own artistic pursuits, but, yeah, also for money. That's how I make a living."

"What kind of books?" she asked, and he told her that he wrote mysteries. "Like our dad?" she asked.

He blanched a bit, then recovered. "Yes and no," he said. "I mean, the mystery genre is pretty broad, you know? There's a lot of territory—"

"But you write mystery novels and our dad wrote mystery novels?"

"Yes," Rube finally allowed.

"And our dad was a farmer, and I'm a farmer," she said.

"Yeah, that's right. Weird."

"Oh, god," Mad said. The thought that her life was determined by her absent father was something she had of course considered, but it was strange to have confirmation from another test subject. She did console herself that, yes, she was also a farmer, but it was partly because her dad had freaking left her mom to run a farm on her own and so Mad had little choice in the matter at first, had to break her back just to keep the farm running. Rube, on the other hand, didn't just choose to become a writer, but he'd also decided to write mystery novels. Still, they were both doing things that their own father had grown tired of. It didn't feel great, honestly.

"Do you write?" Rube asked, and Mad shook her head.

"I barely have time to read," she said. After a few seconds of awkward silence she asked, "And do you have any agricultural interests?"

He smiled sheepishly, looking a little pale. "None," he finally replied.

"Wait! Okay, this might be neat," she said. "His favorite novel was Willa Cather's *O Pioneers!* He read it to me when I was little, and he said it was the greatest American novel. Did he read you that book?"

Rube turned even paler and then got red. "No," he said. "He did not read me that book. He did not, if I remember, ever mention it." He saw her look of disappointment, and he offered, "But he left when I was a kid, so maybe he read it after he left us."

"Like, on the bus to Tennessee?" she asked. "Checked it out at the Boston Public Library and then skipped town with it and owes a million dollars in fines."

Rube seemed ill at ease with her version of sarcasm. He kept smiling, looked around again at the rustic living room, and then said, "Possibly."

"I just . . ." Mad paused, trying to figure out how to say what she was thinking. She didn't doubt Rube. It wasn't about whether or not her dad was his dad. It was that her dad was *not* his dad. "Okay, like, your dad was born in Boston, Massachusetts, and he wrote detective novels."

"Yes," Rube replied.

"But my dad hardly even read and was from Maine, and he was an organic farmer in Tennessee."

"Yes," Rube said again.

"So what does it matter if we have the same dad? We don't have any experiences of him that would connect us. We don't even have our dad. He's long gone."

"That's what I want to know," Rube said, his voice getting a little squeaky. "Maybe there is something that connects our versions of our dad."

"What was your dad's favorite food?" she suddenly asked.

"Lobster rolls," Rube said, already looking disappointed. "What about your dad?"

"Not lobster rolls," Mad replied. "A full slab of ribs. My dad whistled all the time. He would whistle 'Daydream' by the Lovin' Spoonful while he drove the tractor and I would ride beside him. Did your dad whistle?"

"He definitely did not whistle. He didn't drive a tractor, either."

"Did he like sports?"

"Boston Bruins hockey," he replied.

"UT Vols football," I told him. "Hockey? Really?"

"He took me to the Boston Gardens to see the Stanley Cup finals, game four, in 1970, when Bobby Orr scored in overtime to win. It's like one of the biggest memories of my childhood, how happy he was, just screaming, and so I screamed, too, even though I didn't know what was going on."

"He took me to Knoxville when I was maybe seven or eight, something like that. And the Vols upset Bama and he went nuts there, too, singing 'Rocky Top,' and I was just scared of falling down the bleachers, but, yeah, it was neat to see him so happy."

"So that's something, right? Kind of the same?" he asked. But Mad was still thinking about that game, the sea of orange, the absolute shock that reverberated through the stadium when it became clear that they would win, her dad telling her, "This is so great, Mad, this is so great, and we're here! We're here to see it! It's always so good to be there when something important happens." She hadn't thought about it in so long.

"So our father was a kind of good-luck charm for whatever sports team he happened to be rooting for at that stage in his life," she offered.

"Or," he offered, "his kids were good-luck charms for whatever sports team he happened to be rooting for." When she didn't respond, he continued, "You and me. His kids."

"What was his favorite color?" she asked him.

"I have no idea," he admitted. "Maybe green?"

"I have no idea, either," she said. "That was a dumb question. Sorry." Who remembers their parent's favorite color? What a weird thing if your dad was always reminding you, *Hey, this yard sale jacket is green, which happens to be my absolute favorite color.* But, what she was realizing, which was more important than her dad's favorite color, was that she didn't know all that much about her dad. And what she did know felt a little like a dream, a sudden realization that the mug she was holding had been held by her father on the day she lost her first tooth, and how he quickly dumped the coffee into the sink so they could put the tooth in the mug and he could rinse it off. She didn't know *facts* about her dad.

He left before she could compile a dossier of biographical information and habits. What she had was a flickering series of memories that were about ten to twenty seconds long.

At the very least, she appreciated that Rube wasn't trying to fill the awkward silence with more facts about their missing father.

"Okay, I guess this is kind of a dead end," she admitted.

"I think it might need to be more of a kind of organic process," Rube offered. "We'll know more as it comes up, but this feels like the game show version of trying to remember our dad."

Mad was so confused by the turn of events that she couldn't remember who had even suggested that they trade facts about their dad. If it had been her, she felt the need to be a little irritated that he'd called it a "game show version" when, my god, she was just trying to entertain this wild development and keep it contained within her house while a perfect stranger held a leather satchel on his lap like he was trying so hard to sell her funeral insurance. She was getting angry at the wrong person, she knew. Who else could she be angry with, though, since her dad was still frozen in her mind? He was, however, rapidly thawing.

"Do you have photos of him?" Rube finally asked.

"Some," she replied. After he left them, over the course of a few weeks, the few framed photos of their father disappeared from the house, and Mad never asked her mom about it, didn't need to. But she assumed her mom hadn't actually thrown them away. When it was clear he wasn't coming back, they removed the records of him so they could move forward. "A few, of course. And movies. He was obsessed with home movies."

"Yes!" Rube said. "He was always into cameras. He had this, I don't remember the name, but an eight-millimeter film camera. He had a few of them, actually, because he wanted the newest model. You know? There's no sound, and it's on—"

"Oh, yeah, same here. He had a Bell and Howell eight-millimeter with us. I think he actually bought one of the first VHS camcorders before anyone else around here had even heard of them, but then he left." Mad realized that it would be strange if their father had jumped on a bus with a camcorder, as if to document his new life, but she didn't remember it being in their home after he left.

"Did you have them transferred to DVD or anything?"

"What? No. We might have some of them in a closet somewhere. But, you know, thinking about it, Dad was always doing the filming. He's not in them."

"It's so weird that your organic farmer dad was into home video recording," Rube offered, "and so was my mystery writer dad. So I guess some stuff holds over."

JUST THEN, HER MOTHER OPENED THE DOOR, AND HER EYES WIDENED IN such a way that it was as if she'd walked in on Mad having sex with someone on the sofa. "Oh, my," she said. "Madeline, I didn't know you had company."

"Hello," Rube said, nodding.

"Oh . . . hello," she replied. Mad's mother took a full three seconds to look at this person in their living room, dressed like a man who designed golf courses, who owned four different Subway franchises, who was concerned about the demarcation of the property lines for the land he bought to turn into a water park, and she seemed to register that this was not a person that Mad would entertain as a gentleman caller. Everyone was quiet and then she turned to Mad. "Has something happened?"

"Mom, this is Rube," Mad said. She held on to this moment, the last little flicker of time before her family got so complicated, re-shuffled and dealt out in such a way that she had no idea what would come after. "Reuben Hill," she continued, and she saw her mom's demeanor change once again. And Mad knew her mom well enough to know that—oh, shit—maybe she wasn't surprised by this news.

"Hello," Rube said again. "I'm Charles Hill's child. Well, you know, his *first* child."

"Oh, god," her mother replied. "I better sit down."

"Dad was from Boston, Mom," Mad said, as if this was the greatest betrayal, not the secret family that preceded them, and not the possible secret families that followed, and not *leaving them in the first place*, but that he was from Boston, Massachusetts.

"Oh, god," her mother said again. Everyone but Mad seemed to have, like, one phrase that they had to keep using, and it was up to her to fill in the spaces between with something that resembled meaning.

"Dad was, like, a serial dad? He had a family before us. Rube and his mom. And had a family—"

"Families," Rube added.

"Yeah, I was gonna say that. He had a *family* after us *and* more after that."

"Oh, sorry," Rube said. "I see what you were doing now."

"Rube, just let me and my mom talk for a sec," Mad continued.

"Tell me, Rube," her mom said, and Mad just had to resign herself to the fact that no one was going to let her handle this, "have you seen Chuck?"

"Well, Mrs., um . . . is your last name also Hill?"

"No, no. You know, Chuck and I never actually married. We were pretty young and had some interesting ideas about freedom and property and . . . my last name is Daggett."

"Technically, he never divorced my mom," he said to Mad and her mother. "So if he had tried to get married again, he would have been in trouble."

"More trouble," Mad amended. "More trouble than he's in for leaving all of us."

"Yes, of course. *Legal* trouble. But I don't think he married again after my mom."

"Rube?" her mom said.

"Oh, yes, sorry?"

"Be straight with me. Really. Have you seen Chuck?"

"No, I haven't seen him. Not since he left me and my mom for you guys."

If Mad was like her half brother, she would have interjected that, technically, he just flat-out left Rube and his mother. To have left them *for* Mad and her mom, their dad would have had to lay the groundwork in Tennessee on secret trips or been some kind of weird pen pal friend who cultivated a relationship with his mom so that he'd have a place to walk right into when he left his wife and son. But that wasn't the case. He'd left his first family, arrived in Tennessee, and decided he needed another one.

"Mom, did you know about this?" Mad asked.

"Well . . . yes and no," her mother replied. She had now heard—or said—this phrase more times today than if you added up every single use of the phrase in her lifetime previous. She hadn't realized how irritating it was, to be two things at once. You needed to be one thing, always a definitive answer, and she realized that maybe she'd arranged her entire life on this principle.

"Mom, just tell me," Mad continued.

Her mom turned more toward Rube, as if she was being interviewed by him and not her own daughter. "I did not know about you, Rube. I mean, when your partner suddenly leaves you and your child with a working farm and very little savings, you look back less favorably on a person's actions, yes? And so I began to suspect that maybe Chuck had not been entirely honest with me. But I did not know anything about a previous family."

"Oh," Rube said, clearly disappointed, as if he'd hoped that his father, in a moment of weakness, had confessed to his current wife and child that he actually, in hindsight, missed his previous wife and child and—oh, by the way—he had a previous wife and child, and, also, they were so great, just lovely people.

"But," Mad's mom continued, "I did know he started a new family."

"Wait, what?" Mad shouted, unable to control herself. "You knew? When?"

"Well, honey, now, calm down. When your dad left us, you were still a kid. And so, obviously, I couldn't just let him run off and leave us without making sure that he didn't want to come back and, you know, try again. And so for about a year I searched for him in roundabout ways. And then, finally, I got an envelope of money, and it had a phone number written on a notecard and it said to call at a certain day and time, and so I called, and it was a pay phone and your father answered and said that he was sorry, but he was starting over, needed to start over in order to be better this time around. I had no idea what he meant by that. He hadn't been bad to us. But, anyway, he had met a new woman and was starting a family. And that he wouldn't be able to see me again, though, because he had to leave the past in the past."

"He sent you money?" Rube asked, leaning forward, his satchel nearly falling to the floor. "Did he ever call you again?"

"Oh, a few times, but years would go by. Sometimes he'd call on my birthday, but he wouldn't tell me much. We wouldn't talk, really. He'd say, 'Happy birthday, Rach,' and I'd thank him and then he'd hang up. I didn't know about his life and he didn't ask about mine. I think he just wanted me to know he was somewhere in the world. And I didn't mind that, honestly."

"I can't believe this," Mad said. "You never told me."

"Honey, it was better for you, at that age, to think he was just gone, had disappeared, like he'd been abducted by a UFO or—"

"I honestly considered that!" Mad yelled. "And I was worried that the aliens were going to come back for us. I thought he'd been killed by some weird hillbilly mafia. I mean, I thought a thousand different things and it maybe would have been nice to know that he was just walking across the continental United States like Johnny Appleseed or something."

"I didn't want you to think less of your father."

"How could I have thought less of him? He left us. That's the least I could think of him."

It was quiet for a moment as Mad watched her mother try to think of something to say that would make it hurt less. But Mad figured the pain was already here, making itself known in her heart, and so she pushed on.

"Did he ask about me? Did he ever once ask to talk to *me*?"

Mad's mother considered her for a moment and then shook her head. What hurt worse, Mad wondered, to be left behind, or to never be thought of after? It hurt the same, she decided. It hurt exactly the same.

"I feel like maybe I should go. Not leave, actually," Rube offered. "But, like, is there a separate sitting room where I could go if you two wanted to talk about this more?"

"No," Mad said, "that's it. Like, what else can I say? Everyone knows everything about my dad and all the shit he did except for me."

"We all have little pieces," Rube offered. "We have these small parts of him, and so that's why I came. I'm trying to fit them all together. Not just for me, but for all of us."

"So you're just on a fact-finding mission to create an oral history that explains the actions of our dad? You're going to each family and kind of upsetting the order of their lives?"

"I mean, that's certainly a way to put it," Rube said, kind of smiling in embarrassment. "Family history is important, right? I have a sister! It's all kind of incredible and I'm just trying to figure it out."

Mad almost said "half sister," but she knew it wouldn't help anything.

"I have no idea how you and I are connected," Rube said to Mad's mother.

"Oh, I don't think we're anything."

"My mom died," Rube said suddenly.

"Oh, honey, I'm so sorry."

"So I mean, I don't know if it's legal or anything, but maybe you would be like my stepmother, once removed?"

"Oh, honey, I don't think it works like that."

"No, I know. But we're connected, obviously."

"Sure, why not?" she offered.

Mad tried to think of a pop culture equivalent that would explain it. It was like *The Brady Bunch* if the dad had kept running off and his kids refused to let him start a new family without them. It was like *Gilligan's Island* if the island was everyone's dad. It was like *The Parent Trap* if the twins were so damn stupid that they couldn't even *find* the dad to get the families back together.

"So, Reuben, tell me, are you tracking down Chuck? Are you searching for him? Or just going to the affected parties and letting them know what's going on?" her mother asked, like it was the most natural thing in the world, as if the last time a stranger was in this house for this long wasn't at least two years ago. She was talking to Rube as if he was a child who had built a time machine and she was letting him believe it was real for as long as possible before he was sorely disappointed.

"Probably doing both," he answered. "I hired a private investigator"—he turned to Mad—"Which is what I was going to tell you, and she has compiled a pretty detailed dossier of leads and biographical information and public evidence of our dad's existence over the years. It's called skip tracing, and it's usually to track down people who owe tons of money or have broken the law. They 'skip town' and are on the run. It can be easy or difficult based on how much the person wanted to disappear."

"Was Dad easy or hard?" Mad asked.

"Pretty hard," Rube admitted. "He kind of shifted his name and early on forged some documents to get new IDs without altering too much. But then he'd go back to his regular identity and Social Security, so it got a little complicated. But this detective, she's great. Her name is Evalynn Mann. Evalynn Mann, PI. Warner Brothers is actually making a movie about her because she found this millionaire's missing dog and, in the process, broke up this huge international art theft ring."

"Oh, I think I heard something about that," Mad's mother said.

"Well, the issue is that she's kind of stopped helping me. I think maybe the Hollywood stuff might be distracting her from her cases, because I can't get her to reply to my emails or return my phone calls. She has this assistant who says that her role as an executive producer and on-set consultant has made it very hard for her to continue her caseload. But I found you! So it's pretty solid so far."

Mad's mother nodded.

"But no matter what happens, I wanted to meet my brothers and sisters."

"So okay," Mad interrupted, "but how many are there? Three? Six? Thirty? A hundred?"

"Oh, well, from the information that I have, there are four of us. There's another girl, she's in college in Oklahoma, and then a boy, and he's eleven, lives in Utah. There may be more. Evalynn was supposed to keep working on it, but again, I don't think I'm going to hear more from her. And our dad's in California now, if you can believe it. But I can't imagine there are more than that. He's pretty old now." He turned to Mad's mom. "No offense."

"He's older than me," she replied.

"Yes, of course."

"Oh, god," Mad said. But it was a manageable number. It was in the realm of possibility to accept three half siblings into her life. It was nice to know that it wasn't a hundred. A hundred kids? Thanksgiving? It would have been a nightmare.

"My mom died, I think I told you," Rube continued, "and it was difficult, not a good death, or I guess worse than even regular death would be. And I feel lonely? I feel like I missed out on something by not having a family, or not having as much of the family as I found out that I had. So I'm trying to meet them, to hopefully stay in touch." He looked at Mad, who blushed, felt so embarrassed by his outward emotion, how badly he wanted this.

"And," he continued, "I was hoping that Mad would come with me."

"In the PT Cruiser?" Mad asked, her voice cracking, like this was the most absurd part of the situation. "You and me in the PT Cruiser chasing down our father?"

"Yes," he replied. "We'll re-create the migration of our father as he moved westward to start new chapters of his life, and we'll meet the children he left behind, and we'll, you know, get to know each other."

"I can't do that," she said. She was only now beginning to recover from the shock of Rube appearing in her life. For that to continue to work, she needed him to leave so she could keep processing it in her own way, in private, as she collected eggs and drove the tractor and waited for possibly more half siblings to suddenly show up in a retro-styled automobile. "I'm not going with you."

"Please?" he asked, so openly begging, with such desperation on his face. "I can't even explain how hard this was. I drove past your farm for an hour, back and forth, and just was not able to turn onto your road. I kept turning around in the driveway of some trailer a ways off until a lady ran out with a handgun and said she had called the cops, and so I finally came to see you. I can't do that again on my own. I had hoped we'd be able to do it together."

"And then when we meet the next kid? We just ask them to jump in the PT Cruiser and head to the next town?"

"Well, they might not want to go! You don't seem that eager. I was thinking it would just be me and you, but, sure, I'll give them the option."

"You said the boy was eleven? We can't kidnap him!"

"I just want to meet them. The rest is up to them. I guess, depending on luggage and each person's need for their own space, we might have to rent a bigger vehicle at some point," Rube admitted. "You are weirdly hung up on the car, which I didn't request, by the way. It's what the company had at the tier I chose."

"I can't do it."

"How do you even know?" he asked. "Look at me. I'm doing it. I mean, yeah, driving through the mid-Atlantic states, I started to have second thoughts and I had a little freakout at a rest stop, but here I am. And you seem to be a lot more capable than me."

Mad looked to her mother for confirmation that this was insane, but her mother had an expression that was hard to fully explain, except to say that it looked like the expression of someone who was going to tell you that this insane thing *did not* sound insane.

Before her mother could even speak, Mad walked out of the room, taking deep breaths, leaving the two of them in the living room while she stepped into the kitchen and ran to the refrigerator and opened the door, putting her face inside the cool space, trying to calm herself. She noticed a jar of kimchi that she'd bought from some old mountain man at a farmers' market and figured that it had been at least two years ago. Why did she still have that unopened jar of kimchi in the fridge? What was she keeping it for? She hadn't eaten it because the man, right after she bought it, said that if she had heard that his mason jars weren't sanitary, that was an old rival of his and that there was absolutely no truth to those unfounded accusations. But surely she should have thrown it away? Or maybe she was going to hold on to it until the Apocalypse. She and her mother would ride out the end of the world here, just the two of them, and when every single chicken and egg was gone, when the cheese had molded beyond being edible, when they were so weak with hunger that they knew it was the end of their days, they would unseal this jar of kimchi and eat it and immediately pass on to whatever came after this li—

"Honey?" her mother said, having suddenly appeared behind her. Mad cursed and hit her head so hard on the door of the fridge that she saw stars.

"Oh, my god, I'm sorry, honey," her mother continued, awkwardly hopping around Mad, who was still muttering curses. "I had been standing there for *a while* and the fridge was just open for *so long*, and I finally just couldn't take it."

"I was just . . . thinking about stuff."

"Yes, honey, I bet," her mother offered, and of course she would assume that it pertained to her new brother and her not-dead father and her dozens and dozens of possible siblings and stepmothers, once removed. And Mad did not know how to explain that she was thinking about the end of the world, and their inevitable deaths, and why we hold on to some things and not others.

"I'm thinking about my new brother and dad and all that other stuff," Mad lied.

"I think you should go with him, Madeline," her mother said. "He's your brother, and how else will you get to understand all of this? Wouldn't it be better to do it with someone who has just as much to gain and to lose as you do?"

"I don't know him," Mad reminded her. "I don't even know if I want to see Dad."

"You don't have to!" her mother said, as if she'd just thought of it. "You can drop out at some point during the trip if it gets to be too much. You can get on a plane and come back here. But this poor boy, he's lost his mom. He lost his dad a long time ago, like you. But he doesn't have anyone else."

"What about the farm?" Mad offered. "How are you gonna get along without me?"

"Not well!" her mother admitted. "But I'll ask Tracy and Beth and I can get Kimmer's son to help, because he's been asking to do it for a while."

"I think you need more than three people to replace me," Mad said.

"I could never replace you," her mother said, and it made Mad want to cry, the relief of knowing how much one of her parents had loved her. "Just think about it," her mother said. "Rube says he has a hotel for the night, and he can give you time to think about it."

As if conjured by magic, Rube appeared in the doorway. "Hey, I'm not eavesdropping, but I'm just saying I should probably get going. I feel like maybe I tried to accomplish too much today, and I apologize for that."

"You came just when we said your name," Mad said.

"I wasn't eavesdropping, but people are attuned to the sound of their own name, even if everything else sounds like static, so I thought, okay, this is my cue."

"Have you eaten?" her mom asked, just as Mad was about to say, "'BYE, RUBE."

"I have not," he admitted. "I was too nervous to even have breakfast. I'm starving, honestly."

"We should have had lunch by now," her mother said, "so let's eat and then you can head back to your hotel."

"Let me make it!" Rube said. He looked so excited. "I know your farm is famous for your eggs, and I have a kind of specialty with eggs. Shirred eggs! With bacon!"

"Is that a New England thing?" Mad asked.

"Maybe," he admitted. "I think it might be French? But this was a Sunday brunch kind of thing that my mom and I made pretty often."

"Did Dad make them?"

"God, no, Dad never cooked, or not that I remembered. He wasn't overly fond of food, honestly. He ate toast and cereal for breakfast and a ham sandwich for lunch pretty much every single day. A lobster roll as an extravagance on vacation or something." Mad's father, who was, yes, Rube's father in another life, had loved food. He was a farmer, of course, or was when Mad knew him. He cooked constantly, barbecued whole pigs and experimented with soba noodles made with their own milled buckwheat, and perfected yeast rolls with crunchy flecks of sea salt and crushed pieces of lard.

"Well, we'd love shirred eggs," her mother said, and she directed Rube to a high shelf with four dusty, rarely used ramekins and produced a slab of bacon from a local smokehouse, and, of course, their famous eggs, while Mad slumped into a seat at the kitchen table, too overwhelmed to do much else. She watched Rube and her mother discuss the differences between gas and electric ovens, and she wondered if her mother had expected more children. Mad was ten when her father left, so it wasn't like they hadn't had time to have another. Or maybe her dad had insisted on one, or maybe her mother hadn't even wanted her. Who knew? But it wasn't surprising to imagine additions to the family, her and her mother and her brother and maybe another sister, all of them working the farm. There would have been less pressure to marry, to start a family, though truthfully, her mother did not push on this all that much. But it might have been easier for Mad to leave, honestly, if she'd known there was someone else to help keep the farm running. It was too much to think about, not enough time, and suddenly there was a table being set around her catatonic body, iced tea and silverware and fresh butter, and then Rube placed a ramekin with a beautiful egg looking up at her, pieces of red pepper and a dusting of Parmesan, all housed inside of a little bowl-like nest of bacon. It was beautiful.

And they all sat and ate in silence, only remarking on how wonderful it tasted and for Rube to admit that the eggs tasted so much better than what he got back in the city. And Mad felt the reassurance of food animating her body, keeping her tied to the world.

HER FATHER WAS STILL ALIVE. IT WAS 2007. OBVIOUSLY SHE COULD HAVE found out. They had very slow dial-up on the farm, which she used to communicate with vendors and to order things for the farm. She emailed a few friends, just to stay in touch. She knew the internet could do more, but she didn't think she needed any of that. Or maybe she was just afraid to find out how much she needed and how her barely functioning dial-up wouldn't allow it.

In college, when she was studying plant and soil sciences in Knoxville, she finally got a student email address and used the internet regularly in her junior year. One weekend, having finished a mid-semester project in the nearly empty computer lab and not wanting to go back to her dorm and have to talk to her roommate and her skeezy boyfriend, she had made sure no one else was watching her. And then, in the AltaVista search engine, as if she was searching for porn or instructions on how to make a bomb, she had typed "Chuck Hill" and there were a few possibilities that came back to her and she felt her heart racing, all these links that might lead her to a reunion with her father. And she spent the next two hours clicking on websites that never led her to the Chuck Hill who had been her dad on that farm in Coalfield. She tried "Charles Hill" and that made it worse, giving her information about a foreign policy guy who taught at Yale or a detective who had found Edvard Munch's painting *The Scream* after it had been stolen in Norway. So many Charles Hills. At this stage in her life, she had not known that her father could be anyone other than a farmer. She kept searching, using other search engines like Yahoo Search and Lycos and Excite and WebCrawler, as if one of these engines had proprietary ownership of her father's life. But they had too much, even in 1996, when the internet wasn't so omnipresent. Charles Hill was too common, and she wished her dad's name was something like Cornelius Rainbird. When the work-study student in charge of the lab came to tell her that they were closing, Mad nearly shouted in surprise. To have been witnessed searching for her missing father who had never once tried to even contact her was a kind of embarrassment so specific that even now, as an adult, she could easily remember that sensation and feel the heat rising to her face anew.

And, yes, she had checked since then, as the internet got bigger, but each time she'd come up with nothing tangible, no Chuck Hill that was her own dad, and she wondered if he was dead or had changed his identity in order to avoid child-support payments. And each time, when that tiny little desire to find him came back to her, when she gave in and typed his name into a search engine, only to be disappointed, it felt like a betrayal of the life that her mother had made for her, the farm that they now shared, her entire existence. And she would clear her search history, resolve to never try again. If he wasn't going to come back, it was as if he was dead. And if she had found an obituary, real proof, what would it have mattered? It was better to let him live in those ethereal spaces untouched. He was in limbo or he was walking along the information superhighway or he was running a soft pretzel truck in—whatever the hell—Lancaster, Pennsylvania. Anywhere but this farm was beyond what Mad could imagine. She was, she would tell herself, better off without him.

She had occasionally felt the weight of being his progeny, of holding whatever made him leave inside of her. Sometimes, when something good happened for the farm, another magazine feature, she felt the embarrassing desire to make him proud of her. Now she realized that she had been holding too much of the burden, that, depending on how many half siblings she now had, they had all been carrying more than they needed of their father's legacy, holding him up for so long that it made their father weightless, able to walk on water, to escape, to never be bound to anything if it did not interest him any longer.

"I'LL GO WITH YOU," SHE FINALLY SAID, WHICH SEEMED TO SHOCK BOTH HER mother and Rube.

"You will?" Rube asked.

"Yeah, I guess I will. I am going to go with you to, you know, do all that stuff you said."

"Find our dad? Find our siblings? Drive across the country?"

"Yeah, Rube, yes. All those things."

"Have you packed?" her mom asked her.

"Have I packed?" Mad repeated. "When would I have packed? No. I just now decided to go."

"A cross-country trip," her mother continued, "so many different weather possibilities. That's all I meant."

"You can help me pack," Mad offered.

While Rube, having borrowed her mother's apron at some point, washed the dishes, her mom helped her fill a suitcase with whatever she needed. And the house was quiet, the only sounds being those of the actions necessary for any life, to clean and compile and to move through each space and occupy it. And it was not truly a family, or it was not Mad's new family. But the simple addition of Rube, after nearly an entire life of learning to live with subtraction, with less, did not feel unpleasant to Mad. She tried to promise herself to remember this feeling, the strange peacefulness of it, when things got worse.

***

THEY'D AGREED THAT RUBE WOULD DRIVE AND HIS HALF SISTER WOULD handle the navigation. His name was the only one on the rental agreement because he hadn't wanted to talk to the rental car employee and get into the complicated nature of whether or not he'd be able to convince any of his half siblings to join him on the trip, and he hadn't actually met these people yet, and he didn't know if maybe they'd had their licenses revoked or had never learned how to drive (they had no father to teach them, you understand?), and so he was going to be the only person authorized to drive this PT Cruiser for the entire cross-country journey to find their delinquent father.

So Mad had the atlas, though it wasn't that difficult for her at the moment, hundreds of miles due west on I-40 toward Oklahoma, so instead she was reading a novel while Rube stared at the flatness of the interstate, occasionally looking over at Mad to check her response to the book. It was Rube's novel, or one of them. She'd bought it at a Barnes & Noble along the way, and he had never been so relieved that his book was in stock. He was a successful author, yes, but you never knew about these things, and as they'd walked to the Mystery aisle of the store, he was already preparing himself for the crushing humiliation when she looked in the H section and found no trace of him, like he'd made it all up. They had all four of his books, and it made him happy to see how impressed she was, a genuine flicker of admiration for him. She looked at the garish sticker that nearly blocked his own name that mentioned it was NOW A MAJOR MOTION PICTURE STARRING JUDE LAW.

"This was made into a movie?" Mad said.

"They thought *The Blackboard Detective* wasn't serious enough," Rube explained, and Mad said, "I get that," which made Rube cough before he said, "So they called it *The Lottery of the Dead*."

"Oh, okay, I *have* heard of that movie, but I never saw it," Mad said, "so the book will still be a surprise," and Rube didn't mention that the screenwriter had changed nearly the entire plot, including the identity of the murderer, though he did take solace in the fact that most people thought the movie was rotten. He would have liked the money from possible sequels, but it suited him better to only have to worry about the books, and he was far enough away from the experience that he no longer even thought of Jude Law when he imagined his own creation, disgraced private eye turned junior high English teacher, Claude Wilkinson. By the time they made it back to the car, Mad was already reading the novel. He resisted the urge to ask her what she thought, but now they had been driving for almost three hours, and he couldn't even turn on the radio for fear that it would disturb her. He now wished that they'd bought it as a book on tape so they both could listen. Jude Law narrated it; it might have been fun.

He had hoped this time in the car would allow them the chance to talk, to get to know each other, though he also worried that they wouldn't have much to say. But he'd prefer awkward silence to enforced silence. Mad was not overly emotional, though maybe it wasn't fair to say that, since he'd only just met her two days earlier. But the news of their familial bond, their father siring children and abandoning them as he marched toward the Pacific Ocean, didn't produce the kind of response that he'd expected. She had just seemed annoyed. Tired. A little put out.

She had not wept for three consecutive hours and then tried to set their father's remaindered novels on fire until her boyfriend got a fire extinguisher and then broke up with her.

His mother had died of an aggressive form of cancer, a quick but unfortunately painful death. That had been the catalyst. Rube was a writer, and he liked constructing narrative, creating an animating event and then working backward and forward in order to make sense of it. He liked to make a thread that stretched so tightly from point A to point B that no matter where you thrummed the line, it would vibrate in the most pleasing way. It was why he wrote mysteries; it wasn't exactly a result of his father's legacy because his father had no real legacy, had abandoned it, boxes of his unsold novels taking up space in their apartment, his mother refusing to get rid of them.

As a kid, Rube had read them, multiple times, and had found them lacking. They were so dour, so grim. No one was happy. Yes, there was murder, but murder could be fun, right? If you weren't the one murdered, of course. Did it always have to be raining when a possible source was found dead in an alley? Could it maybe be an affirmation of life to follow the clues until you figured out the how and why? He was a boy prone to fits of mania, deep obsessions, but he was honestly still charmed by the world. Could you not have both?

His first attempts at writing were simply retyping his father's novels and making the changes necessary for them to be good. He did it over and over until the books were almost unrecognizable, the murder inexorably tied to a completely different murderer, the detective calmly following the new and more believable clues to an ending that would both surprise and reward the reader. And then it was almost as if his father disappeared from the equation. I could do this, Rube thought to himself. And so he did. But, okay, yes, if not for his father, *would* he have done it? He preferred not to think about it. He made no mention of his father in interviews and no one had even heard of Charles Hill, so he allowed himself the story that his life was his own.

He had done some detective work, of course, but it led nowhere. He didn't have a ton of information to work with. How do you ask your mom, who never married again, to give you the Social Security number of the man who left her for the open road? And, honestly, it felt strange to hire someone to find your dad. And, he understood this inherently, his dad did not want to be found or else he would have returned at some point. Enough time had passed, right? Rube's life was going well. Why invite upheaval and chaos? It would inevitably come, so might as well put it off for as long as possible.

Other than the enormous psychic scarring of him leaving Rube and his mother without even saying goodbye, his father didn't come up in his life that much. Lots of his friends were kids of divorce. Of course, they saw their dads in the summer or on weekends, but a few didn't have any contact. And they seemed to hate their dads more than Rube, who just felt sad that his dad hadn't thought of their family as enough. He eventually assumed that if he and his father would reconnect, it would simply happen. The story would open up to him.

And then his mother died. And Rube had spent the next month cleaning out her apartment, getting it ready to sell, cataloging papers, finally free to search through her private effects and finding there wasn't much to discover, nothing about his dad, other than a framed photo of him that she'd hidden in the bottom of her dresser. He was sitting on some ugly piece of furniture, looking bemused, as if he knew all of this was temporary. The photo went into a box, and Rube used more tape than was necessary to seal it shut.

Rube's boyfriend, though they weren't necessarily serious, but still someone who had a stake in Rube's life, suggested that Rube was prolonging the cleaning of the apartment to avoid closure. "You're saying that I'm delaying the moment when I have to finally accept that my mom is dead?" he asked his boyfriend. "You think that's some revelation? Of course that's what I'm doing. And I'm gonna keep doing it." He went back to the apartment two days later because it would have been his mother's birthday, and he wasn't sure how else to remember her that wouldn't make him dangerously morose. There wasn't much work left to do, everything boxed up and ready for a storage locker he'd rented, so he just sat on the floor and looked at photos of his mom. He was startled when the phone rang, and he remembered that he'd never shut off the phone service, just another thing he needed to do before he would let go of her. He was going to let the answering machine take the call, but then realized he'd have to hear his mother's voice, as if she was in the room with him, and he rushed to the phone and answered, slightly breathless.

"Winnie?" the voice said, which was the nickname his father used for his mom, who had then reverted back to Winona after he left them.

"No," Rube replied, and he knew. Of course he knew. It was his father. He didn't recognize the voice, nothing like that. He couldn't even remember what his father actually sounded like, but he knew this was his father on the other end of the phone. He felt the thread that connected them pull taut for the first time in over thirty years. He spoke, just to make that line vibrate. "This is Rube. Winnie, my mom . . . she died."

There was silence on the line.

"There was a funeral," Rube continued. "She died of cancer."

"Rube," his father said.

"Would you have come if you knew?" Rube asked.

"I have to go," his father said.

"Could I come see you?" Rube asked, but his father had already hung up. He put the phone down and wondered if he'd dreamed this. He had constructed stranger fantasies that he'd imagined to be real. But it had happened. His father had called his mother on her birthday. He had remembered her birthday. And then Rube realized that maybe his father had always called his mother on her birthday. Was that possible? His mom told him that she'd never seen their father after he left. But she had talked to him, he now realized. Once a year? Every five years? Why had it never worked out that Rube had answered the phone when his father had called? And why the hell had his father never called him on his own birthday? He didn't have to sing the song, of course. Rube was not that demanding. All Rube needed was a "Happy birthday, my son," and that would have sustained him for an entire year. It seemed cruel, now that he knew that his own mom was getting birthday calls from this man. His dad had shown up at the worst possible time to now make Rube somehow hate both his father and mother.

He hit *69 and he was connected to the last incoming call, but no one answered and there was no answering machine. He imagined it was a pay phone. He imagined that his father was on the run from the mafia, that his novels had been based on actual experience, and he had been traveling across the country under assumed names to evade them. And then he thought, no, his father had left them out of sheer boredom and sometimes got lonely and called his ex-wife on her birthday. He'd left them behind but sometimes needed a reminder. But not of Rube. And that made Rube so angry that the rest of that day was kind of a blur, though he apparently called his boyfriend, rambled about his father, then he tried to set the remaindered novels on fire, and then the boyfriend put out the fire, a huge mess of white foam everywhere, and said they were over. And then Rube, after weeks of intense sadness, and an adjustment to his medication, hired the best private detective in the business, at a very expensive rate, to track down his father and, as it turned out, his half siblings. If nothing else, his father had given him a mystery to solve. And it was such a stupid mystery that he had created, so unnecessary, but Rube knew how to turn the things his father made into something better. He knew how to make the story work.

In the PT Cruiser, Rube looked over at Mad, who finally seemed to notice her half brother's need for acknowledgment. "This is good," she said. "I mean, I don't read a ton, but this is gripping. And it's fun. It's—you know—funny, kind of. There's murder, but you don't get too sad about it."

"Thanks," Rube said, and he meant it.

"So," Mad started, before she paused, as if she was testing Rube's capacity for emotional honesty. "Is the dad the murderer?" she asked.

"In the book?" Rube asked, slightly startled. "Why would you think that?"

"I mean, he shows up years after abandoning the girl who has just won the lottery, and then she goes to Claude and says she's certain that someone is trying to kill her for the money."

"There are a lot of possible suspects," Rube allowed.

"Yeah, but, I just thought—"

"This is fiction, though," Rube offered, but Mad seemed unsatisfied by that answer. "Do you want me to tell you who did it?"

"No!" she said. "I want to be surprised."

The father was not the murderer. He was just a greedy dumbass who never got the satisfaction of reuniting with his millionaire daughter. Rube knew enough not to be so obvious, or to be obvious in sneakier ways.

She went back to reading the novel, and Rube started to think of another plot, a mystery he'd been working on the last few weeks. It was about a son who murders his estranged father who ran out on him and his mother years before. He discovers the father's whereabouts and then picks up all the siblings he didn't know he had, gathering up a little army of angry and emotionally unstable people, all with their own betrayals and motivations, who want to confront their dad. And they find him living in a mansion with his heiress wife, so wealthy that their dad spends all day long beside the pool drinking mai tais. Rube thought about how, with so many possible suspects, it would be harder to say for sure who actually killed the father. The murder might never even be solved if there wasn't a detective like Claude Wilkinson, who was attuned to the deeper motivations of unbalanced people. He thought it could be a good story. He liked point A (the elaborate plan) and he liked point B (the murder) and what separated these two points was that thread, and you just had to follow it until you reached your destination. The story pretty much wrote itself, he thought. Most stories, he decided, could write themselves if you knew enough to let them happen the way they needed to.

1968, BOSTON, MASSACHUSETTS, 8MM

Close-up on a young boy who is smirking but focused on some task. The camera pans out to show him sitting on the thin orange-and-brown carpet of an apartment hallway as he folds a complicated paper airplane. When finished, he holds it up to the camera and smiles.

Mid-shot of a woman sitting on a lime-green sofa while reading a manuscript and smoking a cigarette. She reaches for the pen behind her ear and marks something on the manuscript.

The next shot is taken over the shoulder of the young boy, who is standing in the doorway of the kitchen. He looks searchingly back at the camera for instruction. He then nods, steadies himself, and holds up the airplane. The camera now focuses on the woman in the distance, still reading, a curl of smoke rising into the air.

The boy deftly flicks the airplane toward the woman, and it catches the air and hovers until it lands in her lap. She drops the cigarette, exclaims, drops the pages to the floor, and then picks up the cigarette and puts it in the ashtray on the coffee table. She looks up at the camera, briefly irritated, but then she softens, smiles. She unfolds the airplane, reads something on the paper, and smiles. She stands and the camera follows her to a desk against the window of the living room. She smooths out the paper, puts it in the typewriter, and types a message. She refolds the airplane, stares back at the camera, and sends the paper airplane sailing toward the camera.

The boy unfolds the airplane and holds up the paper to the camera, which takes a moment to focus. It reads, in awkward, large letters: I LOVE YOU, MOM! There is another line, typewritten, that reads, I LOVE YOU, TOO, RUBE.

The boy folds the paper back into the shape of an airplane and walks over to his mother at the desk. She opens the window, and he tosses the airplane out the window, and the camera follows the path of the paper airplane as it catches the wind and disappears from sight.

CHAPTER THREE

By the time they reached Memphis, Tennessee, Mad realized that they were still essentially strangers. And they were going to add more people to this caravan? Mad wanted to keep moving, to find their dad, but Rube was more content to wander.

It was Rube who asked if they could visit Graceland, and it was Mad who tried so hard to think of a polite way to say no. "Do you even like Elvis?" she asked.

"I mean, he's an icon, right?" Rube replied. "He's a crucial part of American pop culture."

"What's your favorite Elvis song?" she asked him.

"Oh, boy!" he exclaimed, surprised at the question, "Hmm. 'In the Ghetto,' maybe?" And as Mad laughed at the absurdity of that song being his favorite, he changed his mind. "Wait! No, why did I say that? Shit, um, maybe 'Hound Dog'? That's pretty good, you have to admit. Anyway, it's not about the music, exactly. It's just the symbolism of him."

Mad tried to think of her own choice for favorite song by Elvis but all she could hear in her head was Marc Cohn's "Walking in Memphis." Then she could only think of Paul Simon's "Graceland." Did she not know a single Elvis song? He was before her time, but not so far away that he was cool again to people like her. He was just a famous guy who ruined himself through excess and ended up on velvet paintings that hung in the living room of your weird aunt and uncle.

"I've heard the tickets are pretty expensive," Mad offered, trying to keep them on the road, heading west, but then she realized that, if they didn't stop, if they made good time, they would be standing in front of their half sister outside her dorm at the University of Oklahoma, trying to convince her that they were related and that they were looking for their dad, who had also once been her dad. Mad remembered the strange sensation of Rube driving up to the farm, and he had only been one person. If Mad had wanted no part of his plan, it would have been a one-on-one fight, and she could have kicked his ass, shoved him in the PT Cruiser, and sent him on his way. But she thought of this college girl, feeling crowded by these two people who might as well have been old people to her, begging her to get in the car and head west. Why had she agreed to this?

"We can eat," Mad offered, and it was a testament to their growing relationship that Rube seemed to sense that Mad would not set foot in Graceland and so he agreed.

"What should we eat?" he asked.

"Barbecue," she replied.

"Which one?"

"It will not matter," she told him. "They will all be better than anything you've had in Boston."

RUBE HAD STAYED WITH THEM AT THE FARM FOR TWO DAYS, FOLLOWING Mad's mom around and helping with the work while Mad got her affairs in order, which consisted mostly of sorting through her clothes, looking for outfits that suggested that she had her life together and wasn't a scam artist and that this absolutely wasn't about money or a cult. She did not have a lot of outfits that suggested this state of being, because she pretty much only wore blue jeans and then flannel shirts over T-shirts. She decided the best she could manage was to be clean, unrumpled, and so she ironed her shirts and washed her jeans in the hopes that when she walked into the living quarters of a person who was family, they would not be afraid of her. Or, at the very least, they would be less afraid than the circumstances allowed.

They were going to Oklahoma, where they were hoping to meet their half sister, Pepper Hill, who was a senior at the University of Oklahoma. Rube had shown her the folder compiled by the detective, and it was much thicker than the one on Mad, because Pepper was a basketball star. It still wasn't *that* thick because she was a *women's* basketball star, but nevertheless. There was a lot of information on her, even if some of it was purely statistical, even though she was eleven years younger than Mad. She was feeling embarrassed that, of the three siblings, she had the least amount of national press. Rube had his books and Pepper had basketball. Mad had the farm, had been featured in magazines, but farms weren't as sexy as sports and literature. There was no category in Trivial Pursuit for Farming. But, she considered, for a dad who left very little trace of himself as he moved through these families, he had produced exemplary children. Or, no, Mad reminded herself, their mothers had produced exemplary children.

Pepper was a former Gatorade High School Player of the Year in Oklahoma, the only woman to score more than three thousand points in her career, and a two-time state champion. She was Oklahoma's starting shooting guard on the women's team, which was ranked fourteenth in the nation. Mad learned from a profile from her senior year of high school in *The Oklahoman* that Pepper—who went by Pep (of course, this had to be their dad)— had transferred high schools during her sophomore year because the new principal had confiscated her gym key so she wouldn't be able to practice in the mornings and nights. "It's just, like, there's a lot of hours in the day, you know? I spend most of them playing basketball," Pepper said in response, "and my mom knew I'd keep going, just break in, and she didn't want me to go to jail or get expelled, so she moved us to another district. She's a good mom." No mention of a dad, Mad noticed. She wondered if their father had anything to do with Pepper's basketball talent, though she couldn't imagine how he would have influenced her, since he had no experience or interest in it when she knew him. But she figured that Rube was pretty flabbergasted to learn that his insurance salesman father, who wrote crime novels on the side, would turn his next kid into a farmer.

There was a picture of Pepper, in her uniform, but the black-and-white photo was blurry from being reproduced. Still Mad instantly could see a resemblance, the square jaw, the straight blonde hair that Mad shared, and, good lord, the height. According to a scouting report from her freshman year at OU, Pepper was six foot one, an inch taller than Mad and only an inch shorter than Rube. She didn't know what to expect, of course, didn't know if she'd even want this athletic, hyper-driven girl in the car with her as they moved west, but she liked the safety of numbers, to imagine all of them, these tall, imposing children of their terrible father, moving toward him like they were Godzilla, bent on destruction.

AT THE COZY CORNER, THEY ATE RIBS AND BARBECUED BOLOGNA SAND—wiches dripping with sauce and coleslaw. The A/C was broken in the restaurant, a tiny little box of a place, but the food was so good they didn't care. There was no one else in the restaurant, and as they ate, Mad asked Rube a question that seemed too personal for the close confines of the PT Cruiser.

"You mentioned a boyfriend," she started.

"An ex-boyfriend now, but yeah," Rube allowed, still eating.

"Have you been in many relationships?" she asked. "You ever been married?"

He put down the sandwich and wiped his hands on a napkin. He took a sip of iced tea and then looked back at her, as if determining what he could tell her. "I've never been married, no."

"Oh, yeah, okay, I guess I forgot," Mad said, feeling like an idiot. She didn't even fully know what the laws were, if it was allowed in Massachusetts. But all she wanted to know was if he'd been in love, been committed to someone.

"So what about you?" Rube asked her. "Are you . . . do you like guys? Or, maybe, girls? I can't—I guess I don't know."

"Guys?" she replied, and it sounded like a question, though it was meant to be declarative. She had no interest in women. But, honestly, sometimes she wished there was a third option. Or just maybe that she lived somewhere that had more guys to choose from. She repeated herself, more confidently this time. "Guys."

"Okay, cool. It's just, you know, I couldn't place you with the farming and the flannel and the boots and . . . well, it's just good to know. Have *you* ever been married?"

"Me? No. Never married. Never even close to that. I haven't seriously dated anyone since college. The farm just requires so much work. I can't just go out on dates and see where it goes and all that, because there's always something I need to be doing. I don't have time to get to the serious part."

"Are there any handsome farmers who have land that abuts your own farm? Seems like that would be a good fit," Rube offered.

"There are no handsome farmers in our neck of the woods, no. And they wouldn't be interested in our farm, because it's not that big, and we're organic, and we have weird ideas about farming, and they think we're, like, witches who make things grow with black magic."

She did think about a guy from Little Rock, Arkansas, who had come to Coalfield to write an article about the farm for a glossy southern magazine. He was a cute, slightly nerdy boy named Matthew. He had treated her seriously and asked good questions that revealed the limits of what he knew about farming but impressed her that he'd even known to ask. He stayed in town for three days, seriously longer than he probably needed to, and she took him to dinner one night and nothing really happened, but there had been a spark. And he would email afterward, even after the article had come and gone. It was nice to come home after work and relax on the sofa and correspond with him, talking about things that didn't matter, which meant she could share things that didn't matter. But time passed, and she got busy with work and didn't respond as quickly, because it was hard to treat email as something real, and so he stopped writing as much. He'd invited her to visit him in Little Rock, but that had been almost eight months ago, and she'd not replied. It was sad, maybe, but that was the closest she'd been to a relationship in a good long while.

"Do you want to get married?" Rube asked.

"I guess I have to want it more than I want the life that I have right now. And it would be nice if something came along to make me wonder."

"Well, you are very interesting and super capable and quite pretty, so I think you should get online and find somebody."

"I will never go online and find somebody," she replied. "I'd rather just be a farm witch. But I was talking about you."

"Fair enough. Yeah, I've been in a few relationships. It's complicated, I guess." He seemed to consider picking the sandwich back up, but he hesitated.

He told her about how he hadn't known he was gay, that it wasn't something he'd understood about himself from adolescence. But then an older boy in high school had chosen him, had seen something in him that suggested that he was gay. And that meant a lot, in that time period, when things were even worse than they were now. To take a risk like that, you had to feel pretty certain that the other person wouldn't destroy you. Rube just felt like maybe the boy knew him more clearly than he knew himself and he allowed it. They dated in secret, did everything in secret, but Rube liked it, understood how his attraction worked and what he desired, but then the boy went off to college and they never saw each other again.

A few years later, when he went off to Boston College, he dated some, but he couldn't tell his mom because he thought it would break her heart. She had hoped for grandchildren, some way to make their family larger than it was, and then he got a job teaching at a pretty fancy private school. The school had these arcane morality clauses that scared the shit out of him, and so he'd kept that part of himself under wraps. If he did anything, it was always illicit, and it never felt right, like it shouldn't have made him feel so guilty. So it was just better to be alone than to feel that way. He'd lived like that until he sold the novel and could leave that teaching job. And he'd met his boyfriend, who was an editor, and they had been happy, but he still couldn't tell his mom. He'd never told her. And then she'd died. And even if he hadn't cracked up after her death, he doubted his boyfriend would have stayed with him much longer. Rube had kept him at arm's length from parts of his life for so long. Why would you stay with someone like that?

"I keep people at a distance, I know," he said.

"I guess I do, too," Mad offered, but it was easy to do that when you lived on so many acres that you could barely even see your neighbor. But she knew what he meant. If a person wanted her, it made her suspicious, not flattered. It was a part of herself that she hated, to think that she was so deficient that someone was scamming her if they said she was interesting.

"My therapist says that's definitely because of Dad," he offered.

"Oh," Mad said, not sure what to say. She'd never been to a therapist in her life. The chickens demanded so much of her attention that she couldn't even find someone suitable to have sex with every once in a while. No way was she using her free time driving to a city and talking about her freaking dad. No, thank you. But she'd glean what she could from Rube's therapist. She seemed like a lady who might know some things.

"Yeah. She says that he left me and my mom, and so I'm afraid that I'm gonna do the same thing."

"Or maybe you're afraid someone will leave you again," Mad offered.

"That, too!" Rube said. "Yes, one or the other."

"And you think that's all because of Dad?" she asked, genuinely curious. She didn't feel the same. Her dad had done what he'd done, but she didn't think he was the reason she couldn't commit to a relationship with a dude who didn't even exist. Maybe if she met someone online and they got deep enough into the relationship, she'd have a clearer sense of it.

"I think it's at least half of it," he said. "Half of it's that Dad messed me up by leaving. And half of it is that my mom messed me up by staying but being so damn sad that I never forgot about it."

Mad figured that most therapy consisted of focusing on how your parents messed you up, and then finding ways to keep that pain contained within your own body so you didn't pass it on to anyone else or yell too much at the people responsible. But her mom was great. She wanted Mad to leave, to explore, to be happy. Although, if a therapist was present right now, and Mad was forced at gunpoint to say something about the whole situation, she'd admit that maybe having your mom constantly ask you to explore beyond the place that you, with all of your blood, sweat, and tears, helped make into an extremely successful agricultural landmark in the modern American South, you'd feel a little unappreciated, too.

"I can't eat anymore," Rube finally said. "Should we hit the road? Or perhaps there's a cultural landmark that you'd like to check out?"

"We probably should keep driving. It's, like, seven hours to Norman."

"It's already five o'clock. With stops, we won't get there until pretty late."

"We can stop in Arkansas," Mad offered.

"A hotel room?" Rube asked.

"Yeah, Rube," she replied. "Did you think we'd just live in the car? Or sleep under the stars? We'll have to find lodging on this trip. We can't stay in the dorm with this girl we've never met."

"Yeah, of course. I know. But you want your own room, right?"

"I guess it depends on how much a room costs," Mad replied. She did not want to go into debt tracking down her siblings and confronting her dad. She needed to be careful with her money. She had thus far not offered to pay for gas. She had not paid for the tickets to see Elvis's kitchen. She had paid for her own meal here at the Cozy Corner. She bought her half brother's book, those royalties going right into his bank account. She still had to *get back home*. Who knew what expenses might occur. If it meant sharing a hotel room with her half brother, well, stranger things would probably await them.

"Oh, great!" Rube offered. "We can watch a movie and order a pizza."

"Let's just see how tired we are. There is a long stretch of driving that you have to do. And I want to finish your book."

"Yes, sure," Rube answered, but she could see that he liked the idea of it, to be less alone.

And as they drove across the Mississippi, Mad realized this was the farthest west that she'd ever been in her life. Thirty-two years old, and she was only now in the western part of the United States because of a brother that she had never met before and a father who waited at the edge of the country. As they reached the other side of the bridge, Mad closed her eyes, centered herself, even as the car kept moving forward. She could feel the tug of the farm, knew where it was, could see it clearly in her mind. No matter how far she went, she'd not lose sight of it. She opened Rube's novel, took a few seconds to remember what was going on within the pages, and kept reading, eager to see how it all turned out, knowing that, at the very least, when she reached the end, there would be a resolution.

1978, COALFIELD, TENNESSEE, 8MM

Close-up on a hen's eye. The black pupil is surrounded by speckled orange, before the frame expands to reveal a young girl, wearing an Opryland Theme Park cap, smiling, two baby teeth missing, cradling the chicken in her arms.

She kisses the hen, who bristles, and she places it on the ground. She picks up a basket of eggs and walks over to a woman wearing a pair of overalls, who covers her face and shakes her head at the camera. The girl pulls on her mom's arm and the woman relents, smiling. After a few seconds, she makes a goofy face and holds up an egg like she's going to throw it at the camera, which pans over to the girl, who laughs. She takes an egg from the basket and makes the same gesture and the camera slowly retreats, as the woman and girl shake their fists.

The next shot shows the girl holding up the end of a trailer hitch as the mother backs up a John Deere tractor. The mother hops off and helps the girl connect the trailer. The girl then climbs onto the tractor and, after a few seconds, gets the tractor started and pulls out. The camera pans to show a somewhat rickety chicken coop on wheels, painted an electric orange with white trim, being pulled by the tractor to a new location with fresh grass. The girl waves, and the chicken coop jostles and bounces, and the camera pans over to the mother, who is smiling, looking at the girl.

Close-up on the girl's face as smoke swirls around her. The camera pans out to show her reaching into an open smoker and plucking hard-boiled eggs from the grates. She takes one, shuffling it from hand to hand until it cools, and peels off the shell. She looks at the camera, makes a goofy face, similar to the one her mother made earlier, and shoves the entire egg into her mouth. She chews but then laughs, opening her mouth to show the yellow of the yolk stuck in her teeth. She finally swallows, nodding, and then reaches for another egg. She holds it out toward the camera and nothing happens, but then she frowns, gesturing toward the camera, and a hand reaches out and takes the offered egg. The hand quickly retreats from the shot, and the girl watches, waiting for some response. Instead, the camera turns toward the field where the chickens now scratch at the grass.

CHAPTER FOUR

They drove onto the campus of the University of Oklahoma, immediately overwhelmed by the size of the school, with students pouring out of every single building, ignoring the multiple crosswalks and simply moving with the sheer force of youth toward whatever they had to do next. No matter how much information the private investigator had given Rube, Mad now realized how incredibly stupid this plan was.

"Oh, jeez," Rube said, "this was a lot easier with you." And he was right, the ease of driving down some country road onto a property where it was only Mad and her mom, where they had a stand where you could just walk right up, buy some sweet corn, and tell the person behind the counter that you were their half brother. Here there were buildings that required key cards, dorms that were not clearly labeled and all looked alike, parking lots that required stickers or the PT Cruiser would simply disappear from the campus and Rube and Mad would have to enroll at OU and hope to meet Pepper at graduation. But this was how a quest worked, Mad figured, having never left her farm except to go to college and go right back to the farm. You set out with grand designs, expecting glory and riches, and then you ended up surrounded by people who were so much younger than you and did not give a shit about your quest and you realized, oh, god, you weren't even halfway into your quest, and the campus police would arrest you if they heard you talking to the students and saying the word *quest* over and over and over, holding up a picture of a young woman.

As they finally found a parking lot that allowed for guest parking, Rube and Mad started walking aimlessly across the vast expanse of the campus. Rube had a photocopied map, but he seemed unable to reconcile it with the real world. He had his briefcase and was fumbling for the folder on Pepper. Mad finally took the map from him so he could search the briefcase. Rube sifted through the papers until he found what he was looking for, what seemed to be a class schedule for Pepper, as well as her dorm building and campus phone number.

"You have her phone number?" Mad asked.

"Yeah, it's right here," he replied.

"Wait, did you have my phone number, too?"

"Of course. I got it from the private detective. Yours was easy to find, just in the phone book. I think she had to do a bit more work to get a student number from a campus directory."

"Why didn't you just call me?" Mad asked.

"What do you mean?"

"You could have called me, right? And told me that you were my half brother and everything about our dad."

"Yeah, I guess so," he replied, though he was now looking around to see in which direction they needed to move. "So it looks like she would be in this Political Science class, and it gets out in thirty minutes—oh, no, that class is Monday, Wednesday, and Friday, so I guess—"

"Why didn't you just call me?" Mad asked, her voice getting louder. "Why did you drive to tell me?"

He seemed startled by the question, but now he considered it. "Well, because I was starting this journey to find Dad. And, you know, I wanted you to come with me. And I thought you'd hang up on me if I called."

"You thought it would be harder to say no if you just showed up at my house and made eggs for me and my mom and begged me to come with you."

"Mad? Yes! Of course. That's exactly right. That's not insidious. I wanted to see you, face-to-face. No matter what, I would have told you that we were related. But for the trip to find him, I wanted to get a sense of what you were like. If you were unstable or something, if I got to the farm and you were in bad shape and maybe needed a hundred thousand dollars to get out of debt, I could just leave."

Mad wanted to be upset, but what did it matter? She would still be here, in Norman, Oklahoma, searching for their sister. And maybe she needed the shock of having this strange guy crying in front of her. It would have been so easy to refuse him over the phone. She made a point to get over it, to clear her mind. Rube had his methods. He'd found her; they'd find Pepper.

"But, now, Rube? Think about it. There's two of us. Couldn't we just call her? Tell her that we're here and we would like to talk to her about our dad?"

"It worked so well the first time, though," Rube told her. "I really think the visual aspect of it is important."

"It's different. You're a guy, so it's not totally apparent to you, maybe, but when you came to see me, I was working the stand. Customers had come all day long, so when you showed up, even though you looked a little anxious, it wasn't completely unexpected. The fact that you were my brother was shocking, but it wasn't as bad. But, think about it, we are two old people who don't belong on a college campus, and we are going to hang around outside her classroom or her dorm. She will pepper-spray us so fast. She'll get her teammates to stomp us to dust."

"Okay, well, I guess I understand that. But it's not like we'll be sitting on her bed in her dorm when she opens the door. But I get your point. I do."

"So what do we do?"

"It's just . . . we're already here. We're on campus. We came all this way, and it feels so silly to just call her on my cell phone."

"Please call her on your cell phone," she said.

"And then what? I tell her that we are her long-lost brother and sister and—oh, by the way—we're outside your dorm right now, so come on down, we just want to talk?"

Mad realized she was angry at the wrong person. Rube was doing the best he could with the raw materials he had been given. The raw materials? That was their dad's fault. It would have been so much easier if he'd just told each new family, "Hey, I left behind another family, but don't let it worry you because they were real bummers. You guys? I just can feel it; you guys are gonna be great." And then, when he left that family for the next one, the mom and the kid would be at the dinner table and they'd say, "He mentioned this other family, right? One day, maybe we'll meet them." And then, when they showed up to your campus in the middle of the country on a clear day in March of 2007, you weren't completely surprised.

"Okay, how about this?" Rube offered. "We say we're reporters, and we're doing a story about her, and we want to talk to her about her dad, Charles Hill."

"We're going to start out immediately lying to her?" Mad responded. She could not figure out how this was going to end in any other way than her and Rube getting pepper-sprayed and put in jail. Why was this so hard? Why was family so difficult?

"Okay, okay, I'll call, goddamn, and just tell her the truth. I wish we weren't outside on the street with all the kids making noise and cars and stuff. It's gonna sound weird."

"It's the best option," Mad told him, and Rube got his flip phone out of his briefcase and, checking the number on the sheet, dialed. Mad realized she wouldn't be able to hear the call, and she hissed, "Put it on speaker," and she watched Rube fumble on the little screen and hit the SPKR button, which amplified the sound of the phone ringing, a sound that instantly made Mad's heart race. After the third ring, they heard someone answer.

"I'm coming, okay?" the voice said.

"Um, hello, yes, hello," Rube said.

"Wait, who is this?" the voice said. "Courtney?"

"Is this Pepper?" Rube asked. He sounded so formal again, like when Mad had first met him, the weird way he turned into a Mormon missionary or a defeated vacuum cleaner salesman, like he had a pitch all ready to go, but suddenly couldn't remember it and was stalling for time.

"Yeah," Pepper said.

"This is, well, my name is Rube Hill. We have, you know, I think we have the same last name."

"Why are you calling me?" Pepper replied. "I'm late. I've gotta go."

"Go to class?" Rube asked.

"Dude," Pepper said. "I'm going to get on the bus to Austin."

"Austin?" Rube said, so clearly confused.

"I've gotta go, dude, sorry," Pepper said, and then Mad grabbed the phone from Rube and said, "Sorry, Pepper, this is Madeline Hill, and this is really weird, I know, and I'm sorry about this, but our dad is Charles Hill and I think he's your dad, too, and we just wanted to talk to you."

There was a beat of quiet, and Mad listened to the hum of air-conditioning coming through the line.

"We're your brother and sister. Half brother and half sister," Rube clarified.

"What the fuck?" Pepper finally replied. "This is so stupid. This is a joke, right?"

"It's not," Rube said. "We're actually here in Oklahoma. We were hoping we could talk."

"I'm leaving for Austin!" Pepper shouted. "We have a game in two days, you idiot. The NCAA tournament!"

"Oh, shit," Rube said. Mad slapped her head. Why had they not checked this? How were they so stupid? She was a basketball star. It was March. She didn't follow basketball closely, especially not women's college basketball, but she knew this much.

"March Madness," Mad said, before realizing she had said it out loud.

"You guys sound like fucking aliens," Pepper said. "I'm hanging up."

"No, wait!" Mad said. "I know it sounds strange and I'm sorry about the timing of this."

"Spring break is starting, too, you know," Pepper added.

"We didn't!" Mad replied. "We so did not realize any of this or we would have figured out a better way. But if your dad was Charles Hill, and if he left your family, we just wanted to say that he did the same to us. He did it to the guy you were talking to, and then he did it to me. And after he left you guys, he did it again. And we just wanted to meet you and to tell you."

"We're playing Southeast Missouri State," Pepper said, as if she hadn't heard any of what Mad had said.

"We'll be rooting for you," Rube added, and Mad tried to slap him but he put his hands up in defense.

"Are you serious about all this?" Pepper said. Her voice, so deep, had softened a bit. "If you are fucking with me to throw me off my game . . ."

"We're not!" Mad shouted. Some students were walking by them and stopped to stare, but Mad kept going, "We're not, like, spies from . . . what was it? Mississippi State?"

"Southeast Missouri State," Pepper said. "The Redhawks."

"We're not Redhawks," Rube assured her.

"I'm so sorry," Mad repeated. "But we're your brother and sister, kind of. We hope you win."

There was a long pause, silence again. "You're here in Norman?" Pepper asked.

"We're on campus, actually," Rube said. "We're close to the Visitors' Center. There's—let me look—okay, there's a Carpenter Hall, maybe?"

"I have to go meet the bus to go to Austin," she told them. "If you want, you can meet me at the Noble Center, okay? It's the basketball arena. There's this part of it, the Legacy Court. It's like a museum for basketball. You can wait there and maybe I'll talk to you before I leave. I gotta get my stuff. I'm late. I just came back because I forgot my headphones."

"Thanks so much, Pepper," Mad said.

"I go by Pep," she told them.

"Okay, Pep, thank you so much. Sorry. Sorry again. I know this is weird. Thank you," Mad said, but Pep had already hung up on them.

Mad's heart was racing. Was this what Rube had felt when he'd pulled up to the farm? There was a rush to this that felt more than just familial; it was the terror of putting yourself in a position where someone could absolutely destroy you. You had to rely on the hope that something, and maybe it *was* genetic, would keep the person from hurting you, to believe you when you said you only wanted to stand close to them and feel less alone. And Pep was young. She was an elite collegiate athlete. If she wanted to throw them down a flight of stairs, she could. If she wanted to say the cruelest things about Mad's flannel shirt, it would be so instinctual that Pep wouldn't even have to think about it. If she wanted to say that Mad and Rube were *desperate old people* who wanted to steal her fame and her youth and pull her down to their level, she could say it and both Rube and Mad would cry so much. And if she just didn't want them in her life, what else could they do but leave her to the life she'd made without them? They'd have to keep going, knowing that they lacked something, that they wouldn't be whole, but, honestly, Mad was okay with this. A life of farming had prepared her better than Rube, perhaps, who made his living creating stories that would bend to his will. You took what the earth gave you, and you could cultivate it and respect it and work hard, but it decided what you could and could not have. If you didn't die, sometimes that was enough. And Mad knew, no matter how embarrassing it might be to have an entire basketball team call you awful names, that this would not kill her. Rube, however, looked less convinced. But it would be two on one. She did not know basketball well enough to say with certainty, but weren't your odds so much better when it was two on one? Mad grabbed Rube's hand and tugged him toward a reckoning.

THE LLOYD NOBLE CENTER'S LEGACY COURT LOOKED LIKE SOMETHING OUT OF a science-fiction movie, one where citizens of the future would line up to step onto the center court feature and be turned into a cyborg Sooner. There were numerous TV screens above their heads, the blaring sounds of announcers voicing indisputable proof of Oklahoma's basketball dominance, and lenticular images of players who were unrecognizable to Mad, and the swirling star-like auras around the players made them look like Jedi Knights from *Star Wars*. This is all to say that, even if they weren't about to meet their half sister for the first time, this location would be deeply strange.

As Mad and Rube paced nervously around the first floor of the interactive museum, which was populated by only a few other people, they stared at trophies and jerseys and listened to former coaches talk about the almost mystical quality of Sooner basketball. And then their sister, Pepper, appeared in front of them, and Mad almost gasped, after all the holograms and videos and life-size posters, to see a real person before them.

"Okay," Pep said to them, her arms crossed, looking slouchy in her oversize warm-up gear emblazoned with the giant red letters of OU.

"Hi, Pepper," Rube said.

"You guys are tall," she said.

"You're tall, too," Rube offered.

"Blonde hair," Pep observed.

"Like Dad," Rube replied.

Mad saw that Pep flinched a bit, but she recovered, making her face into a mask of indifference again. "Tell me your names again."

"I'm Rube," Rube replied, "and that's Mad."

"Matt?"

"Mad," Rube said, and Mad wasn't sure why she couldn't bring herself to speak. "Like, if you're mad at someone. Dad liked nicknames, I guess."

"You're Dad's kids? You're, like, my brother and sister?"

"Yeah," Mad finally said, afraid that if she didn't talk, she would stay silent for the entire meeting. "His dad," she said, pointing to Rube, "is also your dad, but his dad was a mystery writer and he lived in Boston."

"What?" Pep asked.

"And my dad—who is also your dad and his dad—was a farmer and lived in Tennessee."

"My dad was a farmer?" she asked.

"And a mystery writer," Rube added.

"Yeah, he was," Mad continued, "and we're your half sister and half brother. And we're really sorry about all this. But Dad had other families, and so Rube and I decided to go find him and we're just, like, kind of stopping along the way to meet his other kids."

"'Cause he has more kids?" Pep asked. "Like, after me?"

Rube nodded. "One other kid, at least," he offered.

"He had another kid after he left us?"

"Yes," Rube replied.

"I have to go in a second," she said. "My coach is already a little weirded out that I'm not there. I told her it was a family emergency, but, like, I don't think she knew what that meant." She paused for a few seconds. "I don't know what it means."

"We're sorry about this," Mad repeated. "We knew it would be hard. It's been weird for both of us, too, but we just wanted to meet you. We didn't know it would be at such a bad time."

Pep nodded. It was, she seemed to be acknowledging, a really bad time, but Mad knew that there wasn't a good time.

"We're going to go see Dad," Rube offered. "Me and Mad are traveling to go see him, because we've not seen him since he left us. I mean, he left me and then ten years later he left Mad, but we're going to go see him."

"I can't go with you," Pep replied.

"No, I understand. We would have loved for you to come, though. But, yeah, you've got the basketball."

"It might be a few weeks if we get to the championship."

"Yes, of course," Rube acknowledged, though it seemed like he was thinking about how they might meet up after the tournament and she could join them on the trip. But Mad thought that if this trip took more than two weeks, she would die. She had been a little afraid of another person on the trip, but now she felt sad to leave Oklahoma without adding to their ranks.

"Can I just ask," Rube said, "if you've seen our dad since he left you?"

"Nope," Pep answered. "Never again. He just left and he never came back."

"Maybe he talked to your mom?" Rube asked.

"No way; he's never contacted us."

"It's just that he ended up talking to both of our moms after he left," Rube offered, and Mad saw Pep's eyes blaze with real anger.

"My mom would have told me," she said. She looked around the museum, like it was the first time she'd realized where she was, as if all of these trophies and jerseys were entirely new to her. "I gotta go," she said.

"Maybe we can come see the game?" Rube offered.

"I can't stop you," Pep said. "I thought you were going to find Dad, though."

Mad looked at Rube. They had not discussed this, but how could they have discussed it before this moment? But just like Graceland after Rube had picked up Mad, there needed to be some absurd thing that helped you come to terms with the new discovery of your family. And if Pep wasn't going to travel with them, they could at least be together for a little longer.

"Well, he's not expecting us," Mad said. "There's no set date for our arrival."

Pep smiled a little. "He doesn't know you're coming?" she asked.

"He doesn't even know that we know about each other," Mad replied, and Pep actually laughed.

"Okay, yeah," she finally said. "You can come see me. I do have to go now, though. 'Bye. It was nice to meet you, I guess."

"Nice to meet you!" Rube said. "Oh, wait!" He had a business card that he gave to Pep, who reluctantly took it. "It's got my cell phone number on it. You can call anytime if you have any questions or want to . . . want to talk about him."

"Okay. Cool," Pep said. As she turned to leave, Mad suddenly asked, "What did your dad do for a living?"

Pep smiled again, a lovely smile, and Mad could see how much she looked like Rube at that moment. "He was a basketball coach," she said, and then she was gone, out the door and fading from view, and all that was left for Mad and Rube were the players still trapped inside the Legacy Court, held in place. Mad looked around at everything for a moment longer before they, too, had to leave it behind.

MAD TRIED TO TUCK IN THE ILL—FITTING GRAY T—SHIRT THAT READ LET'S GO, SOONERS! in crimson and cream letters. After their meeting with Pep, Rube had bought both of them T-shirts when they had stopped at the university bookstore. He said it would be a nice way to support their sister as they made their way to Texas to see her first-round matchup, but Rube had guessed at her size, not bothering to ask, and now she had a shirt that made her look like she was wearing a parachute.

That morning, in a motel just outside of Austin, Texas, when she'd tried it on, she did the angriest twirl possible to show her displeasure to Rube, who seemed unbothered. "It will make a nice sleep shirt," he said, and Mad, trying not to yell, said, "But I'm not wearing it to bed. I'm wearing it to an NCAA tournament game in front of thousands of people."

"Well, people are not going to be looking at us," he said, though Mad noticed that Rube's shirt fit perfectly. "This is all about Pepper."

"Yes, you're right," Mad had said, but now, as they pulled into a parking lot near the Frank Erwin Center, she was irritated all over again. What she realized was that she didn't want Pepper to see her and think, Oh, she's clearly not a true fan of the Oklahoma Sooners women's basketball team, but she realized how insane that was. Pepper would not even see them, probably, and she would not care that Mad's shirt was too big because Pepper probably would be more concerned with winning a basketball game. Mostly, Mad just didn't like feeling any more uncomfortable than she already would be, filing into a huge arena to watch a sport that, truth be told, she didn't exactly comprehend. But they were here, right? This is what a family did. They showed up for things they didn't totally understand and wore uncomfortable clothes and they shouted your name nonstop because they wanted you to understand that, win or lose, they loved you. But, of course, maybe it would be weird for Pepper to know that her half siblings, who truthfully had met only a week or so previous, *loved* her.

Mad shook her head. She wouldn't let her own weirdness ruin this moment. She didn't have much experience with family but this *is* what you did. You showed them you cared. Not their dad, obviously. He would not be at the game, not shouting Pep's name, not wearing some giant shirt that somehow seemed to be *expanding* in the heat of the Texas sun. He would be far away. So it was important that Mad and Rube were there in his absence. They had missed every single basketball game of Pep's entire life up to this point, but here they were. And that had to mean something. Go, Sooners!

It was early afternoon and there wasn't as much of a crowd as Mad had expected for a major athletic event. She remembered those games in Knoxville when the Vols had played football at Neyland Stadium and even the parking lot was raucous for hours before kickoff. This was more like a small academic conference on some esoteric subject, with everyone milling around and smiling politely, knowing that, even if they didn't know you, they knew *of* you. There was one lady in the parking lot who was selling homemade merchandise for the game, and Mad stopped to look at one of the shirts draped over the hood of the woman's pickup truck. It had a dog wearing an Oklahoma basketball uniform and a little cowboy hat standing on top of a basketball hoop with the back end of a redhawk sticking out of its mouth. It said BOOMER SOONER in crimson letters. And there were women's sizes, thank god.

"How much?" Mad asked.

"Fifteen bucks," the lady said, and Mad paid her.

"Oh, how cool!" Rube said, butting in. He laughed at the image. "Wait, who's that dog?" Rube asked the woman.

"That's Top Daug," she said—like, *duh*—and didn't elaborate, and Mad hoped that Rube would let it go. Of course they knew Top Daug. Top Daug was, perhaps, their favorite mascot of all time, and that's why Mad was buying the shirt.

"Wait, is Top Daug the mascot for the Sooners?" Rube asked. "A dog? I thought it was a . . . a Sooner."

"He *was* the mascot," the lady said, and now Mad saw the little spark of fire flash in her eyes. Now Mad realized the mistake was engaging the woman, because she now opened up to Mad and Rube. "He was the basketball mascot, but they retired him a few years ago, which was the dumbest thing ever. Now it's Boomer and Sooner and they are—oh, lord—the worst."

"Are they dogs?" Rube asked.

"No!" the woman shouted. "They're horses."

"Horses?" Mad said, and regretted it instantly. "Oh, sorry, never mind."

"Horses?" Rube asked. "Why horses?"

"Well, they pull the Sooner Schooner," the woman explained, and Mad felt like she had dropped acid, but it just kept going, "and maybe that's nice on a big football field, but that's just not going to work on a basketball court."

"Of course not," Rube said.

"Can't have a giant wagon on that hardwood, you know?" the woman said.

"Their hooves, too, I'd imagine," Rube offered.

"So, to me, Top Daug is still the mascot. And he always will be."

"Amen," Rube said, and the woman actually gave him a high five.

Mad was amazed at how her brother was able to navigate these situations without fear. His emotions certainly covered a wider range of possibilities than Mad. She had witnessed the man cry more than once in a very limited span of time; other than her mom, she could not think of another human being who had ever seen her cry. But he also laughed more, seemed genuinely thrilled by, say, a dog eating a bird to express athletic dominance. So as she went back to the PT Cruiser to change into the new shirt, she thought maybe this would be good for both of them. Rube's mania would slightly expand Mad's range of emotion, but Mad's reticence, what she would call stoicism, would perhaps keep Rube from straying too far beyond the acceptable range of his own emotions. Maybe this wouldn't actually benefit either of them, but the point was that it wouldn't hurt them. They'd even each other out in a way that kept them safe. That is, if they made it to California and their father. Or stayed in touch after. Perhaps it was best not to make long-term assumptions about their relationship. Perhaps it was best to just watch their sister's game and hope for the best.

After they picked up their tickets and walked into the arena, gingerly going down the steps until they reached the fourth row at the center of the court, Mad was a little shocked at how few people there were. The arena looked like it could hold at least ten thousand people, but there was nothing close to that with thirty minutes until tip-off. There were huge gaps in the seating, but maybe it was because it was 10:30 in the morning and Texas, though close to Missouri and Oklahoma, required travel for casual fans. What it meant was that the arena would be populated with only the kind of hardcore fan who loved women's basketball so much that they scheduled their lives around it. Mad imagined that was a likelier explanation than her and Rube, who had never attended a women's basketball game in their life and were mostly here to get to see their previously unknown half sister. Mad needed to stop comparing her own situation to other people in the day-to-day moments of her search for her missing family because it would never look good in her favor. She should, even in her own brain, just let it go.

"That's her!" Rube shouted, pointing toward the court, where their sister, Pep, was casually draining three-pointers from the top of the key. Rube was about to wave, but Mad stopped him. "She probably needs to focus," Mad told him, and he relented.

The court, however, was populated with so many people. The players, of course, but also trainers and crew people and little kids who were tracking down stray shots and returning the basketballs to the players. There were camera people and sideline reporters, so much activity in the service of this single game, and there was music blaring over the speakers, graphics flashing on the four giant screens hanging above the court. There was the mascot for the opposing team, Rowdy the Redhawk, the bird being eaten whole by Top Daug on Mad's shirt, standing awkwardly at the edge of the court, bouncing nervously in time to the music. Mad wondered if it was a woman in the uniform, but imagined that, regardless of the sport, it was a man in the mascot suit. She looked for Boomer and Sooner but didn't see them anywhere. But there was Pep, slouching with the kind of casual ease that Mad had noticed from young athletes, the ability to let their bodies completely relax because they were so confident that they could snap instantly back to readiness when the moment required it. She was chewing gum, not talking to her teammates, just waiting until a ball made its way to her, magically summoned from some trainer or over-eager kid, and then she shot, assessed the shot, and went right back to strolling around the court, testing its dimensions, finding the edges of what was hers and what was everyone else's.

And then Rube's cell phone rang, and both of them instinctually looked right at Pep, who, of course, was not holding a cell phone. "Hello," Rube said, and then Mad watched as his expression turned to one of great alarm, and he looked around the arena. "Yes, madam—or ma'am, sorry— Okay. Well, okay. I mean, she invited us. Chip? Ohio? No, okay, maybe we should talk after the— Okay, row two, oh, yes, I see you waving. You want me to— Oh, okay. No, there's room. Good—" And then Rube looked at Mad. "It's Pep's mom," he said, almost hissing. "She's coming over."

"Is she angry?" asked Mad, looking across the court without spotting her. "Is she coming to beat us up?"

"It's unclear," he answered. "She is concerned that we're here. Oh, and Dad went by the name Chip with them."

"Chip? Oh, that's terrible." Her dad, who was a Chuck, did not make sense as a Chip. She imagined that for Rube, who knew his dad as the more formal Charles, especially could not imagine him as a Chip. Their dad, never making sense the minute he left your life.

"She's across the court, so we have some time because she'll— Okay, she's walking across the court. Just striding right across the court and there's no security or anything."

They noticed that Pep had turned to see her mom walking onto the court, but she immediately went back to shooting after her mom waved her off. Pep's mom was a tall woman with brown hair styled like Jane Fonda in *Klute*, a shag cut from the seventies, and appeared to be in her late forties. She was wearing a crimson cardigan sweater with an OU patch sewn on the back, with white pants that had a red stripe down the side. She looked like Mrs. Claus in a hip movie about Christmas. And then she was in front of them.

"You're Chip's kids," she said, a statement of fact. "I can see it right off."

"We're Charles Hill's children, yes," Rube said. "I'm Reuben and this is Madeline."

"Mad," Mad interjected.

"Nicknames, of course," the woman said. "Well, I'm Cathy. Cathy Permalee. And Chip was my husband. He's Pep's father."

"It's a pleasure to meet you," Rube offered.

"Terrible timing, Reuben," she said, looking past him now and fixing her gaze on Mad, who stiffened at the scrutiny. "I was prepared to really hate y'all," Cathy continued in an accent that seemed to blend southern and midwestern inflections and was hypnotic to Mad.

"Oh," Mad said, not sure how to respond.

"But I do like that shirt," Cathy said, pointing to Mad's shirt.

"Oh," Mad said, looking down. "Top Daug, yeah."

"God, I loved that dog," Cathy said, looking out toward the court, wistful, as if hoping that the dog would rappel down from the ceiling of the arena at any moment. She snapped back to the situation. "So, Pep, as you can understand, is under just a crazy amount of pressure, okay? Don't know if either of you played Division One college athletics—"

"Not us!" Rube offered.

"Well, it's real stressful. This is the culmination of Pep's entire career at Oklahoma. Her entire basketball career, which, truth be told, began with her damn dad, so there's a lot going on in her head. And she needs nothing going on in her head."

"She invited us," Rube said. "We didn't want to impose."

"Yes, she told me," Cathy said, shaking her head. "She doesn't have siblings. Not even cousins, actually. She's a little closed off, emotionally, I mean. Had to be, to be as good as she is at basketball. But y'all got her at a weird moment."

"We'll not make any trouble," Mad said.

"Any *more* trouble, thank you," Cathy replied. "But, she also said that y'all asked if her dad had ever talked to me since he left."

"He talked to our moms," Rube said. "And we didn't know."

"Well, he talked to me. Every once in a while. My birthday sometimes. But I never told Pep. It wouldn't have killed her or anything. She's unbelievably tough, but it's just not something she needed to know. And so she asked, and I lied. And I'm gonna keep lying, at least until something changes that makes me have to tell the truth."

"Okay, sorry," Rube replied.

"So drop that, okay?"

"Yes, ma'am," Mad offered.

"And she said y'all told her that you were on some kind of journey to see Chip? To track him down and confront him?"

"We are," Rube said.

"And you invited Pep?"

"Yes, we did. We didn't know about the NCAA Women's Basketball Championship. We were just stopping by to see all of his kids."

"So there's more than y'all?" she asked them, and they nodded.

"At least one more," Rube said.

"After us?" Cathy asked, and they both nodded again.

"Chip," she said softly. "I figured as much, but it still stings. Okay, anyway, Pep will not be going on that trip, okay? I am not going to keep her away from you two. If she wants you to be in her life, that's fine. But she's not driving across the damn country to meet her father after ten years. Not going to happen."

"Okay," they both said.

She took a deep breath and nodded. She observed them a little longer. "He had two whole lives before me," she said, but not to them, "and more after." She then straightened and smiled at them. "Y'all like basketball?" she then asked.

"So much!" Rube replied.

"Well, nice to meet you," Cathy offered, and then, without waiting for a reply, she strode confidently back to her seat across the court. When Mad looked up, she noticed that Pep, who had finished warming up, was watching them. Mad didn't know what to do. She waved. Pep did not wave back.

Mad sat down and leafed through the program, which listed the stats and the players and all kinds of information and she appended to it what she had learned in the hotel room for the last two days, reading newspapers about the Lady Sooners. Pep was the only senior on the team, first-team All-Big-12 for two years in a row, the team's leading scorer and had set the all-time record for threes in the Big 12. She was the captain of the team, but there was also a center named Daedra London who was a freshman and was already a star in the making and, like Pep, a Gatorade High School Player of the Year. She had just won Big 12 Player of the Year and was second in points and led the team in rebounds and had recorded a double-double in every single game of the season, which was apparently a record for a freshman. This duo was the reason that Oklahoma was a dark horse to win the entire tournament, even though they were a four seed. The Redhawks of Southeast Missouri State had needed a good run at the end of the season to even get into the tournament, but they had the leading rebounder in the country and the entire starting five were seniors. The Sooners were overwhelming favorites, and Mad was happy that they'd showed up for a first-round matchup. She could not even imagine what would have happened if they'd appeared at the finals of the

National Championship, holding up a sign that said, PEPPER, WE ARE YOUR HALF BROTHER AND SISTER FROM THE FATHER YOU HAVEN'T SEEN IN TEN YEARS AND THERE ARE MORE OF US AND WE'RE GOING TO GO CONFRONT HIM AND WOULD LOVE FOR YOU TO JOIN US IN THE PT CRUISER while she shot a free throw to tie the game.

"Here we go!" Rube said, nudging Mad, and they both clapped for the Sooners. The arena had filled up a bit, but it was still so surprising to Mad how underattended it was, how little attention anyone seemed to pay to women's basketball. And she felt a little indignant that women always lived in a tier below men and then realized that this was the first time she had ever seen a women's basketball game and, less than a week ago, she could not have named a single women's basketball player in the entire history of the sport.

Daedra London easily won the tip-off, batting the ball over to Pep, who casually dribbled across half court, gesturing to her teammates. She passed the ball, immediately darted away from her defender, used a screen from another teammate just as she got the ball back, and she put up a perfect, high-arcing shot from beyond the three-point line. It looked good from the moment it left her hand and she was already setting her feet to get back on defense when the ball just barely caught the edge of the rim and the ball rattled around the hoop and bounced back into play. Daedra went up for the rebound, fighting with the Lady Redhawks defender, and as she came down with the ball, Daedra landed on the other player's foot and her ankle turned in such a gruesome way that even from the fourth row, Mad knew that something very bad had happened. Daedra collapsed to the ground, already yelling in pain, a time-out was called, and there was dead silence in the arena as trainers ran onto the court. Pep, still stunned by the miss, looked toward the bench, her coach, and then after a few seconds passed and she realized that her teammate was injured, she huddled with her other teammates as Daedra struggled to get up, supported by two trainers. The crowd clapped that she was able to move, but Mad felt like, after what she'd seen happen, maybe they shouldn't let her hobble to the bench, then past the bench, then through a tunnel, and then into the locker room.

"She's not coming back, I don't think," Mad said to Rube, who nodded.

"That was . . . auspicious," Rube offered.

Even after the game restarted, the crowd seemed dead, afraid to cheer in case it might still be attached to the horrific injury they'd witnessed. And in that emptiness, the Lady Redhawks pushed the pace, driving to the bucket at will. And the Sooners, probably still thinking about Daedra, couldn't get back on track. Pep missed her next five shots, committed a dumb foul trying to steal the ball, and then missed three more shots.

"She's missed nine straight shots," Rube offered, as if maybe the official scorekeepers for the game might not realize what was happening.

"Well, I think she's realizing that her best teammate is probably out of the rest of the tournament, so I'm sure she's trying too hard to make up for it."

"And, well," Rube said, "maybe us showing up?"

"Rube, please," Mad replied. "Please don't. I'm already feeling like shit, okay?"

"Well, I just wanted to put it out there. It's hard not to think about it."

"All she has to do is hit one shot," Mad said, and she felt her entire body begin to tense. Her chest felt tight, and she had to keep taking these deep inhalations to try and get air into her body. There was no way she could have ever done this, played in front of this many people. But she also knew that this was the tenderness of wanting a person you care about to avoid this kind of pain. For the first time in her memory, she thought about what it would be like to have a child, to have that child tell you that they wanted to play basketball, then having to attend years and years of games, each time hoping your child doesn't get hurt or ruin themselves. And maybe you felt that same tension just watching them go to school, to the arcade with friends, sitting in their room with their headphones on. Maybe every single moment of loving someone you helped make was connected to this low-level terror that hurt your heart. Is this why their father left them?

In the time it took Mad to consider all of this, to nearly have an anxiety attack in this arena while Technotronic's "Pump Up the Jam" played on the loudspeakers during a time-out, Pep had missed four more shots, picked up two more fouls, and was sent to the bench by her coach, an intense woman in an all-white pantsuit with electric-blonde hair who spent the entire time-out screaming at Pep, who took it without flinching, staring straight ahead. When the half ended, the Sooners were losing by twenty-five points and Pep was 0-13. They watched as the Sooners players limped back to the locker rooms, displaying the most aggressively defeated posture that Mad had ever seen, while the Lady Redhawks looked like they were moonwalking off the court.

And as if summoned by dark magic, while Rube was using the restroom, Cathy Permalee appeared right behind Mad, which almost made Mad scream when she turned to find the woman standing over her.

"Sorry," Cathy said. "You're pretty darn easy to scare."

"It's been a weird week," Mad lamely offered.

"Tell me about it," Cathy said, sitting in Rube's empty seat.

"I'm so sorry," Mad said again.

"Lots of time left," Cathy said. "Pep is resilient. She's driven. She'll figure it out. They might not win. Losing Daedra is pretty damn bad, but it won't stay this bad, I'll tell you that for sure."

"I hope so," Mad said.

"So my husband was your dad—shoot, sorry—*is* your dad. Pep's father, Chip, is your father . . ."

"Chuck," Mad said, filling in the gap that Cathy left.

"I'm not going to get used to that," Cathy said. "Chip was not a Chuck."

"Same here, but, you know, the opposite," Mad replied.

"He was such a strange man. He was not cruel, except for, of course, leaving me and my child and never coming back. He was a good man, and he loved us. Do you understand?"

"I do," Mad admitted. "I feel the same way. For the time he was with us, he was a good dad. Honestly, he was the best dad. I just don't understand why he left."

"I don't, either."

"Pep said that he was a basketball coach?"

"Oh, yes, he was. He was very good at it. He coached the women's basketball team at Pocola High and they won a state championship his third year at the school. And he coached Pep's rec league teams when she was a little girl."

"He was a successful basketball coach?" Mad asked. "Because, I don't know if you know, but he'd never played basketball before he came to Oklahoma."

"Well, that is very strange, but I believe that Chip could have willed himself to becoming a successful basketball coach. You know, he told me and people at the school that he had played at Ohio State. He said he'd been injured his freshman year and didn't get a chance to play and ended up quitting the team in his junior year because he couldn't play anymore. And, you know, I just didn't call Ohio State and ask for the roster to see if a redshirt freshman named Chip Hill was on the team. What a strange lie for him to tell, but also what a strange thing for a wife to fact-check when you love your husband. But after he left us, I wanted to find him and I did a little research. Nope, never played at Ohio State. So you're telling me that he never even played basketball, period and, yes, that checks out. Do not tell Pep anything about this, but I hired someone, and they told me that the Chip Hill that matched the Social Security number I had for him was still married in the state of Massachusetts. He told me he had been married long before, but said it had been brief and ended in divorce. Certainly never mentioned kids. There was a lot that didn't add up, and I decided I didn't want any of it to come back on me and my businesses and, of course, Pep. So I ignored it. And now you're here."

"That's bigamy," Mad said. "He never actually married my mom because they were hippie farmers. But if he was married to Rube's mom and you at the same time—"

"Well, we never actually got married," she admitted. "His idea. Or maybe I was okay with it. I wasn't much for marriage, but I did like companionship. Still gave Pep his last name, though, and then ran off. I am not candid with many people, but I'll probably never see you again, so I'm just going to say this. When he left, I felt like a fool, like I had been stupid for loving him. He hurt me, and I didn't like that feeling, and I wasn't going to track him down because I just wanted to forget. Wasn't good for Pep. Probably wasn't good for me. But there you go."

Mad suddenly realized that Rube had been standing in the aisle for perhaps a few minutes. He was holding a huge bucket of popcorn and a giant soda.

Cathy saw Mad staring up at Rube, and she turned and nodded at him. "I took your seat," she said. "We were gabbing."

"Sorry about the game," Rube said, but Mad and Cathy both said, in unison, "Still a lot of time left."

Cathy stood and shimmied out of the aisle. She looked at

them, appraising them, and said, "If you find Chip, and you get a sense of what your true emotions are about the situation in that moment, mention me to him. Tell him that Cathy says hi. Or if it goes bad, tell him that Cathy says to eff off forever."

"Okay," Mad said, smiling, though she could not imagine saying either thing to her dad.

As she walked away, Rube raised his eyebrows. "I missed a lot, didn't I? There was, big surprise, no line in the men's room, but the concession line was so damn slow."

"I'll fill you in later," Mad said. There were only a few minutes left before the second half began.

AS SOON AS THE SECOND HALF STARTED, PEP PLAYED WITH A KIND OF RUTHless efficiency that nearly took Mad's breath away. In less than two minutes, she had hit three consecutive threes, all from different spots on the court, one time with two players guarding her. With Daedra out, the lineup went small, trying to speed up the game, and Pep was now guarding the Redhawks' best player, a power forward, the leading rebounder in the nation, and Pep, even with three fouls, played the woman straight up, using her shiftiness to get inside to grab rebounds and move right into transition. She hit two more threes, and they were now down eleven points. The crowd was starting to amp up, fans for both teams realizing that maybe the noise that they generated might have some effect on the outcome. Rube yelled, "WHOOP!" after every shot that Pep hit, but Mad couldn't speak, could not take her eyes off of her sister, who had turned into an assassin.

Every time it seemed like the Sooners could get the deficit to single digits, the Redhawks would storm back, and with five minutes left to go, the Sooners were still down ten points and Pep had scored thirty points without missing a shot in the second half.

With four minutes left, Pep hit an off-balance runner that some-how banked in, and they were down by eight, and the entire Soon-ers bench was stomping and clapping. The Redhawks coach called a time-out, and it was strange to see how the demeanor of the teams had changed, how hard it can be, when you feel that shift in fortune, to turn it back.

"Can they do this?" Rube asked. "I mean, is this rare? Is this how the games typically go?"

"I don't think this is normal," Mad admitted, but she wasn't sure. She could not imagine that it was a regular occurrence for a team to come back from a twenty-five-point deficit and win. She imagined that someone scoring thirty-four points without miss-ing a shot after missing their first thirteen shots was unlikely, something that people would take notice of. She wondered what the announcers on ESPN were saying. It would have been nice to have that context, but Mad also knew it might be worse to have ex-perts explaining things to her, to take away any doubt that maybe Mad just wasn't attuned to the intricacies of the game. And with Pep doing what she was doing, Mad did not want to be anywhere else but in this arena, watching her sister.

Pep stripped the ball on the next possession and threw an outlet pass the length of half of the court for an easy layup. They were down six. Another miss, and Pep ran three different defend-ers into screens, her legs just constantly moving, and hit another three. And finally, after showing no emotion for the entire game, she screamed, pumped her fist, and sprinted back on defense.

With a minute left in the game, Technotronic's "Pump Up the Jam" playing again for some reason during a time-out, the Soon-ers were still down by three. The Redhawks had the ball, dribbling the shot clock down before hitting a jumper to go back up by five. With forty seconds left, Pep was now constantly double-teamed, but she shook off her defenders and raced to the corner of the court and put up an off-balance three that hit nothing but net, and both Mad and Rube screamed with elation.

"I think she can do it," Rube said, and who would disagree? The Redhawks were basically leaving every single player except Pep open, and even though her teammates could not hit anything, seemingly shocked by Pep's outburst, they were still in this game. On the inbound, the Sooners intentionally fouled and sent the Redhawks to the line. The player hit both, calmly, like they weren't in the midst of one of the most epic collapses in basketball history, and there were now fifteen seconds left and Oklahoma was down by four. Pep took the ball up the court, time ticking off, but the Redhawks swarmed her and she hit a teammate cutting for an easy layup. There were now five seconds left and they again intentionally fouled. Even though the attendance felt paltry at the start of the game, so many empty seats, Mad felt like the arena was now shaking from the noise.

Mad had never wanted anything more than for Oklahoma to win this game in her entire life. It was partly for Pep, but it was also to absolve her of the guilt of maybe having caused this series of events. Beyond all of that, she just wanted to be present for something so surprising that you could not believe it if you weren't there. She wanted something magical, and she was starting to believe it was possible.

The Redhawks player, who had previously hit both free throws under pressure, missed the first shot and she hung her head immediately, like this was her fate and she could only play it out. Mad watched Pep, and her sister's hands were at her sides, her fingers wiggling like she was casting a magic spell, so much energy and wildness vibrating inside of her. The player set for the last foul shot and it clanged badly off the rim, bounced off the hands of a Redhawks player, and somehow ended up with one of Pep's teammates. The clock was ticking, and Pep raced to receive an outlet pass, and the entire Redhawks team looked like the Keystone Cops, just wildly moving in all directions, bumping into each other. Pep tried to get close enough for a desperation heave and just as she was in the motion of shooting, just past the half-court line, the buzzer went off, and then Pep released the shot, which banked off the backboard and fell in. Rube and Mad, who had been standing, threw their arms into the air with elation, not sure of what had exactly happened. Every player on the court except for Pep fell to the ground like their batteries had been yanked out of their bodies, exhausted, the game over. The referees frantically waved off the shot, signaling that it had come less than half a second too late to count, and Pep stood at half-court, defiant, looking up at the scoreboard as if to confirm something she couldn't quite accept. She nodded, brought her closed fists up to her forehead, centering herself. And she then walked to each teammate, pulled them up off the court, hugged them, and walked past the cacophony of celebrating Redhawks and their fans, down the tunnel, and disappeared.

"Fuck," Rube finally said.

Mad still could barely breathe, her chest so tight, the sadness of not getting what you wanted, the acceptance that life goes on. It was a lot. You live on a farm your entire life, spending your life with chickens who have an interior life that is a mystery to you, and then you set off on a quest to find your missing dad and you feel the static electricity of touching someone who shares your DNA, and you maybe ruin their life, and you maybe ruin your own life. Isn't that a lot? Isn't that maybe too much for Saturday afternoon in the Frank Erwin Center in Austin, Texas?

"Do you think Dad watched the game?" she asked.

"I don't know what would be worse," he replied. "But I hope he did. I hope he saw what Pep did without him."

The crowd was starting to filter out of the arena, making their way down the aisles, but Rube and Mad couldn't bring themselves to move. Cathy was no longer in the section with the other Sooner fans, and there was still a fair amount of activity on the court, sideline reporters finally getting to do their job. There was another first-round game coming up, and Mad watched as fans dressed in their own unique colors, toting signs, had arrived early to watch warm-ups, and it was strange to see all that unblemished anticipation right after such a crushing disappointment. She almost hated them, somehow wanted both teams to lose, and then she got a handle on her emotions, which never took long if she tried hard enough, and she hoped that the two teams stayed tied, overtime after overtime after overtime until the sun burned out and the world ended.

"I guess it's time to go," Rube said.

"Where?" Mad asked.

"West," he said, like they were Lewis and Clark. "Just keep going, right?"

"She was amazing," Mad said.

"Really amazing."

"I like her, our sister."

"Me, too. But we have to keep going."

"I know. But, like, maybe just a few more minutes. There's still a lot of Redhawks fans milling around and I don't want them to make fun of my shirt."

"I totally understand," Rube told her. He put his arm around her, the first spontaneous sign of affection between them, and it didn't seem as strange as Mad imagined it would be. She leaned against him. It was good to hold on, to steady each other as the world spun. And then they would go. They would keep going.

JUST AS THEY PULLED OUT OF THE PARKING LOT NEAR THE ARENA AND BE-gan driving back to the hotel, Rube's phone rang. "Shit," Rube said. "Hold on." They were stuck in traffic and he was trying to turn against the light, so he handed the phone to Mad. "Could you answer it?"

"Hello," Mad said. "This is Rube's phone, but this is Mad."

"I wanna come with you," Pep said.

"Wait, what?"

"Can you come get me? Like, right now?"

"You want to come with us? You want to go find Dad?"

"Yeah," Pep said. "But you gotta come get me, like, right now."

"Okay, shit, okay. Where are you?"

"I'm hiding right across from the arena. I'm at the School of Nursing Building. There's, like, a bridge or something, and I'm standing near it."

"Oh, Pep, are you . . . you're not . . . you're not going to jump off the bridge, are you?"

"What? Are you fucking crazy? Of course not."

"Okay! Okay, sorry," Mad said. At this point, Rube tried to get the phone back.

"Let me handle this," he said. "I have experience with this kind of thing." Mad didn't want to get into it with her brother, but she thought he was referring to his own breakdown after the death of his mother and she wasn't sure that was the kind of expertise required in this situation. And, plus, Pep had emphatically stated that she wasn't going to do anything.

"Hello?" Pep said.

"Yes, I'm here," Mad said, slapping Rube's hand. "Hang on, Pep. Rube? Turn around. Go back to the arena. Look for the School of Nursing."

Rube nodded and Mad stayed on the phone with Pep. "You want to come with us?" she asked. "You're sure?"

"Our season is over," she said. "My college career is over. I might never play basketball again. I don't want to go back to

Oklahoma right now. I don't want to get on the bus with my team and sit there the whole time thinking about all this. I told my coach about my dad, about the situation . . . well, kind of. Broad strokes, you know? And I told my mom and she is mad at me, but she can't stop me. So I'm coming with you. I want to see Dad. If you guys will take me with you, I'll come."

"We do want you to come with us," Mad said. "I'm sorry it's like this, though."

"Just hurry," Pep said. "I feel weird out here, just standing here in the middle of the day in my tracksuit, and I think the cops might think I'm up to no good."

"Okay, we're almost there," Mad said, without checking to see if it was true. "You were so good, Pep. That was like nothing I've ever seen."

"We lost," Pep said.

"Still. You were incredible."

"For half the game, yeah. But, thank you. I was really good. Yes."

"I see her," Rube said. "Tell her I see her. I'm waving. Tell her we're in a PT Cruiser."

"I can hear him," Pep said. "I see the car. I'm running to it right now. Don't worry about parking. Just let me get in."

"Do you have luggage or, like, your duffel bag?" Mad asked.

"No, I just peaced out of there. It was so fast, and—here, just let me—"

Mad could hear Pep breathing hard on the phone and then she saw her, running from the bridge over to the street, and Rube slowed down so that Pep opened the door and jumped into the car in one fluid motion and then they just kept going, caught in the flow of traffic.

"That felt like a bank robbery!" Rube explained. "I'm the wheelman and Pep was the robber and, Mad, you were, like, the lookout."

RUN FOR THE HILLS   91

"I'm starving," Pep said.

"Okay," Mad replied. "We can get something."

"Drive a little," Pep said. "Then take me to whatever fast-food place you can find. I don't have any money, by the way."

"It's on me," Rube said.

"I'm going to eat so much," Pep announced, and then she slumped into the seat, looking out the window, no doubt realizing that she'd jumped into a PT Cruiser with two people whom she had not known existed a few days previous. It was a lot to think about, Mad understood. They drove in silence, and Mad, still the lookout, searched for a place suitable for her sister to feast.

AFTER FIFTEEN MINUTES OF DRIVING, THEY FOUND A PLACE CALLED DAN'S Hamburgers, a diner where they could sit down and reimagine the future. Mad marveled as Pep confidently, without any money, strode up to the cashier and ordered a double cheeseburger ("with hickory sauce?" the woman asked, which Pep allowed), an order of onion rings, a grilled cheese sandwich, a Coke, and a strawberry milkshake. "Thank you," Pep said to Rube, and then she went to an empty booth and sat sideways, taking up the entire bench, propping her head against the window.

Rube looked at the cashier and said, "One small Coke, please," and Mad felt like she should order food so Pep didn't feel strange, so she ordered some curly fries, and Rube paid and they both turned to Pep, who still seemed dazed by the events of the day. Mad tried to calculate every single thing that had happened to her since the morning, and it was overwhelming, so strange that eating a ridiculous amount of fast food in a booth with your newly discovered family was not even at the top of the list.

Mad also considered just how young Pep was, only twenty-one years old, and realized that Rube, at forty-four, could have been her father. She hadn't done the math on it, and with all the things she had learned recently, she wasn't even sure if she knew how old her father really was. He could have been some bush-league Greek god or a vampire. You had to keep an open mind, not adhere too closely to what you thought was true, when it came to her father. You had to accept that your father might have been an ageless con artist who had sold his soul to the devil. Anything was possible.

But if she did the math correctly, her father was twenty-three when Rube was born, and thirty-four when she was born, which meant that he had been—oh, god—forty-five when Pep was born. And there were more kids! At least one more. Even if Mad had started at twenty-three, she did not have the ability to leave her family and set up new ones for the rest of her natural life. There would have been a biological cut-off point if she had been the one having the children. And she wouldn't have attempted it, even if it were possible, as evidenced by the fact that she was thirty-two years old and standing in Dan's Hamburgers in Austin, Texas, with her half siblings, no children of her own, living with her mom on a farm surrounded by chickens, sleeping in her childhood bed.

"We have to go over there," Rube said, "even if you're scared of her."

"I'm not scared of her."

"I am," he said. "Though I was also a little scared of you when we first met."

"She's scarier than me," Mad admitted.

Just then, Pep looked up at them and arched her eyebrow, as if knowing they were talking about her, but, like, why wouldn't they be? Who else would they be talking about other than the girl who literally hopped into their still-moving car and asked them to kidnap her?

"You go on over," Rube said. "I'm going to wait for the food to be called."

"I think they might bring it—"

"I'll just wait for it," he said. "Go on."

Right when Mad sat down, Pep said, "I'm going to be honest with you," and Mad nodded so that Pep could continue. "I'm honestly, like, trying to make sure this isn't a dream."

"I don't think it is. I mean—oh, god—it's not a dream. Okay? This is real."

"I keep thinking that maybe I died when I went back to my dorm, right before you guys called me. I think that maybe the elevator collapsed and I'm dead and everything that happened after is, like, my body making peace with it." Pep looked completely and totally emotionless as she was saying this, like she was testing the limits of reality and was not going to freak out over her own death if she didn't have to. "And so meeting you guys and learning about my dad and playing in the tournament and Daedra breaking her ankle and losing that game and getting in the car with you and sitting at this restaurant, it's all just a dream. I know you were worried about me on the bridge, but actually I was kind of thinking about it then. And I was like, how would I know?"

Mad was about to console her sister, but then she thought for a second. She remembered that moment when the PT Cruiser drove to the farm. Maybe, in the seconds before Rube appeared, she'd had a brain embolism and died. And that would mean that all this was her brain making peace with it. And Rube had come and told her this story about their dad and then met their sister and traveled to see her play in a huge arena in a NCAA tournament game and now here she was. And—oh, god—maybe Rube had died when he'd set fire to his father's books, and they were all part of *his* death spiral dream.

"I'm pretty sure this is real," Mad finally said, but she had never sounded less sure of anything in her entire life.

Rube showed up with a tray piled high with food that was

almost entirely for Pep. "What are you two talking about?" he asked.

"Just getting to know each other," Mad said, and Pep nodded.

Rube pushed the food over to Pep, who immediately took the largest bite of a burger that Mad had ever witnessed, and the hickory sauce that drenched the burger spilled down Pep's chin like she'd bitten into a blood capsule, and Pep smiled, chewing slowly, nodding in affirmation of something that seemed so important.

"I think this is real," Pep finally said to Mad, and then she wiped the sauce off her chin with a napkin.

"What's real?" Rube asked. "The burger?"

"Yeah," Pep said. "The burger is real. I know it is. I know it now."

"I was over there for, like, eight minutes," Rube said. "Did something happen?"

"Did you guys not order anything to eat?" Pep said, now suspicious again.

Mad reached for the curly fries. "No! I got these curly fries. I'm eating."

"I wasn't hungry," Rube said, confused.

"Try a fry," Mad said to Rube, pushing a fry in his face, and Rube ate it.

"Mmmm," he said, as if trying to decipher from Mad's facial expressions what was going on. "That's real, yes."

The burger was gone, and Pep had moved on to the onion rings, alternating between sips of the Coke and the shake.

When Pep finished her shake, took a deep breath, and leaned back in the booth, she then told them about her dad. He'd come to Oklahoma and was doing community outreach for a church, doing construction work, working in kitchens, and he met her mother, Cathy, who was a waitress at her parents' diner, which actually wasn't that different from this one that they were now sitting in. And they got married, and then her mom and dad got a Sonic franchise, and it did well, and then her dad, who had been a star player in high school, started coaching youth basketball in the area and ended up getting a job at the little high school in Pocola when the head coach had a heart attack and retired in the middle of the season. Pep was smiling now, talking about him.

She told them how he completely changed the way the Lady Chiefs played basketball, getting rid of all the set shots and stationary plays and instituted a wildly aggressive and attacking style of play that was a little flashy, teaching the girls to do no-look passes and fallaway jumpers and cutting quickly to the rim and doing finger rolls. He had the center sometimes play as a point guard. Pep said she would come to all the practices when she was four and five and six and the girls all treated her like royalty because her dad had led them to their first winning season in six years.

She said that her mom kept buying more Sonic franchises, and she now had eleven, and that meant they had a lot of money, lived well, and their dad was coaching and it was a good life. He won a state championship when Pep was eight, and then, less than a year later, before the next season started, he was gone. She came home from grade school and her mom said that their dad left a note that he had to go away. "And Mom," she continued, "who I think was as clueless as I was, was getting all these questions from people because, you know, he was a big deal in our little town, and she finally said, after three months, that my dad was in rehab and that he was going to then spend a year working on a ranch in Wyoming to try and stay sober. And I never understood why she'd make up a lie like that, because my dad didn't even drink that much, but now I guess it was easier to say this bad thing instead of saying, like, 'my husband left us without warning and we don't know where he is and I'm realizing I don't even know all that much about him.' And then my mom admitted that she and my dad had never actually been married. Like, they were just living together. She said my dad didn't believe in marriage, that he'd had a really bad first marriage a long time ago when he was young and it hadn't lasted, and so he didn't want to do it again. And my mom was actually okay with this, partly because she was an independent lady and always had been and didn't want him to have ownership of her businesses. I never knew. They celebrated their anniversary, but it was just the day they met. I guess they just kind of forgot?"

So the only person he'd ever actually married was Rube's mom. And he was, perhaps, still married to her. Well, no, she was dead. He was a widower. If he was still alive. It made Mad so confused to think about it.

Pep took another breath; it was clear that she hadn't talked about this. Of course not. Neither had Mad. Neither had Rube, except to his therapist and, Mad allowed, his private detective. It was strange, but it was almost easier to tell the story of their dad when you knew that every version ended the same way.

"And Mom was emphatic that if my dad didn't want to be with us, then we wouldn't think about him or waste any time feeling bad about it. And she was good at it, or it looked like it to me. But I did want to feel bad about it, you know? And I loved basketball because he'd made me love basketball, and it wasn't like I was going to stop just because he'd left. I was so good at it. So I don't know. I guess I just had to pretend he'd never existed. And no one in town asked about it because it was just so insane that my dad had left us and never come back. I don't know how to explain it."

"We get it," Rube said.

"And we're really going to find him?" Pep asked.

"He's in California," Rube said. "At least, that's what I think."

"This is so weird," she said. "But, like, you said there are other kids?"

"Yes," Rube said, "there's another kid in Utah. He was in Utah after he . . . you know . . . after he left you."

"So we're going to go see him?" Pep asked.

"I think so," Rube said. "It's tricky. I mean, he's still a kid, you know? We can't, like, take him with us. But we can meet him and his mom and, like, let them know what's going on."

"That feels pretty heavy," Pep said.

"I guess it is," Rube allowed. And then Mad realized that they would be knocking on the door and asking to talk to a child. Three adults standing on the porch, explaining that they all had the same dad but that he had different names and different professions and how would they not get arrested? She'd been so focused on Pep, the terror of meeting someone and telling them the truth. She hadn't even expected any of this to work. But they had to be careful now. They were getting closer and closer to the blast impact of their father, people who were still getting over the fact that he had left them.

"We gotta, like, call the mom," Pep said. "We have to get permission, you know?"

"I mean, yes, of course," Rube said. "We will call her."

"But not like you guys called me," Pep told them. "Because that was fucked up. You had clearly not practiced. You gotta practice, you know?"

"We'll practice," Rube said, his skin blushing so hard and Mad realized that, of course Rube had not thought this through. They would practice. They would go through the proper channels. They would have a parent or guardian present at all times. Maybe they could use puppets or something?

"Maybe I should do it," Pep said. "You guys are, no offense, older. I think the mom will handle it better if I talk to her."

"Well, these are all good points," Rube allowed, "and we can figure it out later. But we should probably get back to the hotel. It's been, good lord, such a long day."

Mad remembered that Pep had no luggage, and she wondered if Pep would feel weird sharing clothes with her. She wouldn't ask right now. They would figure it out. Every step of the way, even if there were awkward moments and disaster and everything seemed doomed, they would work together and somehow they'd get to where they needed to be. There was, Mad was realizing, strength in numbers.

**

HER NEWLY DISCOVERED HALF SISTER HAD OFFERED TO SHARE CLOTHES with her, but Pep preferred having her own wardrobe. And this was perfectly reasonable under the circumstances, but Pep also had to admit that she wasn't used to sharing. On the court, yes, as a teammate in basketball, she was selfless and performed her specific role with intense focus, but in her own life, what was hers was hers alone. She was, or had been until just now, an only child. So, no, she did not want to borrow Mad's clothes, which were nothing but denim and flannel and a gigantic Oklahoma Sooners T-shirt and another one that only reminded her of the intense failure of the last collegiate basketball game of her entire life. And, even if she wanted to share the socks and panties of a woman she had just met, she needed a toothbrush, right? It was a good thing, she decided, to assert some individuality within this new dynamic, to demand some basic human privileges so it didn't feel like she was joining a cult.

Pep felt bad because it wasn't her siblings' fault that she had jumped into their car without her travel bag. It wasn't their fault that she had run off without even taking her wallet. She wished she'd at least remembered her iPod and headphones so she could listen to music in the car when they drove to Utah to meet *another* sibling. She had wanted to call her mom again and ask her to wire her some money, or to call a teammate and ask them if they remembered to grab her duffel bag from the locker room when they left and maybe they could meet her somewhere in the western United States and return her ID and credit cards to her. But that would mean answering the numerous calls from all of these people and explaining what was going on, what she was feeling, why she was doing what she was doing. She had no idea why she was doing this. She had no idea what was going on. To admit this to the people in her life who most cared about her was so unpleasant that she decided it was better to beg her siblings for money so she could buy some sweatpants.

Before she had called Rube and Mad, standing on that bridge, Pep had called her own mother to say that she was going to find her dad. And her mom, who was so capable and pragmatic, tried to explain why this was a bad idea, that she had just experienced the end of her college basketball career and she was struggling to come to terms with that. She called what Rube and Mad were doing "a road trip" and even though she kind of hated those two weird people who had appeared on her college campus, she didn't appreciate her mom thinking they were two weird people. It seemed unfair that after the game had ended, this crushing disappointment, her brother and sister got to jump in a car and go find their dad together, and she had to go back to Oklahoma and sit in a crowded lecture hall with kids who didn't even really care about women's basketball if it didn't result in a championship that they could celebrate with couch burning and drinking. She would be all alone, wondering where they were, if they had found their dad. And so she told her mom that she was going with them, and she spoke as harshly as she'd spoken to her mother in years, and it made her mother relent, to make Pep promise to be careful, to call her with updates. And Pep had agreed because she wanted to get off the damn phone with her mom and find Rube and Mad. And she had not called her back.

While Mad stayed behind to talk to her own mom on the phone, like any good daughter would, considering their moms were the ones who had not run off and started a series of new families, Pep and Rube went to a mall, and she quickly picked out a wardrobe that wasn't too expensive and provided enough options to allow for all the new experiences she would be walking into. The key was comfort, flexibility, so that if she had to jump right back out of that moving car or run across the vast desert plain to chase down their half brother, or get into a fistfight with her dad, she was ready for it. And she was grateful that Rube, who was paying for all of this, didn't seem to think any of this was weird and in fact seemed fairly excited about it. He acted like it was an important milestone, to take your half sister to a store for clothes and then to a drugstore for tampons and a toothbrush and a hairbrush and then to an electronics store for a charger for her phone. Each time, when the cashier rang up her purchases and Rube handed over his credit card, Pep said, "I'll pay you back," and Rube just smiled and nodded, and Pep thought that, no, she probably wouldn't pay him back. Her presence was the payment, right?

She thought about her dad all the time, but it was because she thought about basketball all the time. Her fundamentals, at such an early age, had been shaped by the calm voice of her dad, who never shouted at his players or denigrated their abilities. She loved that, as a little kid, the way the older girls respected her dad, listened to him. Even now, in high-stakes college games, after having been coached by top-flight AAU and high school and college coaches, she found that she fell back on the things her father had taught her. It was why, when he left, she had felt so confused, so distraught. He loved basketball. She was so fucking good at basketball. Why wouldn't he stick around to see her play? And when he'd left, what had also confused Pep was that he didn't take anything with him that she thought would have mattered. His huge binders of plays and strategies, his books on basketball theory, his freaking whistle that the girls had bought him, plated in gold, when they won state. All of it he left behind. And for a few years, she would pore over those plays, drawn up in his own precise handwriting, and she remembered how much he loved this, charting out the flow of a game and then seeing how it worked in real time and how much he would adjust with each new substitution, every time a player graduated or quit. It was like chemistry to him, or alchemy, and it was still how Pep thought of the game, this alchemical mixture that required human bodies to make it work. And she made sure that whatever she did on the court turned to gold.

Pep had been mystified by her siblings' lack of awareness of how the internet worked, how little they had searched for him online, but Pep was of a generation that had lived with the internet and with technology, and so she searched often for him. She had been confident that he would turn up, that she would find some article from a newspaper in Minnesota about a new high school basketball coach named Chip Hill, but she never found it. She would search "chip hill basketball girls," but it was a dead end.

Another thing he had left behind, and Pep had always convinced herself that it was on purpose, a sign to her and her alone, was his key to the high school gymnasium. And Pep wore that key on a string around her neck at all times, would let herself into the gym at all hours of the day and night, shooting baskets sometimes until the sun came up and it made more sense just to sleep on the bleachers before classes started. And then one day, when a new principal had come to the school in Pep's sophomore year, he had noticed her one evening as he was leaving the school, and he told her that this was a liability issue and it wasn't safe for her to be in the gym without supervision. He said that she was technically trespassing and that trespassing was an infraction that could result in suspension. He demanded the key, so Pep threw it across the hardwood, where it skittered to his feet, and when she went home that night, crying uncontrollably, which was so unlike her, her mom pulled her from the school and they rented a house in another town, and she had not even returned to Pocola for her books, which for all she knew were still in her locker. The coach and principal at Howe agreed that she could have a key to the gym, could come whenever she wanted, because she was an All-State player as a sophomore and they had been losing to Pocola since her dad had taken over as coach. And every single time they played her old school, even though she had nothing against her former teammates or her coach, she absolutely lit their asses on fire. And she knew her dad would have approved.

And now, driving back to the hotel room, preparing for what came next, she thought back to her last game, that final shot. She had been so angry with herself after the way she had collapsed in the first half, how terribly she had played once her teammate broke her ankle. But she had locked in, partly because she knew that her brother and sister were in the crowd, watching her, and she wanted them to know how good she was, how fucking amazing she was at this game. And she lit it up, turned into a killer. And during the time-outs, when her coach was scrambling to adjust to the situation, as her teammates shouted encouragement, she wasn't listening at all. She was thinking about her dad. He had always said, from the very beginning, that winning and losing did not matter in sports at all. In so many ways, he had told his teams, the outcome is out of your hands. Sometimes the other team is just too good and you're going to lose. Sometimes you get unlucky bounces; small, tiny reversals that change the entire trajectory of a single game or even a season. And so you could be happy when you won and sad when you lost, but that ultimately would not matter. All that mattered was that within the confines of that game, on the court, you did everything that you could and you played as well as possible, and you pushed yourself to excel and to get better and to thrive under the pressure. Because sports, he told them, was fleeting. There would come a time when it would go away, when you wouldn't be able to play it any longer, not in the same way, with the same intensity. So you held on to it in the moment, put everything you had into playing alongside these people you loved, and you wanted to keep doing it after the game was over, that was what mattered. Every single game, he told them, every moment of your life, is just putting in the effort so that you can hold on to what you love for as long as you possibly can.

And he had left her. And he had left Rube. And he had left Mad. And he had left this kid in Utah. And what did that mean? Had he not loved it enough to hold on to it? She wanted to ask him. She wanted to know the answer.

The game was almost over, one more free throw and then she would have one last chance to score. And she would never know, would she? In that moment, in the scramble for the rebound, when she set her feet, got that pass, and scampered up the court for that final shot, had she held on to the ball just a split second too long on purpose? Had she hesitated, knowing she was absolutely going to drain this shot, because she wanted the game to be over, the tournament to be over, the season to be over, her career to be over, so that she could join her brother and sister in that car and track down their dad? She didn't think so. Her dad had said it all the time, how there are tiny factors that you can't account for that will change the outcome of a single game. And all you could do was know that you'd put in the effort to make it worthwhile. And it had been. Pep knew that much. It was worthwhile.

1994, FORT SMITH, ARKANSAS, DIGITAL STANDARD—DEFINITION VIDEO

Opening shot of a sign attached to a white picket fence that reads: PLEASE KEEP OFF THE GALLOWS. RESPECT IT AS AN INSTRUMENT OF JUSTICE. The camera pans up to follow a set of stairs behind the fence before pulling back even more to reveal a huge white structure that, if it wasn't referred to in the sign as the gallows, would look like a bandstand or stage. The sound of wind constantly flickers in the background, but there is also a rhythmic, steady thumping sound. There is a woman's voice that suddenly exclaims, "Eighty-six executions in twenty-three years! That's simply too many executions. My god. Arkansas. What can you do?"

The camera spins 180 degrees to settle on a young girl wearing maroon track pants and black Air Jordan 8 sneakers. She has a white long-sleeved Nike T-shirt that reads MR. ROBINSON SAYS ALWAYS USE YOUR ELBOWS! She is bouncing a basketball on the dirt and the same woman's voice says, "Pep, the ghosts of Fort Smith do not want to hear that racket." The girl rolls her eyes and practices her jump shot, letting the ball roll off her fingertips and arcing above her before falling back into her hands. "I'm staying off the gallows," she tells her mother.

The next shot is inside a gymnasium, as the girl, who looks younger than the other players, calmly dribbles past her defender and then puts up a floating shoot that easily falls through the hoop. She looks over to the camera and nods. After a miss, she catches an outlet pass and, rather than dribbling in for a layup, stops at the three-point line and pauses for a second before putting up an awkward line-drive shot that passes through the net with such force that it makes a ripping sound, and the filmmaker can be heard shouting his approval. The girl looks at the camera, nods, and then smiles, holding up three fingers.

After the game, as the people file out of the gymnasium into the parking lot, the setting sun has turned the sky a deep shade of pink. The girl is carrying a trophy nearly the same size as her. The camera follows the girl and her mother as the two of them hold on to each other, until the camera loses focus and the scene ends.

CHAPTER FIVE

Mad was moving into uncharted territory. In terms of geography, she realized she was the only one who was new to the western part of the United States. Pep had been to Salt Lake in 2004 when they played the Lady Utes. Rube had been to the same city on his first book tour. They had both been to California multiple times. They most likely could not count the number of times they had been on a plane. Their work made travel necessary, while Mad could barely imagine an overnight trip to Nashville, the amount of planning and worry rendering the whole enterprise not worth the effort. And, yet, here she was in the PT Cruiser, with her brother and sister, and the number of times that she had the urge to jump out of the moving car had lessened considerably in the last few hours.

Rube and Mad had been chastened by how Pep had regarded them with incredulity about their plan to simply show up in Utah and ask to see a child. In their defense, the plan had been working (weren't all three of them in the PT Cruiser at this very moment?), so they hadn't realized the need to adjust in order to account for the variations of their circumstances. For instance, their sibling was a child, a minor. He was young enough to be the son of either Rube or, Mad shuddered to realize, herself. This was the unintended consequence of their father's continual reinvention. By the time they discovered their father somewhere in California, they would not look like a group of siblings. They would look like a nuclear family, with Rube as the dad and Mad as the mom and Pep and this boy their children. And their father, Mad realized, would look like their grandfather. She imagined all of them sitting for a portrait at the JCPenney, the resulting image, in a gold frame, confusing every single person who looked at it.

The boy that they hoped to meet, hopefully without accruing some strange criminal charges that would hamper their desire to enter into new careers if they followed in their father's footsteps, was named Theron, and he was a fifth-grader at Beacon Heights Elementary. That was pretty much all the information that they had, and it was embarrassingly comforting to Mad to know that she was not the least famous sibling in the family. Theron was not the youngest brain surgeon in America or the star of a TV show about the youngest brain surgeon in America or even just in med school studying brain surgery. Yes, she'd had a twenty-one-year head start, but she had definitely accomplished more than little Theron. He was just a regular kid in Salt Lake City, Utah, and Mad was not going to be intimidated by him.

A FEW DAYS EARLIER, IN A HOTEL ROOM IN ALBUQUERQUE, NEW MEXICO, THE three of them listened on speaker as Pep called the number provided by Rube's private detective in order to speak to Trista Goudy, a thirty-five-year-old woman who had been their father's fourth partner. Trista Goudy was the anchor for *Good Morning, Utah* for KTVX, Channel 4 in Salt Lake City. There was an image from a local magazine that the detective had included in the materials, and Trista was blonde and put together in the way that all people who spend a lot of time in front of cameras must be. She was wearing a pearl necklace that looked like it had fifteen layers to it, just a ridiculously ostentatious piece of jewelry, and her eyes were disconcertingly wide open. Perhaps it translated more effectively if you were looking at her while she was seated behind an ostentatious desk that looked like a sci-fi movie and she was talking about a gunman on the loose in the early hours of the morning.

"Goudy residence," a child's voice said.

"Oh, god," Pep replied, looking frantically at Mad and Rube.

"Hello?" the voice said. "Who's there?"

"This is Pep—Patsy, excuse me. This is Patsy Kleinfeld, and I'm looking for your mom. Or, like, Trista Goudy? I'm trying to get in touch with Trista Goudy."

"Oh, okay," the voice said. Pep balled her hands into fists, so exasperated with herself for getting rattled, but then she relaxed.

"Hello," a voice said, and it was clearly Trista.

"Hi, yes, hello," Pep said. "Is this Trista Goudy?"

"Are you selling something, or, like, is there a problem?" Trista asked.

Pep looked at Mad and Rube and shook her head, defeated, realizing that, despite her earlier confidence, there was no good way to do this.

"My name is Pepper Hill, and I'm calling because my father was Chip Hill. Or maybe you knew him as Charles Hill or Chuck Hill or something like that. But, anyways, he was my dad and he left our family. And he ended up with you."

"Oh, sweetie," Trista replied. "He's not here. He left a few years ago. And I'm not sure where he is."

"Oh, no, we know that. He left you," Pep said, nodding, but Trista's voice took on a strange tone as she replied, "Well, no, not really. I left him. How old are you?"

"I'm an adult," Pep replied, her voice cracking just the slightest bit. "I'm twenty-one."

"Oh, okay," Trista said. "Well, your dad and I were together, but it didn't work out. I did not know about you, I promise. And, look, I'm so sorry, but this is a lot to do over the phone, and I was actually about to head to an appointment. Do you want to leave me your number? Would you like to talk about this? Or did you just want me to know?"

"I have two other siblings," Pep said. "From earlier families. My dad, I mean. He had a bunch of kids. We all have different moms. Um, it's harder to explain than I thought it would be. They're actually here with me."

"Hi!" Rube said. "Sorry, I know this is awkward."

"Yes! It is," Trista said, her voice beginning to show signs of irritation or suspicion. Up to this point, she had been doing a good job of managing the situation.

"And you have a son," Pep said.

"Tom," Trista replied.

Mad wondered why you'd even saddle a kid with a weird name like Theron and then just start calling him Tom. Like, name him Thomas, right? Though perhaps Trista had demanded Theron. Maybe it was a very popular Mormon name or something, not that Trista was Mormon, or there was no evidence other than the fact that she lived in Utah. The point was, Mad realized, maybe the moms picked the names and their dad amended them to something he liked more. She should ask her mom. Why had she not asked her mom a very simple question like, "Hey, is Madeline a common name in your family, Mom? What is the origin of my name, Mom?" Why did she not ask? Why did she not want to know everything about herself, how she was made?

"Wait, how do you know this?" Trista continued.

"We've been searching for our father," Rube said. "It's not been easy, but I've managed to find out more information about him, which is how I found out about you and Tom."

"Because Tom's dad is also our dad," Pep continued.

There was silence, and Mad realized how suspicious this

would seem, to randomly call someone and mention the name of their child. She thought Trista might hang up at any moment.

"Could we meet with you?" Mad asked suddenly.

"Is that another one of you?" Trista asked, and they had her back.

"Yes, sorry. But that's it. There are three of us here."

"And we're driving across the country," Pep continued.

"We're in New Mexico," Rube said. "I started in Boston, which is where our dad started his own life. And I picked up Mad in Tennessee and then Pep was in Oklahoma."

"Wow, that's a long way to come," Trista admitted.

"And he's in California," Rube said, "if you didn't know."

"I didn't," Trista admitted. "Well, okay, if you have been driving across the country, I feel like I can't stop you. You're not going to make trouble, are you? I know it may not seem like a huge deal to you, but I'm a well-known person in Salt Lake City, and I have worked hard to build this life and achieve these things, and I don't want a bunch of Carl's children showing up and making a big scene."

"Carl?" Mad asked.

"Yes, Carl Hill."

"We're not going to make a scene," Pep replied. "We just want to talk to you and get some information, and we'd like to meet Tom."

"Well, I'd have to ask Tom. He is very much an independent-minded person, and he would have to agree to that. I try to let Tom kind of determine his own path, because—it's complicated—but I let other people guide my life when I was a kid and it did not go well. Why don't you leave me your number, and I will be in touch once Tom has made a decision."

"Thank you, Trista," Rube said. "This is all very reasonable and we're so grateful." He gave Trista his phone number and she wrote it down.

"Safe travels," Trista replied, and then she hung up.

Pep looked at Mad and Rube, shaking her head. "I did a bad job, didn't I?"

Rube shook his head. "You did great!" he said. "We got what we wanted, didn't we? Don't worry about the execution, okay? Worry about the result, and the result is that we get to meet our brother."

"Maybe," Mad offered. "He has to decide."

"How do you not worry about the execution?" Pep interrupted, still thinking about Rube's comment. "I actually don't think the end result matters as much as the execution."

"Pep?" Rube said, still smiling. "I'm just trying to make you feel better because you seem a little shaken up by the phone call. You said your name was Patsy Kleinfeld. I didn't want to make a big deal about it."

"If you start a new life," Mad offered, "you could be Patsy Kleinfeld."

Pep frowned. They were all getting accustomed to having siblings who might gently tease you in order to make you feel better. Mad was getting accustomed to saying anything that might be playful. They'd figure it out. They still had a long way to go. By the time they made it to the Pacific Ocean, they'd have so many inside jokes and complicated handshakes that their dad would be terrified of them.

MANAGING FOOD PREFERENCES WAS DIFFICULT. MAD WAS NOT USED TO EAT—ing anything that she hadn't made herself, and most of it things she had grown. And Rube ate at a rotating set of familiar restaurants for almost every single meal back in Boston. Pep, on the other hand, who would one day inherit an obscene number of Sonic fast-food franchises, seemed to exist entirely on food that was prepared

in under sixty seconds. Gas station breaks consisted of Mad decid-
ing between a brown banana or a five-dollar package of unsalted
almonds, while Rube bought things that required two hands,
fancy cups of yogurt or packages of hummus with a separate com-
partment of pretzels, so that the two women had to sit in the PT
Cruiser while he fastidiously enjoyed his expensive snacks because
Mad and Pep were still not allowed to drive the PT Cruiser. Pep, on
the other hand, walked out of the gas station with multiple bags of
Skittles and every single item that had spent its time in the store
spinning on metal rollers. If they stopped for a meal, Mad voted for
barbecue, because she was interested in the brisket and sausages
out west, felt like it was a meal that someone invested time and
effort into making, while Rube wanted an eclectic café, and Pep
always voted for Sonic, though she admitted that there weren't as
many this far west. So they rotated. Mad worried that if the child
somehow joined the expedition, it would delay her own food choice
by one extra meal. When your whole world consisted of a retro-
styled compact car increasingly populated by your previously unknown half siblings, traveling further and further into uncharted
territory, you relied on anything that kept you tethered to the person you had once been. And for Mad, in this moment, it was eating
some kind of meat that had smoked for hours and hoping that the
restaurant made their own coleslaw. She did admit, however, that
Sonic had amazing drinks, strange soda combinations with tiny
bits of crushed ice and cherries and slices of lime tossed in. And
sometimes, yes, it was nice to eat a congealed salad served by a
very old lady. You could expand your horizons as long as you occasionally got to run right back to the only thing you really knew.

AS DUSK SETTLED AROUND THE PT CRUISER, HAVING MADE IT THROUGH THE
traffic of Albuquerque, Mad suggested that they stop for the night.

Pep had been reading Rube's second novel, having deemed the first one to be satisfying, but she was now asleep in the backseat. Rube focused on the road, but Mad's suggestion had made him involuntarily yawn.

"We're making such good time, though," Rube told her. "I feel like we should keep driving."

"We've been in the car for so long, Rube," Mad said, but she could see a flicker of irritation from him.

"Let's just keep going. It's about two hundred miles to Durango, in Colorado, and then we're basically a day's drive to Salt Lake. I just want to get there. You can go to sleep, I'll listen to the radio."

"I'll stay up," she said. Her legs ached, and even sharing an uncomfortable hotel bed with a sister she barely knew was preferable to being stuck in the PT Cruiser. But she understood Rube's need to keep moving. The closer they got to the end, the harder it was to wait. They had spent most of their lives without their father and now they were as close as they had been to him since he left. They didn't want to lose him now.

She watched the highway, the constant movement. She tried to place Coalfield in her mind, to think of the roads they had taken to get to this very point, retracing her movements, and it instantly made her fall asleep, the sheer distance she had traveled in this passenger seat, fixed in place, getting closer and closer to her father.

A WRECK WAS THE WORST WAY TO WAKE UP. OR, NO, THE WORST WAY TO wake up was seconds before a wreck. You have time to tense your body, realize you might die, and then you hit something. This was how Mad was waking up right now, violently shifting in her seat with the sound of her brother saying, "Oh, shit, shit, shit, shit, shiiiiiiiiiiiii—" And then Mad sitting up, the seat belt restricting her with such force, it felt like she'd dislocated her shoulder, and Pep yelling, "I don't have my seat belt on—" And Rube saying, "Oh, god, we're going across—" And Mad asking, "Where are we?" as if that would somehow save her from dying. How did all this happen in a split second?

Mad watched as the PT Cruiser slid across the forty feet of grass that made up the median, the car sliding wildly as it alternately sped up and slowed down as Rube struggled to control it, and she turned to see a car in the opposite lane coming toward them at great speed. "Rube, please!" Mad yelled, and Rube said, "Oh, god! Hold on, wait. Wait—" And Mad heard the sound of the oncoming car's horn blaring. And then it was silent, a complete absence of sound, the lights of the car blinding her, and then the PT Cruiser went back off the road, bumping and shaking as it came to an awkward stop on the other side of the interstate.

"Holy shit," Pep said. "We almost died."

"Are y'all okay?" Mad asked her siblings, but no one spoke, because they probably didn't know the answer yet. Mad sensed only this surge of adrenaline that was still moving through her body. She actually felt, to be honest, like she would never die, that nothing would ever hurt her, that she was impervious to pain. She knew that in an hour or even a few minutes, this rush would wear off and her entire body would hurt, but right now, she was just going to live in this moment of not being dead.

To have died in the PT Cruiser? Good god, how humiliating. To have died on some stretch of interstate in New Mexico, in search of her missing father, would have been too embarrassing to mention at the wake, all three of them lined up in caskets at some nondenominational church, their father never even knowing what had happened to them, their moms trying to explain to well-wishers exactly what the circumstances of their deaths were.

No matter how bad being alive could feel, it was way better than the embarrassment of death.

"The engine completely stalled out," Rube said. "I was pressing the gas and then all the lights came on, and the engine just died, and then when I took my foot off the gas, it sped back up and I lost control."

"I thought we were going to die," Pep admitted.

"I know," Mad said, "it sure seemed like we were."

"I mean, for a few seconds, I just thought we were going to die," Pep said again.

"Yes, okay," Rube said. "But we didn't. Okay? We didn't die. We're okay."

"Rube," Mad said, trying to decide if it was even worth it to ask if he'd fallen asleep, "are you okay?"

"I think so," he said. "The car just went haywire."

"You fell asleep!" Pep yelled.

"No!" he replied, "I just told you. The engine went crazy. Did you not hear me say that? The engine went dead and I said, 'What in the world is happening?' to both of you. Do you not remember?"

"I was asleep," Mad said. "I didn't hear anything except when you said 'shit' like a hundred times."

"I was asleep, too," Pep offered. "But then I woke up and was like, 'oh, we're gonna die' and I didn't even have my seat belt on."

"Pep, please. We didn't die, okay? And, guys? I didn't fall asleep. I promise."

"Nobody stopped," Mad observed, looking out the window.

"I'm going to take a look at the damage," Rube said, and then he groaned as he unbuckled his seat belt. "Oh, man, my shoulders hurt."

In the aftermath, now that Mad was assured that the three of them were still alive and had no visible injuries, she walked through a checklist of the accident. They had not hit another car.

They actually, as she replayed it in her mind, hadn't hit anything. They had shot sideways across a grass median, had almost been completely T-boned by an oncoming car, and had come to an abrupt stop on the other side of the interstate. Was it possible that the car was completely fine?

"Oh, no!" she heard Rube yell from outside the car. Mad stepped out of the car, the traffic rushing by them, but though cars were slowing slightly or moving lanes, no one had stopped to check on them. She looked at the entire front bumper of the car, which was missing.

"Where did it go?" she asked.

They looked around for a few seconds and then Mad saw it in the median, twisted in the shape of an S, standing upright in the dirt.

"Should we try to get it back?" Rube asked, and Mad shook her head. "Let's not push our luck. We need to call the police and a tow truck."

"Guys!" Pep yelled. "Get back in the car. You're standing next to cars going sixty miles an hour. Get back in the freaking car!"

The two siblings climbed back into the PT Cruiser, which, Mad realized, had kept them safe. She was sorry to have been so mean to the PT Cruiser. She highly doubted it had random mechanical issues. Rube probably had just fallen asleep at the wheel.

"I'm going to call nine-one-one," Rube said.

"What do we do?" Pep asked.

"We just have to wait for the police," Mad replied, but then she heard Rube speaking to emergency services and telling them the highway number and somehow the last mile marker.

"Mad," Pep continued, once Rube was continuing the call, "I mean, like, do we keep going?"

"Wait, what did you say?" Rube said, holding the phone away from his mouth. "Pep? What do you mean?" Then he was back on the phone, "No, sorry, sir, just checking on my sister. Yes, of course."

"Should we stop?" Pep asked. "Do you think this is a sign?"

"I think—" Mad leaned closer to whisper to Pep, "I think Rube fell asleep."

"It's just," Pep said, "maybe this is our chance to turn back before something bad happens."

Mad thought about how far she had come, how many miles, how much awkwardness and anxiety and sadness she had experienced, and it made her unspeakably sad to think of quitting now. But there was also a part of her that understood what Pep meant. They had each other, the three of them. If they didn't meet their brother this time, they could wait until he was actually old enough for it to mean something. But they knew each other existed, her and Pep and Rube. This was a makeshift family. Maybe it was enough.

Just then, Rube hung up the phone and turned to face them. "We're not stopping, okay?"

"Calm down," Pep said to Rube. "Jeez. That was a scary situation. It still is." Mad watched Pep's demeanor change now that Rube was asserting himself.

"Why didn't you have your seat belt on?" Rube said. "You could have been hurt."

"You almost killed us!" Pep finally yelled. "That was insane."

"It was the car!" Rube said. "The engine cut out and then kicked back in. It was a mechanical error. Look, how far have I been driving? Hundreds and hundreds of miles. I'm a super responsible driver. This was not my fault."

"I said we should have stopped earlier," Mad said, unable to stop herself.

"Mad, please," Rube said.

"Or you could have let me drive sometime," Mad continued.

"Oh, my god, I've told you, like, a thousand times that you aren't on the rental agreement. Imagine if the engine had done this while you were driving. I'd be on the hook for the car! I'm paying for everything alrea— Sorry. Shit, sorry."

"That was mean," Pep said. "I don't even have my wallet and she's a freaking farmer."

"Pep, that's not—" Mad tried to interrupt, but Pep was still going. "And you just show up and turn my entire world upside down and I lose that game and, god, if I'd been hurt right now, I couldn't even play basketball anymore."

"Your season is over, though," Rube said.

"Professionally!" Pep shouted. "I might get drafted for the WNBA. It could happen. Definitely, I can play overseas if I want, in, like, Russia or Belgium or even Turkey."

"Okay, well, I didn't fully realize that, but you're okay. Right? You're okay," Rube offered. "Even though you weren't wearing your seat belt, which is its own kind of miracle."

"Rube, please," Mad said.

"I heard you guys, okay? You think this is some kind of sign? Well, the fact that Pep didn't go flying out of the car is a sign. We'll get another car and we'll keep going."

"Maybe we should fly?" Mad offered.

"Do you know how expensive it would be to fly to Salt Lake City and then fly to California?"

"I don't have an ID," Pep reminded them. "I don't have my wallet, because I ran away so fast that I forgot to even bring a freaking toothbrush."

"She can't fly," Rube said to Mad. "We'll get another car, unless you want to take the bus."

"Hey, the cops are here," Pep said, and they looked up to see the flashing lights of a highway patrol car.

"I didn't fall asleep," Rube said. "That's a fact."

An officer walked cautiously to the PT Cruiser and tapped on Rube's window. Rube gestured that he would need to open the door, and the officer allowed it.

"Do any of you need immediate medical assistance?" the officer asked them, and the siblings stared at each other and then shook their heads.

"Miraculously, Officer, I think we're relatively unscathed," Rube said, and Pep whispered, "Why are you talking like that?"

"License and registration, please." Rube informed him that this was a rental car, but that he was the person responsible for the vehicle.

The officer also seemed to notice the weird formality that Rube was exhibiting, and looked at the three of them, a strange grouping, the ages not lining up, and his eyes narrowed. "What are you three up to tonight?"

The three of them looked at each other, struggling to explain who they were and what they were doing. Mad realized that the longer it took them to reply, the more it seemed like they were smuggling drugs across the country. But she still couldn't speak, couldn't begin to explain to this officer of the law what was going on.

"Mad and Pep are my sisters," Rube finally said. "We're on our way to see our dad. Kind of a surprise. We haven't all been together in a pretty long time."

Even before Rube had finished explaining, the cop seemed convinced that they hadn't kidnapped Pep and had lost interest in their story.

Mad felt her breathing even out. They were siblings on a road trip. It wasn't that strange, right? To hear it out loud, to any random person, they were brothers and sisters spending time together. It almost made the fact that they had nearly died in a horrific car wreck worth it just to hear one of them say it out loud and not be met with disbelief.

The officer looked across the interstate and shook his head. "I am trying to figure out how in the world what happened here . . . happened."

Rube again explained the theory that the engine stalled and the officer nodded. "And you haven't been drinking have you?"

"Nary a drop, Officer," Rube said, shifting right back into the voice of a time traveler from the Victorian era, and then he turned to Pep. "You're making me incredibly self-conscious."

"Okay, I'm going to run this, fill out some paperwork, and we're going to need to get a tow truck out here, and you'll need to stay with the car until then."

The three siblings sat in silence, listening to the rush of traffic, their heads aching from the flashing lights of the patrol car.

"Please come with me," Rube finally said. "I'm begging you."

Pep looked at her phone. "I think I'm going to call my mom," she told them. "Maybe she can come get me."

"Oh, god," Rube said, and he looked like he was going to cry.

"Rube," Mad said, touching his shoulder. "It's okay. We're okay. We'll figure it out."

"I'm going to tell you something," he continued. "It's personal. I'm trusting you."

"Rube, I'm not sure—"

"I had this plan that I was going to kill Dad when we found him."

"Rube!" Pep said.

"Not in front of you, obviously. Kind of when no one was looking. Or poison him? I don't know. I'm not a murderer, so I didn't think about that part, but it was just something I kept thinking about after my mom died."

"Hey, the cop is coming back, just for your information," Pep said, tapping Rube on the shoulder.

Rube turned to the oncoming officer, who said, "Okay, here's where I need you to sign, and then you can get an accident report through the mail if you contact this number. Or you could even go online and get it, which is listed here. And a tow truck will be here in about five minutes. I'll stay here until that happens, okay?"

"Yes, sir," Rube said.

"And I need you to sign this, which states that you refused medical assistance at this time."

Rube signed everything and the officer looked over the paperwork. "Are you a religious man, sir?" the officer asked.

"Not really, no," Rube admitted.

"I'm not either, honestly," the officer replied. "But you got lucky tonight."

"I don't feel super lucky."

"Tomorrow you will."

"I hope so."

And then it was the three of them again. Rube checked to make sure the officer was back in his patrol car. "The point is, I just had this fantasy."

"Rube, this is so dark," Mad told him.

"But then I met the two of you. And it was, like, I felt like I had this family and it was a good thing, and I didn't feel that kind of impulse anymore. I'm not going to kill our dad. I never was, probably."

"Good," Pep said.

"But I stopped thinking about it once we were on the road, the three of us. And I'm just scared if you guys leave."

"We won't leave you," Mad said. "We were not talking about leaving you, Rube."

"It felt like it."

"We almost died. We're shaken up. We're in the middle of nowhere."

"I don't even have my ID," Pep added.

"Pep doesn't have a wallet or ID or her iPod."

"Everything was just going forward, and now we've stopped. Whether you like it or not, we're stuck for a little while. That's it."

"Both of you will go home to your moms and to your lives. I'm lonely. I've liked this trip so much. Even if we turned around, I'd be grateful for this. But I don't want to turn around. I need to find him. I don't know that I'll try again if I quit. I just need to see him."

Mad turned to look at Pep.

"Okay," Pep said. "Yes, I get it. I like to finish what I start. I'd probably regret it if I left."

"I'll keep going," Mad said.

"Do you feel like I'm taking advantage of things to make you stay on this trip?" Rube asked.

"Rube, I said I'll keep going," Mad told him.

"Oh, god," Rube said. "Where are we going to find a hotel? And a rental car place? The closest airport is probably all the way back in Albuquerque. Shit, I have to tell the rental car company where to get their car."

"Do you think we need to go get the bumper?" Pep asked him.

"I got the most expensive insurance package they offered," he replied. "I don't think they have to have the fender back."

"It's still standing straight up," Pep observed. "It's like it got planted into the earth. Oh, hey, the tow truck is here."

"Thank you," Rube told his sisters.

"It's okay," Mad said. "Thank you for not killing us. You kept your wits when the car went crazy."

"You screamed so loud," Pep said, "but it was pretty impressive."

"I love you," Rube suddenly said. "Both of you."

Mad was not used to these kinds of proclamations of affection, but before she even let her mind work through the complications of what to say back to this person who was only recently revealed to be her half brother, she just said, "I love you, too, Rube."

"Me, too," Pep said. "I love you."

"How weird," Rube said. "Sorry, I didn't mean to say it. I wanted to say it at a more opportune time, like looking out toward the horizon as the sun came up. But thank you."

"We've had our big family fight and now we've made up," Pep said. "That's how it works, I think."

The tow truck operator checked on them and when Rube informed him of the apparent issue, the man nodded. "I've not heard of that happening, honestly. But I also don't see many PT Cruisers out this way."

At this point, even Rube seemed to realize that, damn, he had probably fallen asleep, and so he didn't press the issue.

"I'm gonna get you guys situated, and then I can drop you off at a hotel for the night. I can't imagine you'll be driving this thing anytime soon."

They all stepped out of the car, stood as far away from the scene as was possible, and sat down on the dry ground. The lights of the tow truck and the patrol car were flashing around them, but Mad and Pep sat on either side of Rube and they looked up at the sky, which was filled with stars, millions and millions of tiny lights, and they allowed themselves this moment, to feel so small and alone in the universe, before they had to keep going.

THE PT CRUISER WAS NO LONGER A PART OF THEIR LIVES. THE AFTERMATH of the wreck had been such controlled chaos, and she was grateful for Rube's love of procedure and his ability to hold on to forms and receipts and insurance account numbers and credit card resolution hotlines. But they had also been in the middle of nowhere, so they had to make do with what was available to them. And what was available to them, at no extra charge, the rental lady informed them several times, was a Chevrolet HHR. When it arrived, actually driven to their run-down motel by an employee of the rental car company, the siblings marveled at the fact that, somehow, the Chevrolet HHR, which had been described as a "retro-styled, high-roofed, five-door, five-passenger, front-wheel-drive wagon" looked like a freaking PT Cruiser.

"Oh, god, no," Pep had shouted when the wagon pulled up. "This is a stretched-out PT Cruiser. How? How is this possible?"

"It's not even the same brand," Rube marveled. But it looked the same, that weird future-retro look that felt like a Dick Tracy cartoon, like a stream of freakish villains should be pouring out of it.

"It's all they had," Rube reminded them.

"I'll drive," Mad said. This time, Rube had put both of them on the rental agreement.

"To new beginnings," Rube said, as they headed back onto the highway, and Pep told him to please shut up.

1999, SALT LAKE CITY, UTAH, DIGITAL 8MM

Opening shot of a small CRT monitor, the image flickering. It shows a weather map of the state of Utah, swirling colors of yellow and red moving on the computerized screen.

Into the frame steps a young boy, wearing a blue suit and a red tie, his hair slicked back. He is pointing at the town of Moab on the map and says, "Today's temperature in Moab is going to be a chilly negative-fifty-eight degrees Fahrenheit." He looks awkwardly off screen and shifts his body to uncover parts of the map behind him. He then points to Salt Lake City. "In Salt Lake City, though, we'll be experiencing a balmy one-hundred-and-sixty-four degrees!" He pauses and then remembers to add, "Fahrenheit."

He looks offscreen again and nods, and the image behind him changes. "Okay, let's look at our five-day forecast, and it appears that we're going to have flooding on Wednesday." He points to a cartoon image of Noah's Ark. "But then on Friday, no rain, but the sun isn't going to rise at all." He points to a cartoon image of the sun, asleep in bed, the alarm clock showing little squiggles of sound. "All in all," the boy continues, gaining confidence, smiling, "a typical week in the great city of Salt Lake. Back to you, Mom—or, wait—back to you, Trista."

The camera pans to a woman in a lavender pantsuit who is clapping, smiling. "Thanks, Tom," she says, "and thanks to our cameraman and technician for those wonderful weather graphics."

The camera pans back to the boy, already taking off the tie and jacket, who is laughing, pointing at the camera. The shot fades to black.

CHAPTER SIX

As they pulled into the driveway of a very nice house in a wealthy neighborhood of Salt Lake City, Mad marveled at the variations of their father's living situations. He'd gone from an apartment in Boston to a farmhouse in Coalfield, to a modest two-story home in Oklahoma (though Pep had mentioned a few times that after their father left, they rented a pretty sweet McMansion in a neighboring town), and now she tried to imagine her dad, organic farmer Chuck Hill, reclining on a leather sofa inside this huge home. She reminded herself that he wasn't here any longer, had moved on, so she didn't need to try too hard to imagine it. That was the thing with their dad. When you imagined him in his new iteration, he was already gone, had moved on, so everything wavered in your brain like a ghost or a wisp of smoke.

Rube got his trusty satchel while Mad and Pep stepped out of the car and stretched out the miles. This was Rube's third time doing this, Mad's second, and Pep's first. Mad knew from the experience of finding Pep that it was hard not to consider your own moment, just before you found out the truth. Of course, Mad understood that life was made entirely of moments where you could see the break, the before and the after. Their father leaving them was one. One day he's there and the next day he's not, and you remember that moment so clearly, because even then you know it matters. And they were about to do it to this little kid. Maybe it was okay. They would show him that he was less alone in the world. Ultimately, that had to be good. She tried to convince herself that a life needed these moments, where you felt the split of who you were and who you became. Without those moments, what was your life? Just an unbroken line that went from birth to death? Though that actually seemed kind of nice, Mad admitted, how lovely the sound of that unbroken string would sound when you thrummed it, a single sound that died when you did. Wait, what in the fuck was she talking about? She couldn't stop thinking of birth and death on this trip, but she needed to focus on the middle, which, you know, she was still living inside of.

She wondered if Rube and Pep were having these spiraling thoughts inside their own heads. All that time on the farm, just animals and crops, you sometimes made two versions of yourself so you could have a conversation, but it made her feel a little crazy when it was happening in the presence of actual people. Instead of waiting, she just started walking up to the front door, leaving Pep and Rube to chase after her. She rang the doorbell, held her breath, and when the door opened, she had to look down to see a kid standing in front of her. Theron. Her brother.

He had buzzed-short black hair so you could see the paleness of his scalp and was wearing a huge T-shirt featuring the movie poster for *The Phantom Menace* that went to his knees. As the siblings regarded him, this boy who did not look like them, he gestured for them to come in. As Mad looked more closely, it was like Theron was their opposite, with black hair, so petite, and instead of the square jaw that the other kids possessed, a much more feminine and thin face. Where the Hill siblings looked rough and weathered, Theron looked like a pixie. "Hi. I'm Tom," he then said, as if he'd been waiting for them to introduce themselves. His voice, strangely, was scratchy and deep, like a cartoon frog, and it shocked Mad into responding.

"Oh, yeah, sorry," Mad finally replied. "Hey. I'm Mad. And that's Rube and that's Pep."

Tom's eyes widened when he saw Pep, as if he recognized her, and Mad watched his breathing quicken. His eyes flashed, like a cartoon, little sparkles of an epiphany, and he then calmed his breathing. It was eerie to watch, and Mad suddenly felt out of her depth.

"And is your mom around?"

"No," he said. "She's in a meeting."

"Oh, jeez," Mad said, looking over at Rube. "I think she told us to be here at four p.m." Trista, they learned, worked weekday mornings on the show from 5:00 to 8:00 a.m., hours to which Mad was accustomed on the farm but seemed like torture to Pep and Rube, and so they'd planned a time when Trista and her son would both be at home. But now here they were, in an empty mansion with a little kid who did not look like them, no adult supervision. It felt like a scam. Why was Mad afraid of this situation while Tom, blinking up at them with genuine curiosity, seemed entirely in control?

"Well, is she coming?" Pep asked.

"Yeah, eventually," Tom said. "Are you hungry?"

"What? Um, no," Mad said, but then Pep said, "Do you mean, like, a meal? Or just like finger foods, or—"

"Snacks," Tom said calmly. "Like, I have Pop-Tarts or there's—"

"I'd like a Pop-Tart," Pep said. Mad and Rube stared at their sister, who just shrugged. As Tom led them into the kitchen, Pep turned and said, "Okay, first, I am hungry. I think my eating schedule is very different from you guys, but, also, this is an easy way to get things moving, right? So we don't just stand in the hallway for seven hours in silence?"

"Yes, it's a smart tactical move," Rube said, "well done. But I am very concerned that Trista is not here. Like, I feel like she's gonna show up with cops and pretend that we broke in. Or just shoot us. How conservative is Utah? It's pretty conservative, I would think. I think they'd believe her."

"We've got four kinds of Pop-Tarts," Tom announced. Because he was so small, his arms and legs so thin, the T-shirt like a dress on him, she kept thinking he was much younger, but she remembered that he was eleven. He was a preteen, she thought, though she didn't know the exact ages of that category off the top of her head. When she was young, you were just some dumb idiot child to the adult world until suddenly you were a teenager and an object of concern and pity.

"Ooh, man, you've got Splitz!" Pep shouted. "It's two flavors in one."

"Do you want one?" Tom asked, smiling.

"Heck yes," Pep said, and Tom handed her a weird Frankenstein Pop-Tart that was half blueberry and half strawberry, and Pep ate it so quickly that it felt like a magic trick. "Hmm," she said, pausing for a second after she'd finished. "I can't really tell the difference in flavors."

"You literally ate it in three bites," Rube said, amazed. "How can you tell?"

"You have to alternate sides," Tom calmly explained, and everything about this kid made Mad think he was a fairy creature, his croaky voice and tiny body, handing out magical pastries. "First you eat one side, savor it, then you eat the other side, and you go back and forth like that until it's just the middle and you finally eat that and you get both flavors."

"Ooh, I like him," Rube whispered to Mad.

Tom grabbed a few more packages of the Pop-Tarts and gestured for them to follow him into the living room. He tossed the snacks on the coffee table and then jumped into a huge papasan chair with a bright orange cushion, and the siblings cautiously walked over to a giant white leather sofa and sat down, Rube and Pep on either side of Mad, the leather squeaking in a way that made Mad think that no one ever sat in it.

"You're my brother and sisters," Tom said, and it felt like they were on a talk show from the seventies. Mad had never tried acid, but each new meeting with a sibling felt like a different possibility if you took acid.

"That's right, Tom," Rube offered. "I'm your oldest brother, and my name is Reuben, but I go by Rube."

"Nicknames," Tom said, nodding, like he was familiar with this concept.

"And I'm Madeline, but I go by Mad," she said. "We met earlier."

"In the hallway," Tom answered, nodding again.

"And I'm Pepper," Pep said. "I go by Pep."

"How old are you?" Tom asked.

"I'm twenty-one," Pep said. "I'm a senior in college."

"What's your major?" Tom asked.

"Oh, I'm a health and exercise major with a minor in business," Pep replied.

"Will you be a doctor?" Tom asked. "Like an exercise doctor?"

"I don't know," Pep said. "I play basketball and I guess I might coach after I finish playing, but I could go into training or physical therapy or something. I honestly don't know."

"You play basketball?" Tom asked.

"She's a star," Rube offered. "She's, like, one of the best college basketball players in the country."

"Wow," Tom said. "Do you like the Utah Jazz?"

"Not really," Pep said.

"Me, either," Tom offered. "My mom's boyfriend, he's the sportscaster for Channel Four, gave me a signed Andrei Kirilenko jersey, but I just threw it in the closet. I was gonna give it to you if you liked the Jazz."

"I kind of like the Hornets, because they've been playing in Oklahoma City," Pep offered.

"I don't follow basketball," Tom admitted.

"So your mom has a boyfriend?" Rube interjected, trying to get the discussion off of basketball, even though Mad kind of wanted to know why a team in Utah was called the Jazz, which seemed weird as hell to her.

"Oh, yes, Mitch Manning. He played football for Utah. His favorite movie is *Pearl Harbor*. One of his fingers is permanently crooked because it got broken so many times. He got arrested once for drunk driving. His wife died in a skiing accident. I absolutely cannot stand him."

"Oh, wow, that's a lot to process," Rube replied. Mad felt like this was a good test. Five details about a person and you decided if you hated them or not. She also thought she would dislike Mitch Manning. She tried to imagine the five details about herself. Then about her siblings. It was less fun then.

"Maybe we should stop asking you so many questions and you could ask us anything you want to know about us or about our dad—who is also your dad, of course—when he was with us. Or with us individually, because, up until this year, we didn't know each other existed."

"I don't have any questions," Tom replied. "Mom said you guys wanted to meet me."

"Oh, well, nice to meet you," Rube said. "Tom, sorry, do you understand the situation? Your dad was my dad. He was my dad first, though it's not like a contest. And then he left my family, and he made a new family and Mad was born. And he left Mad and her mom and he made a new family and Pep was born, and—"

"And then he left her?" Tom offered.

"Exactly, okay, I guess you do understand. Yeah, he left Pep and her mom and he ended up here in Utah, and that's when he had you."

"Are you guys not from Utah?" Tom asked.

"No," Pep said. "I'm from Oklahoma. And she's from Tennessee, and he's from Massachusetts."

"Boston?"

Rube looked at the boy. "Yes, I'm from Boston."

"And Coalfield? Coalfield, Tennessee?"

"Wait, what?" Mad replied. "How do you know that? Did your mom tell you?"

"I . . . never mind."

What in the world had Trista told this kid? Had she said, "Three adults will come a knockin', and these three random adults are related to you in ways that are too complicated for me to explain. Give them an hour of your time. And then you will never see them again"?

In the resulting silence, Pep reached for another package of Pop-Tarts and ate one, this time exactly in the manner that Tom had instructed. She nodded her approval to Tom, who smiled and bowed his head knowingly, and now he seemed a little like Yoda to Mad, that weird voice in that little body.

"And so then he left Utah and he's in California," Rube continued, and at this news, Tom's eyes widened and seemed to radiate light.

"He's in Hollywood?" Tom asked.

"Oh, well, maybe at one point? He's in Northern California, or that's the last address I have for him. If nothing else, that address will either lead us to him or to someone who might know where he went. And, after all of this, we'll see him."

"You're going to see my dad?" Tom asked.

"*Our* dad, yes," Rube continued. "We're all on our way to go see him. None of us have seen him since he left us."

"I haven't seen him since he left us," Tom offered, as if finally, in this moment, he understood the connection between himself and these three people sitting in his living room. "He left us almost two years ago and I haven't talked to him since then."

"Oh, god, I'm sorry, Tom," Rube offered.

"I miss him," Tom finally admitted and his voice softened. "I love my mom. She's my mom. But I miss him a ton. He kind of understands me a little better than my mom. She's really busy. She doesn't like many of the things that I like. I think I scare her a little bit. Just a little."

"That's not true," Mad jumped in. "We talked to your mom on the phone. She loves you a ton. She sounded so proud of you."

"She thinks I'm kind of weird," he told them. "I'm a filmmaker."

"Oh, wow, I think that's amazing," Rube said. "I'm actually a writer."

"A screenwriter?" Tom asked.

"No. I write novels."

"Oh, okay." He was clearly disappointed.

"One was made into a movie, though!" Mad offered, and Tom smiled again.

"Do you have connections in the film industry?" the boy asked Rube, who smiled and nodded.

"Kind of? I mean, I have an agent and I know a few people."

"I'm more of an indie filmmaker," Tom admitted. "I'm a low-budget independent filmmaker."

"Oh, wow," Rube replied.

"You, like, make movies right now?" Pep asked, struggling to keep up. "Like, you're eleven and you make movies? With a camera?"

"Oh, yeah," Tom said. "I have a Sony Digital-Eight Handycam. It was Dad's, you know? He's a filmmaker, too. But he isn't a low-budget independent filmmaker. He called himself an 'experimental filmmaker.'"

"Wait, what?" Mad asked. "That was his job?"

"Well, yeah, kind of. He was a cameraman. Did you not know that? He was a cameraman for the news. He worked with Mom at Channel Four when she first got started there. And then they had me, and he stayed home with me. He did commercials and he did these, like, industrial shorts for companies, and he had a whole little production company. Did he not make movies when he was with you?"

"Well, yeah, he did," Rube admitted, and Mad also remembered that both versions of their dad loved cameras and making home movies. It was the constant of their childhood, their dad filming everyone else, always off camera.

"He said he worked on this movie, *Code of Silence*, in Chicago, as a camera operator."

"Well, it's possible. When did that movie come out?" Rube asked.

"In 1985? It had Chuck Norris in it."

Rube looked at Mad, who shook her head, because her dad had left before that, and Pep shrugged, not sure of the exact dates of her dad's life before she was born in '86. Even with all four of them in the same room, they had trouble piecing it together. They needed a chart of the years, a single line that represented their father's life, with brackets to indicate each child, as well as their moms. Instead of a family tree, with roots that reached deeper and deeper into the earth, it would look like a shark, constantly moving forward, with remora fish attaching themselves to him for as long as they could. Mad looked over at Tom and said, "I think it's, like, chronologically possible, actually. Who knows?" Mad truly believed in the possibility that their father had a brief foray before he married Pep's mother where he was a camera operator on a Chuck Norris film before he decided coaching girls' basketball was the right path.

"I wouldn't care if he lied," Tom admitted. "It's okay."

They were all quiet for a moment, each thinking of their version of their father.

Tom seemed to be considering them, the truth of what they were telling him. And then, pulling his shirt even tighter over his knees, he said, "I want to show you something. I believe you. But I need to show you something." He stood up and when Rube also stood, Tom gestured for him to stay in the living room. And then Tom scampered out of the room and up the stairs.

After a few seconds, Pep asked, "Do you think he's running away? Or calling the police? Or his mom?"

"I mean, any of those are possible," Rube admitted.

Tom returned with a padded CD wallet and he unzipped it. "I found some stuff in Dad's studio after he left. I burned them onto these discs, but I have the originals, too."

"What are they?" Rube asked, but Tom went over to the entertainment center and opened it up to reveal an enormous TV and all manner of electronics. He powered up the DVD player and placed one of the DVDs in the machine. On the screen, a silent image flickered, this fiery orange static hovering on the edges of the image like it was being conjured by memory. Mad stared at the movie, a boy folding a paper airplane.

"That's me," Rube said, his voice cracking. "That's our place."

It was so strange to watch Rube as a boy, to see the ways in which he had grown out of being that boy, the things he held on to. Mad looked at what she assumed was his mother, glamorous on the sofa, smoking a cigarette. They watched the whole home movie, such a brief little vignette, so perfect, though maybe to Rube it was shattering.

Tom turned it off when it finished, and he held up another DVD, which was labeled 1978, COALFIELD, TENNESSEE, 8 MM, and Mad tensed for what would appear. When the screen again came to life, she watched an image of herself as a child, holding a chicken, and it broke her heart. "That's me," she admitted to her siblings. "That's our farm." She watched her mother, so beautiful, the real and fake exasperation she had for her husband. She watched herself drive a John Deere 4010 tractor, which they still had and maintained, though they'd since bought a new tractor. How in the world was she, a child, allowed to drive such a huge tractor? She was barefoot. She uttered a brief squeak of recognition when her father, previously hidden behind the camera, reached out for the egg that she had offered him.

Tom stopped it. "Me next?" Pep asked, nodding. He held up one that they all understood would be Pep, and after a few moments, the camera panned over to her, bouncing a basketball. "Holy shit," Pep exclaimed. "That's just across the border in Arkansas. I remember this." They watched her dominate on the court, so easy for her even at that age, and Pep said, "I still have that trophy. I really earned that one. I was two years younger than everyone else in that league. I've never seen this before."

And once it was finished, Tom turned off the DVD. "These were movies that Dad made."

"Home movies," Rube said, "of us."

"Short films," Tom replied. "I didn't know they were home movies. I found them. I didn't know. I thought it was his early stuff. I thought all of you were actors. He's not really in them, you know? And he left it behind, and I was trying to figure out how to use it in a movie, little pieces of it. And then you showed up. And I saw Pep, and I knew who you were. I remembered you. But I wanted to be sure. I thought maybe I was making it up, like a fantasy or something. I don't know."

He put another DVD into the player and they watched Tom, a tiny boy in a suit, pointing to a weather map that showed insane variations of temperature, little cartoons of disaster presented in such a straightforward manner.

"Dad came up with this," Tom told them. "He did all the special effects. Isn't it cool? It's a home movie, I guess, like yours, but it's more like a movie. It's a movie of all of us. He was maybe making a movie about all of us."

The siblings tried to keep watching as the images changed to the food court in a mall, but they couldn't pay attention.

"Dad kept those," Rube said, confused. "He took them with him when he left us. Each time, he took them."

"I guess to remember us?" Pep offered.

"Maybe," Rube allowed.

Mad wondered how often their father, when he was alone, when he could allow himself to remember all the people he'd left behind, would watch these little home movies.

"Are there more?" Mad asked.

"Not of you guys," he admitted. "These were in a box by themselves."

"Why did he leave them?" Rube wondered. "He took them with him each time he left us."

"Maybe there were more," Pep said. "Maybe he took other ones with him and left those."

Pep was probably wondering the same thing as her, Mad figured, if somewhere in their own houses, there were home movies of their previous sibling sitting in a box. What a bizarre feeling, to think that there were clues that they'd never discovered. But then Mad corrected herself. She could not imagine him leaving that kind of evidence behind in those years. He had gotten lazy now, or forgetful. Or was just so tired of hiding it that he wanted it to be found. Or he finally wanted to let it all go, that he was so far from that version of himself that there was no point in holding on to it. Because he was never going back.

She wanted to watch the video again, all by herself. What a strange thing to have denied herself, the pleasure of memory, of living inside a moment that, however mundane, held some piece of who you had once been. That chicken she had been holding, which she had not named or cared about more than any other chicken, was long dead. How lovely to see that chicken again. How lovely to see herself again.

"You can have them," Tom told his siblings. "Dad would want you to have them."

"No, he would not," Mad suddenly replied, which made Pep and Rube laugh. "But we'll take them."

Tom returned to the chair and considered his siblings, as if accepting for the first time that they were tangible people and not the manifestations of a dream. He now seemed a little more at ease with them.

"And you're all going? To see Dad?" he asked them.

"Yeah," Pep answered. "They picked me up and then we wanted to meet you and then we're heading to California."

"Can I come with you?" Tom asked.

"I don't think so," Mad replied, because she wanted to answer before Rube, who would definitely have said that this child could come with them. "You've got school."

"Does she not have school?" Tom asked, pointing at Pep, who frowned. Rube and Mad actually turned to Pep, who said, "It's spring break. Or, wait, maybe it's over. It doesn't matter. I'm taking two classes. I pretty much have graduated already."

"Fifth grade isn't that hard," Tom said. "It doesn't matter. I never miss school. And our school says you can have excused absences if you're doing something that—what do they say?—it's, like, if it's . . . um . . . oh, culturally enriching. And this would be, right?"

"Yes, absolutely," Rube answered.

"Tom," Mad interrupted. She wondered why it mattered to be reasonable. She wondered why she would even think of herself as reasonable at this stage in the journey. "Maybe you and your mom could, like, caravan with us. And that way you'd have, you know, proper parental supervision."

"She can't miss work," Tom replied, and his voice was getting croakier as he got more excited. "She is, like, the most famous morning newsperson in Utah. All these people would go crazy if she wasn't on TV. And she wouldn't want anyone to know why she was leaving. She doesn't ever talk about Dad at all, and I'm not supposed to talk about him to people. She's embarrassed about it. She couldn't come."

"Well, I just don't think you can come without a parent with you," Mad said.

"We're going to go see my dad, right?" he continued. "He's my parent, yeah? You guys are just taking me from one parent to another parent."

Mad could already feel herself weakening because the psychic vibrations coming from Rube and maybe even Pep were overwhelming her. "I mean, maybe Dad has joint custody with Trista," Rube offered, and Mad groaned. She leaned over to Rube and whispered, "He has joint custody and just hasn't seen this kid in years?"

"Well, it's murky legal territory, at the very least," Rube replied.

"If my mom signs a permission slip," Tom said, "that would be okay, right?"

"Tom, when is your mom getting back?" Mad asked. "Like, she is coming back, right?"

"Yeah, she'll be back. I'm gonna go get a piece of paper and you guys can help me write up a permission slip, okay?"

"No, Tom, that's not—Rube, you should call Trista—that's not how this works," Mad said.

"Why did you come here, then?" Tom asked. "You were just gonna leave me behind? That's not fair."

"It does kind of suck," Pep admitted. "Remember when you guys were gonna leave me?"

"No!" Mad said, now defending herself, like it mattered somehow. "You said you didn't want to go, and then you, like, dove into the car as we were leaving."

"No, I know. I just mean, when I realized I'd missed my chance, and you two were together and I was by myself, it felt pretty bad."

"It feels awful," Tom insisted.

Rube had his phone out, and Mad asked if he was calling Trista, but he said that he was actually looking online for examples of a document that transferred authority of a child to a sibling.

"Okay, Rube, can you make a permission slip?" Tom asked. "And, Pep, could you help me pack? And, um . . ."

"Mad," Mad said, and Tom nodded and then continued, "Mad, maybe you wanna wait for my mom to get here?"

"No!" Mad now shouted. "It's a long drive. I feel like maybe we're at capacity, you know?" She looked at Rube and Pep for support, but she knew it was over. "I don't even have a bag," Pep said. "And look at him! He's little."

"I'm tiny," Tom said.

"The Chevrolet HHR has a seating capacity of five individuals," Rube informed them, like he'd memorized the manual.

"I meant more, like, you know, *emotional* capacity," Mad weakly offered.

"There's four of us!" Tom said, smiling. "Does Dad have any more kids? We could fit one more kid!"

"Where the hell is your freaking mom?" Mad asked, but Pep and Tom were already running upstairs, and now Rube was holding up his phone for Mad to look at it. "It's actually just the most simple thing in the world," he said. "It's just a child travel consent form. It doesn't technically even have to be notarized. It's actually kind of wild. Plus, it's easier because we are his siblings, so it's not that big of a deal."

"What is this website?" Mad asked.

"Hmm, it was just the first site that came up. Let me see. Oh, it's called easychildlawdepot-dot-com. They even have a template you can download. Wait, hmm, it might require a membership. How much is it? Let's see."

"Rube! Please. Don't you think this is insane? This is too fast. We've met him. He knows we exist. We can get to know him. Send him birthday cards. He and Trista can come visit me on the farm one day. We don't have to do this all at once."

"You saw him. He wants to see Dad again. We all do. That's what we're doing, right? And why not have all of us? I know, I know, I know. When we started, I just said it was good to meet each other and we'd see what happened, but once Pep came along, it just seemed like all of us needed to go to Dad."

"Just try to think about this for a second. If it goes bad for us, okay, whatever. We're adults. We've made a life for ourselves without him. Tom is young and has only just lost Dad. If Dad is a jerk, or if Tom freaks out, what if it ruins his life?"

"It's better if he's with us, right? We'll all be together."

Pep and Tom came back down with a duffel bag and then some camera equipment. Tom was filming them with his Handycam, which made Mad immediately feel self-conscious. She stopped talking, deferred to Rube, who waved at Tom, who waved back. "This isn't for anything," Tom assured them. "I'm not gonna, like, make a documentary about this. Dad just said it was good to film random things and maybe you could use it later. I have a lot of little pieces and I like putting them together."

"I'm working on the permission slip, and I think it will work out," Rube told the boy.

Mad felt exhausted. Why resist? Their dad was pulling them toward a reckoning, and it felt like the sooner that happened, then the sooner she could see what was left of her life, how to get back to Coalfield. They'd nearly ruined Pep's life in only a few days, and she seemed okay. Maybe all of them had a preternatural gift for self-preservation. Maybe they couldn't be hurt. Or maybe they kept their emotions so deeply inside of themselves that it just took longer to reach them.

She accepted the possibility, even wished for it, that nothing would change. They would meet their father again, have it out, ask him the questions they wanted to ask. He would impart some kind of wisdom or reveal that there was no meaning to anything, and then they would each return to their lives, those separate compartments spaced out by so many miles, and everything would go back to the way that it was, except that strange emptiness they'd felt when their father had left would now be replaced with certainty. Maybe the secret to pain was to acknowledge it, to admit that it hurt so bad, so you didn't have to pretend that it didn't. And maybe it didn't go away. Maybe the secret to pain was to respond to it in ways that made the pain worth it. Maybe she was trying to rationalize the fact that she was taking a child, one who was clearly very fragile, to the farthest edge of the country to meet a father who might not even exist. She finally turned to Tom and his camera, and she waved, smiled. Pep was holding the duffel bag, and Rube was now carefully printing out a legally binding contract, and Tom was making a movie, and what else could she do but be a part of it.

"Do you get carsick?" she asked Tom, who replied, "Sometimes, oh yes."

"We'll take care of you," she told him. She looked past the camera. "Do you believe me, Tom? Do you believe that we'll protect you as best as we can?"

Tom turned off the camera. He looked down at the floor for a few seconds and then he regarded his oldest sister. She waited, would wait forever, and then Tom nodded. "I do believe you."

"Okay, then I guess we're going to do this," Mad said, and it was at this exact moment that Trista walked in through the front door, holding a giant box from a bakery, tied in ribbon. Tom's mother regarded everything going on, as if she had suddenly been awarded custody of three additional children, frowned, and then said, "Tom told me that you weren't going to get here until five. He asked me to get this cake. He said it was one of your birthdays."

"Oh," Mad replied. "Pep, is it your birthday?" Pep shook her head. "I think there was a miscommunication along the way. Like, crossed wires."

"How long have you been here?" she asked.

"Not long!" Pep offered.

"I'm going to California, Mom," Tom told her. "With my brother and sisters. To see Dad."

"Why did I buy a cake?" Trista asked.

"To celebrate!" Tom replied. Trista shook her head, exhaled, and resigned herself to making sense of things once she was no longer holding a birthday cake that celebrated nothing real. It began to dawn on Mad that perhaps Tom was the kind of child that exhausted responsible adults, that having a pixie living in your house with unlimited access to Pop-Tarts and forever working on a low-budget independent film was perhaps not as magical as it might seem. And this scared Mad because, up until this very trip, she had been a responsible adult.

Rube sheepishly walked up to Trista and offered to take the cake, and as he awkwardly took control of the box, he handed her a piece of paper.

"What is this?" Trista asked.

"It's a consent form to allow your child to travel with us, his biological half siblings. I've actually put down Mad's name as the actual responsible party who will be charged with caring for Tom."

"Rube!" Mad shouted.

"It was purely random. Alphabetically, you know? Mad comes before Rube or Pep. That's all it is."

Trista regarded Mad, which made her shrink under this beautiful woman's scrutiny. Even though her hands were clean, Mad always felt like she had dirt under her fingernails, worried that the smell of chickens and manure was always in her hair. Men did not intimidate Mad, they never had, but beautiful women who announced their femininity with confidence made Mad want to die. And now the number one morning news anchor in Salt Lake City and quite possibly all of Utah was staring right at her.

"I'm thinking that you are the most responsible child of Carl. Am I correct?" she asked Mad, who could only nod.

Trista was now actually looking at the contract, as if it were a real document, as if she were considering signing it. "Can we talk privately?" she asked. Mad could only nod again.

"Tom?" Trista shouted. "I'm going to talk to Mad, for a few minutes. You and your siblings can sit tight. You could show them your movie, okay?"

"Can we eat this cake?" Tom asked.

"Yes, that's fine," Trista replied, already leading Mad down the hallway and into what appeared to be the master bedroom.

"Sorry about the state of the house," Trista said. "It's been a crazy day, obviously." Mad observed the bedroom, which was spotless, as if she had just checked into a penthouse suite in a hotel.

"Oh, it's no problem," Mad said, realizing there was no furniture to sit on except the bed, so she stood awkwardly while Trista took off her jewelry and hung it on a bronze tree sculpture on her dresser. "And, obviously, we're not going to just take Tom with us to California."

"Well, it's actually not the worst idea," Trista replied, still looking at herself in the vanity mirror.

"Well, I mean, even if it's not, like, *the worst* idea, it's not something we'd do without asking you or considering how it might affect Tom."

"Mad. And, just let me understand, is your name short for Mattie or Madeline or Mary, or what?"

"Oh, sorry, yeah, that was Dad's thing. Mad is short for Madeline."

"Okay, so, Mad, I am going to tell you some things that literally no one else knows."

"Oh, god, no, you don't need to do that," Mad replied.

"No, I'm going to do it. It's important to me. I feel like I need to tell someone, and . . . here you are."

"Do you think maybe Rube might . . . it's just that he's the oldest."

"No, it's you. I'm going to tell you."

"Okay. Could I sit down on the bed? I feel a little dizzy."

"Yes, sit. Okay, here is the thing. I met your dad at a very vulnerable time in my life, okay? I had a pretty bad childhood and I don't want to get into it. That's not something I'm going to tell you about. Not today, at least. But I had worked so hard and I majored in journalism and I got this great job at Channel Four, and I had become a reporter. It was a big deal."

"Okay, yeah, I would think so. And I'm sorry about your childhood. God."

"Yes, thank you. Okay, and there was this man. He was, well, I guess since you're not from Salt Lake City it's not going to be a big deal, but it was George Nielsen."

"I'm sorry, but I don't know who that is."

"No, you wouldn't if you aren't from around here, but just take my word for it. He's the most famous news anchor in Utah. And he comes from, well, just the richest family you can imagine. Super handsome, like Tom Selleck. And he liked me. And, we had a thing. And he was married with kids and all that. And I guess I thought maybe he was going to leave them for me. But of course, he wasn't and I was so damn stupid and I think he thought I was some kind of con artist because he couldn't believe that I truly thought he was going to leave his wife for me just because he got me pregnant. And, well, you can imagine what that kind of guy wanted me to do, right?"

"I can guess," Mad offered.

"And I didn't want to do that. It was a very difficult time for me. And I was doing well in my job and not because of George Nielsen, I'll tell you that much, because it was so much harder because we had to hide it from everyone. Anyways, I'm rushing through this, but Carl, your father? He was a cameraman at the station. And he was so good and he was kind to me and he helped me and, god, I don't know. This handsome older man had just wrecked my life and then there was this handsome older man who was helping me on the job and I broke down and told him everything. And he said that he'd help me if I wanted to keep the baby. He said he'd claim paternity of the child if that would help. He said he'd raise the kid as his own. It was sudden, but I just kind of wanted something. I'd been so close to getting what I wanted, and I didn't get it, and then I didn't want to have nothing, you know? I wanted to have something, even if it wasn't exactly what I'd wanted. So I said yes. And we got together, but we never actually got married. Neither one of us wanted to go that far. It was more like pretend, you know? We pretended like Theron was his kid. And I'm a little ashamed about this, but Carl, your dad, you understand? He went to George Nielsen and he got in his face one night in the parking lot, when no one else was around. I knew nothing about that, but anyways, George ended up giving me just an obscene amount of money. I had to sign all these legal papers to say that I'd never go after him for child support and that I'd never do anything to suggest that we'd had an affair. Honestly, I think he's done it before, because the lawyer didn't seem all that surprised. But that money set us up. And I had Theron. And I got to keep my name, because that was important, and Theron took my last name, too, which Carl was fine with, honestly."

Mad couldn't help herself and interrupted, because it seemed like maybe they had crested the wave of the worst stuff. "Can I just ask if my dad came up with the name Theron, or . . ."

"No, I chose it. It means 'hunter' and I liked that. Of course, Carl started calling him Tom, and it stuck. He liked to do that, just kind of tweaking things. But, you know, he ended up quitting at the station and started doing commercial work and had a production company, but he also took care of Tom, which was huge for me. Because pretty soon after that, George Nielsen got a really, really big job in Denver, and he left the station. And I won two regional Emmys and then I got the *Good Morning, Utah* spot. Pretty soon, I'll be the evening news anchor, I'm fairly certain, or I might even look at something national, or that's what the higher-ups are suggesting. And I couldn't have done that without Carl. And I grew to love him in some kind of way. And Tom loved him so much. But I was just moving in a different direction, and it felt like my life was taking off, and Carl just seemed like nothing much was happening. And, I hate saying it because I'm thirty-five in this industry and I know all about ageism, but he was getting so old. He was working on his films, and a few of his shorts won some awards, but he seemed content to just kind of settle into life, and I think he wanted me to settle into life. He was ready to retire, I guess. And I couldn't. I can't. And we drifted apart and I told him that I needed more, and that I wanted to be on my own. And, I don't know. He said he understood. And I assumed he'd stay here in Salt Lake. I thought we'd share custody of Tom. Our relationship was ending, but I didn't understand what was going to happen. And a week or so later, he just disappeared. And that hurt Tom so much, but what could I do? We just kept going, without him. And I told people we'd separated, and, honestly, the single mother reporter was a much better hook. That's crass, but it is what it is."

It was so strange, to realize that their father had not left of his own accord, that Trista had asked him to leave. Oh, if her mom or Pep's mom found out, the jealousy they would have felt. And Tom was not his biological child. Which meant that Tom was not their biological half sibling. Nothing was lining up in the way she'd expected, and now they had asked if they could take Tom with them to California.

"And then you show up. And you tell me about Carl and that kind of makes sense, you know? And you want to take Tom to see him again. It would be so good for Tom. And for me, too, honestly. I know that's selfish, but I'm in this new relationship with someone. His name is Mitch and—"

"Mitch Manning," Mad said without thinking.

"Wait, do you know Mitch?" Trista asked, confused.

"No, not exactly. Tom told us about him. Said his favorite movie is *Pearl Harbor.*"

"Oh, yeah, Tom *does not care* for Mitch. And, honestly, it goes both ways. So maybe this is a good chance for all of us to get a little distance and just see where we stand when it's over."

"Wait, so you'd like us to take Tom to see our dad so that you and Mitch can have some time alone?"

"Mad, please. Don't say it like that. I want Tom to get some closure. I didn't know where Carl was. I had no idea. He just left. It will be good for Tom. And I'm with Tom all the time, except for when the housekeeper is with him in the mornings, you know, because I have to be at the studio at like three in the morning, but it's just the two of us most of the time. And maybe without Tom around, I can figure out what it is that I want. I can just think for a little bit."

"Well, Rube has this form for you to sign."

"No, I know. I saw it. It looked pretty good. I'll sign it."

"And you're going to let us take your son?"

"I'm going to let you take your half brother to visit his father."

"I'm sorry," Mad said. "I don't want . . . I don't want to think you're a bad mom."

"Oh, why do this? We were getting somewhere."

"No, I know you love Tom. And what do I even know? I don't understand any of this. But Tom is so young. He's a child. Why would you even allow it, considering what could go wrong?"

"You and your brother and your sister," Trista replied. "Do you feel like maybe you've been ruined by what happened with your dad?"

"Ruined? God, that's pretty heavy. I feel like . . . maybe not Pep?"

"Mad? Do you wish you'd found your dad sooner? Do you think it would have been easier for you?"

"Yes, it would have been. Even if it had been awful, I don't think it would have been worse than not knowing."

"I left my family, okay? They were not good people. I don't want to go back, ever. But your dad wasn't bad like that. Tom loves him. I still love him, in my own way. I want Tom to see him. I just can't do that yet. Maybe not ever. But Tom should find him."

"You're not a bad mom. I'm so sorry I said that."

"I had a sister," Trista said. "I left her. She was so cruel to me. I've never seen her again. You found each other. You found Tom. I want to believe this is a good thing."

"Okay," Mad finally allowed.

"And don't tell Tom any of this, okay? Nothing about George Nielsen."

"I mean, at some point you'll tell him, right?"

"Of course I will. Someday. Just not now."

Mad thought about how much it would crush Tom to find this out. She couldn't imagine it. It was a pain that seemed impossible to fully accommodate at any age. To be left by your father, only to learn that he wasn't even your father, Mad tried to imagine it. To have traveled so many miles in search of a person who hadn't even made you. But maybe that was the point. How had he truly made any of them? He had left. His absence is what had shaped them, and maybe the actual biology of it was second to that fact. And what finally might have pushed Mad toward this possibility, to allow this young child to accompany them, was that, when he finally learned the truth, he would be less alone in the world because of this moment.

"Thank you," Mad said. "I'll take care of him."

"Please," Trista said. "He's so good. He's the best boy."

Trista stood up and gestured for Mad to stand up as well. And when she did, Trista embraced her firmly, and Mad stood there, frozen. It was hard to understand what was being communicated in this hug, but it seemed important to receive it.

As they walked back into the living room, Mad saw Rube and Pep sitting on the sofa with Tom, all of them transfixed by the TV screen. Rube was softly crying, one hand covering his mouth. Pep noticed Mad and her eyes widened. "Oh, Mad. Look." She gestured to the TV. "It's Tom's movie."

"It's not finished," Tom said. "It's a work in progress."

Mad turned to see their father on the TV screen, sitting on a bucket in what looked to be a messy basement. He was in profile, facing Tom, who was also sitting on a bucket. She looked at her father, still so startlingly handsome, even though he had aged, his hair longer and now silver. But it was her father. And he was right there, talking to Tom, gesturing with his hands.

She listened, the sound of her father's voice, which she had not heard since she was a little girl, saying to Tom, "You just have to believe me, okay? I'm you. Do you understand? I'm you."

"Dad," Mad said softly, and she realized that she was crying. And she looked at Rube, and his eyes were red and filled with tears, though he was now smiling. And she looked at Pep, who was trying very hard not to cry. And she looked at Tom, who was beaming, so happy to have captured their father in this way, to show his brother and sisters the person that they had been searching for.

"I made this," Tom told Mad, and she smiled.

"It's so good," she said. "It's beautiful."

***

TOM BROUGHT THE HANDYCAM WITH HIM. HE DIDN'T LIKE DOCUMENTARIES, because he thought they were a little stuck-up about the truth, because, as his dad had told him, all stories are fiction and to pretend otherwise is an artistic failure. But Tom decided that he wasn't actually going to make a documentary. He was going to record his brother and sisters and, whether they liked it or not, he was going to make them a part of his movie. Or one of his movies. He had some ideas. That's what he loved about being a low-budget independent filmmaker. You could make it something completely different when you edited it. After the thing had already happened, you could sit down, work it all out, and you could make it become what you really wanted it to be.

He'd packed a duffel bag with a half dozen gigantic T-shirts and some underwear and tube socks and high-top sneakers, his standard uniform. His new sister, Pep, had helped him, marveling at his wardrobe choices. "So you just, like, wear big, huge T-shirts? With, like, cartoons on them?" He nodded. It was hard to explain, but he'd always liked the bagginess of huge T-shirts, how they were basically dresses, and how nice it felt to know that, if danger arose, you could disappear inside your shirt, turn into a ball, and let it all pass by you. The more garish the image on the T-shirt, the easier it was to get away with the fact that you didn't have pants on.

And now he was in the backseat of this car with Pep while his oldest siblings drove and handled the map. He liked Pep, who was handsome and stern and boyish, unlike himself, who was beautiful and wide-eyed and girlish. In fact, all of his siblings were handsome and boyish, with square jaws and big hands and feet and skyscraper-tall, whereas he was so light that a huge gust of wind would get under his giant T-shirt and turn it into a parachute, sending him into the atmosphere. That, he decided, would be a good image for a movie, these three sturdy siblings holding on to the leg of the youngest child as he hung in the air like a kite. He took out his notebook and wrote down: *bigfoot kids hold on to kite kid.*

For the first hour or so of the trip, though they tried to be casual and to respect the fact that he was a little kid and they were all adults, they asked pointed questions about his dad, who was also, he guessed, their dad, but he didn't think so. They asked the following questions.

Rube: Did your dad like books? Did he like mysteries? Did he ever mention the city of Boston, Massachusetts? Did he ever use the name Harry Bucket or C. A. Hill?

Mad: Did your dad ever do any farming? Did he have a garden? Did he mention a preference for organic food over processed foods? Did he ever mention the city of Coalfield, Tennessee? Did he have a southern accent?

Pep: Did your dad like basketball? Did he mention a preference for zone defense or man-to-man? Did he ever eat at Sonic Drive-In? Did he ever mention the town of Pocola, Oklahoma? Did he say that girls could do anything that boys could do and maybe even better?

The answer to all of these questions was either *"no,"* or "I'm not sure," or "*could we stop at a Sonic Drive-In so I could try a cherry limeade?*" And though he felt bad to see how his siblings tried to hide their disappointment, he was also a little happy. Their dad was his dad, but his dad wasn't really their dad. He had been just Tom's dad.

He turned on his camera and looked at Pep through the view-finder. She was reading one of their brother's novels, a mystery. Tom had skimmed it but felt like it wouldn't make for an interest-ing film, or not the kind of film that Tom wanted to make. But Pep seemed pretty invested, her mouth softly sounding out each syl-lable as she read, and he recorded her for about eight seconds. He then turned the camera on Rube, the eldest sibling, who was staring straight ahead, but he was nodding and tilting his head from side to side, almost like he had water in his ears and was trying to get it out without anyone noticing. He noticed that Rube had the most tics, whereas Pep and Mad were like stone, barely moving. It would be nice to line them up so that they were all in profile, and film them for ten minutes and see how they blinked and breathed and ges-tured. And then, if he put the camera on a tripod, and maybe got a step stool, he'd stand next to them, like Mount Rushmore.

Mad was the hardest for him to see, because she was in the passenger seat, directly in front of him, so he tried to catch her reflection in the window, but it wasn't easy. She was looking at a road map, then out at the landscape, as if making sure that the map wasn't lying to her. She was the most mysterious to him. Rube was a little silly and Pep was young, like him, but Mad seemed like she held all of her weirdness so deeply inside of her that he would have to work hard with the camera to find it. But he didn't mind. Mad noticed him holding the camera on her, and she turned around. "Are you putting me in your movie?" she asked. "It's more like I'm taking your picture," he said, "but it's just a video."

She nodded. "Okay," she told him, "but if the picture is longer than a minute, that feels like I'm in a movie and it'll make me feel weird." Tom accepted that this made sense and agreed.

He and his father had been working on a film together, though, truth be told, it was mostly Tom. When Tom was way too young, his dad had shown him a bunch of No Wave films from the eighties, low-budget and gritty. Tom had not known what to make of them, but his father seemed so intrigued. "All those years when I was dreaming of Hollywood, trying to think of some grand block-buster," his dad told him, "I should have been doing this." His dad pointed to an image of a young, weird-looking woman with short curly hair and giant sunglasses, walking through New York City, which looked like a garbage dump to Tom. It was like an alien planet to him. He could not imagine wandering around Salt Lake City with such a lack of purpose. You'd get eaten by a black bear or a cougar would steal your hot dog right out of your hand. He imag-ined that what his father liked was the idea of looking interest-ing while surrounded by dirty stuff, as opposed to looking boring while surrounded by mountains and red rocks. And so Tom turned the basement into his own little studio, emptying box after box of old electronics and hand-me-down clothes and arranging them in a way that suggested that a very small bomb had gone off. And then he set up his Handycam on a tripod and started digging through all the old stuff and talking to himself. He wore his huge T-shirts and underwear and a pair of his mom's old rhinestone cowboy boots, and he kept picking up a dead phone and placing orders for cars. With a paisley tie as a headband, he'd bark into the phone that he wanted a "really fast car by tomorrow morning" and then, pretend-ing to hear a voice over the line, would reply, "They're all on fire? Oh, no!" and then hang up the phone. After he had about three hours of footage, he showed it to his dad, who smiled, clearly so happy. His own dad's work was mostly silent, abstract, with lots of jittery cuts after long periods of unbroken images, but he seemed to appreciate the frenetic energy of Tom's work.

"Who are you playing?" he asked Tom, who shrugged.

"Just me, I guess," he replied.

"Well, okay, so is this place in the film just your basement?"

"No, it's, like, my bomb shelter, but way in the future, and I just appeared there like in a time machine. And everyone else is gone. And I can only talk to people on the phone."

"Can I be in your movie?" his father asked, and it made Tom so happy that he almost started crying.

"Yeah, you can be in it. Everyone else is gone but you."

"But it's your movie, okay?" his dad told him. "So who can I be?"

"You'll be me," Tom said, working it out in his head as he talked. "You're me in the future. And sometimes you come into the room to check on me and talk to me, but if we're in the same place too long, you'll disappear, so you have to leave the bomb shelter sometimes so we don't cancel each other out."

"Okay," his dad said. "I like that. I can be you."

"But," Tom continued, "I don't believe that I'm you. I think maybe you might be lying to me. I think that maybe you're someone else and you just want me to think that. So sometimes I pretend that you're a stranger."

"That's good, Tom," his dad said, and Tom could tell that his father was thinking of his own version of this movie, how he would make it in his own style, but it made Tom feel a measure of pride to believe that his idea was one that his father would be compelled to steal.

And they had made the movie, improvising everything, his father looking at all the footage to see where he might come in and add something. There would be a few scenes where his dad would try to convince him that they were the same person, but he would let it go if he sensed the boy getting agitated. And then they had improvised a scene where his father had held on to Tom's shoulders and said, "You just have to believe me, okay? I'm you. Do you understand? I'm you." And then, when Tom pretended not to believe him, he continued. "I'm going to go away for a bit. I feel like I'm disappearing a little. I think I've been here too long. But when I come back, I'll bring something that will prove that I'm you, okay?" Tom had nodded. He wondered what in the world his dad was going to bring into the basement, maybe a picture of Tom as a baby? Or maybe he would wear one of Tom's giant T-shirts, with a special design, but it would look like a normal T-shirt on his dad's body. Maybe they would have the same shirt on in the scene. That's what he'd do, unless his dad had a better idea.

But later that week, his dad was gone, disappeared. His mother said that their dad needed to sort some things out. That they were taking a break from each other. And that it didn't mean that his dad didn't still love Tom, which, like, Tom had never questioned for a single moment until his mom suggested as much. "I think, Tom, it's hard to explain, but it's like me and your dad aren't the same people we were when we got married, and that's not a bad thing, but it's not a good thing to stay together just because we used to be together." Tom thought that maybe people should stay together because they had a kid and that kid needed his mom and dad, but he could tell that his mother was struggling to explain her own feelings. And she was still here. She hadn't left him. For whatever reason, his dad had left them.

When Tom asked where his dad was, his mom shrugged. "I honestly don't know at the moment, sweetie," she said. And so Tom went into the basement, set up the camera, and picked up the telephone. "Hello?" he said, but of course there was no answer. "Is anyone there? Is everyone dead? Am I still there? Am I coming back? You were going to show me something. I'm here. I'm waiting." He dug through boxes, turning back to the phone for a moment as if he'd heard a sound, but there was nothing. No one ever called him back.

HE HAD GONE FROM FEELING LIKE HE WAS ALL ALONE, ORPHANED BY HIS OWN father, to suddenly having three siblings, who were now ferrying him to meet his dad once more. That felt like an interesting movie, but he had come in a little too late. He didn't know these three people. They were, unfortunately, old. They had all experienced a life before their father left and then a life after he left them. But not Tom. His father was still so fresh in his mind, and when he saw him again, it would make the brief absence feel worse, he thought. Or would it be worse for Rube, to see his dad after thirty or forty or fifty (how old was his brother?) years and realize he was nothing like the man he'd remembered? It was messy, to think of things as a narrative. He didn't think of things as a beginning, a middle, and an ending. In his life, he mostly didn't know if things were ending or starting. He was a kid, for crying out loud. Everything felt like a beginning and an ending at the exact same time. There was no middle. It was all beginnings and endings, over and over, until you got old and had enough footage to determine what the story was about. Life made him feel funny, honestly, and he didn't feel comfortable in it. He didn't feel comfortable in his own body, even. So instead, he imagined that someone was filming *him*, that he was in someone else's movie, and he tried to act how he thought would make for a pleasing story. His mother said this was worrying, but she spent most of her time on TV. She walked through the world like a camera was always trained on her, so some of his weirdness had to be because of her. But he didn't know for sure. He looked at his siblings, who were made of the things he was made of, and he wondered who made them the way that they were. Maybe, when they all saw their dad again, all the versions of him wrapped up in a single body, it would make sense. Whatever happened, he would film it. They could all watch it later.

ad was shocked to see fields of alfalfa as they drove through Nevada, huge swaths of green. It always made her happy to see something growing, land that wasn't obscured by buildings. But it made sense, with all the cattle in Nevada, but alfalfa was not something she saw much of in Tennessee. It was always clover, and her mother, when she was sixteen, had been selected as the Queen of Crimson Clover for the annual Crimson Clover Festival. There was a framed news photo of her mother, eyes wide, holding a bouquet of clover, a crown awkwardly tilting atop her hair. She asked Tom to use his camera to record the swaying alfalfa, hoping she could show it to her mother when this was all over. They were so close to the end, weren't they?

They stopped at a gas station outside of Reno, where they'd spend the night, and Mad watched as Tom stepped out of the car, stretched his arms to the sky, his giant T-shirt reaching above his knees, and then he sighed. "Can I have anything I want in there?" he asked, pointing to the convenience store.

"Yeah," Pep replied as she jogged past them, avoiding a car that was pulling into an adjacent pump. "Yes!" Tom said, but Mad told him that there was a limit to what they could spend on gas station snacks.

"But what's the limit?" he asked, genuinely curious. Trista had given Mad an envelope with five hundred dollars to pay for any expenses that Tom accrued during the trip, but the money seemed so arbitrary. How much did it cost to take a kid from Utah to California? What was the right percentage for his share of the hotel room? And would they get a single room, still, or would Pep and Tom get their own now? Or would Rube and Tom share one room and Pep and Mad the other? Then Mad added up what she'd spent so far on this trip across the country and was sheepishly reminded of how much Rube was paying for all of them. She had not paid for a single hotel room, and, especially after that awkward moment after the car wreck when Rube had yelled about the money, Mad felt like she needed to instill some kind of financial responsibility in Tom, so she told him, "You can spend ten dollars total."

Tom frowned, as if he was adding up an imaginary bill in his mind, but finally nodded. "Okay," he said. "Do you want to give me the ten dollars?" Mad told him to just come to her with the food and she'd pay for it. And so Tom waddled across the parking lot, his video camera strap slung across his shoulder, and into the store.

Rube pumped the gas and regarded her. "We're getting close," he said. "Did you think we'd get this close?" She shook her head.

"It's Woodside, California. That's the last address I have for him."

"And we're all together now?" Mad asked him. "It's only the four of us?" She had not told Rube that Tom wasn't their biological half sibling. She felt bad for not telling him, but she worried that Rube might treat Tom differently, or that he wouldn't let Tom see their father when they found him. She'd tell him later. And Pep. Or maybe their father would tell them.

"Yes, as far as we know, there are four of us. No more. I mean, well, maybe more in California."

"If we show up and he's got septuplets or something . . . ," Mad said, trailing off.

Rube turned his attention back to the pump, now that the car was topped up. They walked into the store to look for their two youngest siblings. Pep was drinking a slushie, electric red and already staining her lips, and holding a packet of Big League Chew and some peanuts. "Where's Tom?" Mad asked.

"He went to use the restroom," she said. She looked around and then continued, "Oh, yeah, he's over there."

Mad walked over to Tom, who was standing on the precipice of a separate room, which was flashing with all manner of lights, a kind of arcade, and Mad steeled herself to negotiate the cost of video games in his allowance. She stared at the back of his giant shirt, which was on backward, showing a cartoon character named Johnny Test, playing an electric guitar with lightning bolts coming out of it, the catchphrase "Say wha?" in huge letters. He was filming the room but turned off the camera when he saw her.

"Hey there," she said, and Tom immediately turned to her, pulled on the pocket of her jeans, and said, "Go put ten dollars in that machine."

"Wait, what?" she said. "What machine?"

"The Diamond Doves machine," he said, gesturing to a glowing slot machine with different fruits in the manner of cathedral stained-glass windows, with the phrase FIVE TIMES PAY in bright letters, which Mad could not understand. She had never gambled in her life.

"Is this a real slot machine?" she asked. Was gambling legal in a gas station?

"Ten dollars," he said. "Go do it."

"Why do you want me to do that?" she asked.

"'Cause I can't go in there!" he said, in the loudest whisper she'd ever heard. "It's illegal for me to go in there. But you're over twenty-one, right?"

Mad nodded. "Yeah, by a lot of years," she replied.

"Just, okay, just go in there, okay? Put ten dollars in the little tray there and pull the lever. Look, you can win a ton of money."

"No, you can't, sweetie," she said. "The odds are crazy."

Pep appeared beside them, which made Mad jump. "Hey, what's the holdup?" Pep asked. She had, Mad noted, already re-filled the slushee cup.

"Tom wants me to gamble," Mad said, "but I told him we shouldn't."

"How much?" Pep asked.

"Ten dollars," Tom replied.

"Here, give it to me," Pep said, "I'll do it."

"Hey, now, no," Mad said.

"Don't think," Tom advised. "Just go do it."

Mad wondered where Rube was, probably using the restroom, but then she decided the quickest way to move on was to drop ten dollars, a lesson learned, so she finally nodded, saying, "Okay, ten dollars."

"Go!" Tom said, turning his camera back on, framing the scene.

It took Mad a second to get the machine to accept the ten-dollar bill, which kept spitting it back at her, like a sign, but then the machine got louder, started to whirr and whistle. She looked at the buttons, but she couldn't quite figure out what to do. She saw a button that said, "Play Max Credits" and hit it, which made the reels spin, though this was a video display and not like the slot machines Mad remembered from movies. And it seemed like the lines of possibility were greater, with strange zigzags on the glass screen, but she watched as the reels lined up and she couldn't de-cipher that anything had happened, certainly no matches, and she turned, holding up her hands, but then Tom shout-whispered, "It's saying you get a *bonus*! It's another spin."

Mad turned to the machine and pressed the button and the

machine spun again, but this time there were three symbols that all had the diamond dove symbol, sea-green cartoon diamonds with wings, and the machine went *ding-ding-ding* and Pep was now beside Mad, who turned around to see Tom, his face wild with happiness, and he pulled his T-shirt down to cover his legs and he crouched there, rocking a little, still filming her.

"I think you won!" Pep said. A light atop the machine went off, and the screen showed birds wildly flapping their wings. "Holy shit!" Pep continued, "You *did* win!"

"I won," Mad said, keeping her emotions in check. "I won. I won four thousand dollars." She turned back to Tom, his face obscured now by the camera, still filming her. She gave a thumbs-up, smiled. The machine spit out a slip of paper, and she took it. She and Pep jogged out of the arcade, the machine still making a racket, and she showed the slip to Tom, who returned the camera to his side.

"Four hundred thousand dollars!" he shouted, which made the only other person in the gas station turn to look at them. It was an old lady, and her eyes widened in shock.

"No, Tom, look, it's not four hundred thousand dollars. It's just—I mean, not *just*, but—it's four thousand dollars."

"What is happening?" Rube said, finally walking up to them. "I couldn't find you. I went back to the car. I thought you guys ran off."

"We gambled," Mad admitted. "We played the slots."

"In a gas station?" Rube asked, confused.

"Mad won four thousand dollars!" Pep told him.

"Well, I mean, Tom won it, but he's not twenty-one, so I was kind of like his proxy or something."

"That's a thousand for each of us!" Tom said. "And I still have the money that Mom gave you."

"You're gonna share it with us?" Pep asked.

"Yeah," he said. "Of course. You would, right?"

"I mean, yeah," Pep admitted, "but you're a kid. I didn't know if you'd share."

"Of course," he said, smiling. "We all get a thousand dollars. So where's the money?" he asked.

"It's just this slip of paper. They don't do the coins anymore, I guess. I just . . . okay, I take it to the front counter." Mad walked up to the teenager at the register, who saw the slip of paper and instantly seemed nervous. "You win something?" he asked Mad, who nodded sheepishly. "I never gamble," she said, as if this guy would judge her. "Beginner's luck, I guess."

She handed him the slip and his eyes widened even more. "Oh, holy shit. Um, I gotta . . . let me . . . we don't have that kind of money."

"Oh," Mad said. "So what do we do?"

"Trade it in for lottery tickets," Tom offered. "Look, these ones say you can win five hundred thousand dollars."

"Oh, no, it doesn't work like that, little dude," the cashier said to Tom. "But, honestly, it's an outside company who handles the gambling machines. We can do, like, up to three hundred or something like that, but I've never seen anybody win this much."

"How do we get our money?" Pep said.

"You might have to come back in a few days," he told them, and Pep leaned over the counter. "We're traveling through, okay? We are not going to be here in a few days."

The force of Pep's insistence, plus the wildness of Tom's excitement, his T-shirt swaying as he spun around the store, made the cashier reconsider his options. He picked up the phone, looked through a little folder under the counter, and then made a call. He turned away from them, walking as far as he could get for privacy, but they could make out some of it. "Yeah," he said, "four grand, dude . . . well, yeah, the ticket is right here. . . . No, this chick is adamant that they want the money now . . . okay . . . yeah . . . four grand, dude."

When he hung up the phone, he turned to them, nervously smiling. "Okay, so somebody is coming with the money right now."

"Wait, like, someone is bringing the cash here?"

"That's correct. He has some tax forms or something and then he'll give you the money, in cash, and then you and your kids can get back on the road."

"I'm going to get another slushee," Pep said. "The cola one, this time."

"He thinks we're the parents," Mad said to Rube.

"We are," Rube said. "For now, we are."

A battered Honda Civic pulled up twenty-five minutes later, and a man stepped out with a bank pouch. "You the lucky lady?" he asked Mad, who nodded. He had a sunny disposition for someone who was about to fork over thousands of dollars, but she imagined that this happened once a year, if even that, and he must be making so much more off of people who had been forced by their newly discovered half sibling to bet ten dollars on a slot machine and subsequently lost and then poured nine hundred and ninety more dollars into the machine without success. It was interesting to Mad, that they could both be happy over the outcome, such a rare thing. She filled out the forms, and the entire family circled around the man, Tom's camera trained on the scene, as he counted out hundred-dollar bills into Mad's waiting palm. Even the cashier huddled with them as they counted—"Three thousand eight hundred, three thousand nine hundred, four thousand!"— and Mad held the stack of cash with both hands and backed out of the convenience store, running to the car like they'd just pulled a robbery, Pep and Tom, still filming, and Rube chasing after her. They were all laughing, and then Tom said, "I think this is the luckiest thing that's ever happened to me!" and who would disagree? It was maybe the most she had ever felt like she belonged to a family, the happiest she'd ever been that she had people related to her there to witness the event. It was such a great sensation, and she knew it was magical and improbable and that most families don't win four thousand dollars on a gas station slot machine. But that absolutely did not matter to her at this moment. She had a family, a large family, and they were all filthy rich. As they drove to Reno, she handed each family member a thousand dollars, and she let Tom hold on to his portion, which he fanned out in his lap over and over.

She stared out at the fields of alfalfa, marveling at the fact that she was riding in a Chevy HHR with her three siblings, farther from home than she had ever been in her life, somehow wealthier than she'd been before she started the trip. If they turned around right now, if they just put the car in reverse, dodging the oncoming traffic, all the way back to Tennessee, it would honestly have been enough for her. Everything in this moment was lovely, no harm done, but she knew it wouldn't last. What else could they do? They had to push their luck.

CHAPTER EIGHT

Finally, here Mad was, in the same state as her father for the first time in more than twenty years. There was a pleasure in this fact, not the proximity to her father, necessarily, but the notion that she was so close to him and he had no idea. After so many years of uncertainty, a kind of constant low-level mystery swirling around her, she knew something that her father did not know. If she could only maintain this feeling of superiority for as long as she could, if she could somehow walk undetected into her father's home, could stand just behind him until he sensed something charged in the air, and then reach out her hand to tap him on the shoulder, it would almost make the twenty-plus years worth it. Almost.

Woodside, California, was not what the kids had expected when they thought of their father, questing further and further from his origins, but unless their dad planned to sail across the Pacific Ocean or hike to Alaska, it was a place to settle. It was also abundantly clear that it was rich as hell, the houses looking like things that railroad magnates had lost, thanks to the steady dilution of their fortune and then sold to venture capitalists who did things with money that would make the old-money folks want to kill themselves if they weren't already dead. It was interesting to chart their father's progression across the country. He had started in a metropolitan city, and when his first bout of restlessness and ennui hit, he sought out rural spaces, agriculture, "real" America.

And then he went to Oklahoma, the vast plains, an opportunity to consider the questions of life on this planet. And then he went to Salt Lake City, which had the word *city* in the name, a place, though still mountainous and wondrous with nature, where you could get sushi if you wanted it. And then, perhaps realizing how little time he had left on this mortal coil, he decided to pick one of the richest places in the world, populated with people who owned wineries and horse farms and made artificial hearts, and decided it was time to relax. This was all conjecture, of course, but their father, in his absence, encouraged, perhaps even demanded, conjecture.

They could see the Santa Cruz Mountains as they left behind the coffee shops and dog boutiques and stores that were probably just fine, but made Mad grumpy on principle. And then they arrived at the address, and they were looking at a mansion so large and ornate and old that it looked like the cover of a romance novel, or the painted backdrop to a movie from the forties. If their father was inside this mansion, everything made a little more sense. Forget about familial responsibility. Just set aside the ethics of abandoning children and lying to everyone who ever loved you. If you started out in an apartment in Boston, Massachusetts, and you intuited that your real future lay here, in a mansion on the edge of the Pacific Ocean, maybe you had to go find that mansion. She was still so mad at her father, but, truly, this was a breathtaking mansion.

"Our dad is rich," Tom said.

"There's a gate," Pep observed. "We can't even get in. Who is going to let us in? Dad's just gonna hide in there if he sees us."

"Oh, god," Rube said. "Wow. I am losing my nerve."

"No, Rube, please," Mad said. "Look, there's a little box. We just talk into that box. He opens the gate. We finish what we started."

"Once he closes the gate back, we're trapped," said Rube.

"Dad is not going to trap us," Tom said.

"He doesn't even want us here in the first place," Pep offered.

"We won't know until we talk into that little box, Rube," Mad said, and Rube nodded. He drove up to the box and rolled down the window. He pushed the button.

"He might not even be here," Rube said.

"Why would anyone leave this place?" Tom wondered.

"Hello?" the voice said. It was a woman's voice, cautious, and instantly everyone in the car seemed to relax a bit. They could delay the shock of seeing their father for a few more seconds. And the astounding length of the driveway would give them a few minutes to prepare. They just had to get in.

"Yes, hello," Rube said. "My name is Reuben Hill and I am trying to schedule a meeting with my—well, with our—I have associates with me who are also involved in this—"

"Who is this?" the woman asked, so confused.

"Why do you always talk like a fake lawyer when you get nervous?" Pep asked. "It's so weird."

"I'm here with my brother and sisters and we're looking for our dad. His name is Charles Hill and this is the address I have for him. We want to speak to him. We want to meet him."

There was silence. Mad wondered how long they would stay here, waiting for an answer. Forever? How could they turn back now. They would ram this car into the gate, over and over, until they gained entry. They had wrecked one car already. What was one more?

"You're Charles's children?" she finally asked.

"Yes," Rube replied. "There are four of us."

"You have no ill intentions? You are not trying to hurt me?"

Mad once more thought about Rube's initial desire to kill their father, and she hoped, in his strange state, that he didn't mention that he had only considered killing his dad, but that now he had no murderous thoughts toward him and that he'd never once, even in the early stages of the fantasy, thought about killing innocent bystanders. She prayed this did not happen.

"I'm so sorry, ma'am, but we don't even know who you are. We understand why you would be shocked or concerned, but we're just trying to find our father."

"I will let you in. I'll meet you at the front door. I'm trusting you."

"You can trust us," Tom said from the backseat, and Mad resisted the urge to shush him because she sensed that would only make things worse, to hear the harsh shushing of a small child just as you're about to push the button that protects you from intruders.

The gate slowly opened, and Rube inched the car forward.

"Is Dad going to be out on the front porch, too?" Pep asked. "Is he here?"

"We're so close," Rube said. "Is everyone okay?"

"No!" Pep yelled. "Of course not. But we have to keep going, right? Let's just do this."

When they pulled up to the house, which did not recede in grandeur the closer they got to it, there was a woman who seemed to be in her forties, fit in the way that rich people were fit, just the slightest bit of frailty embedded in their good health. She was wearing a wildly floral long-sleeved maxidress, like something Joan Didion would have worn in the seventies, and was standing at the front door.

"I'm scared," Mad admitted. She did not like to be in the presence of wealth, but who did? Even rich people probably didn't like being around other rich people on their home turf. But at least they had a Rolex or the security of an Ivy League education to protect them. Mad was a farmer looking for her lost father like someone out of an old John Ford movie.

"There's four of us and just one of her," Rube said.

"And Dad," Pep added.

"And maybe another kid," Tom said.

"We have to get out of this car," Rube said. "The longer we sit here, the more suspicious it looks."

And so they exited the car, all of them in perfect unison, all four doors opening at once, and they regarded this rich woman and tried to smile.

"You're looking for Charles Hill?" she said. They all nodded. "And you are his children?"

They nodded again. "From different mothers?" They nodded. "From different places in the continental United States?" How much nodding was going to be involved in this meeting. Why didn't they just say, *yeah!*? But it was too late. They were nodding. They were going to keep nodding.

"And you think he's here?" she asked. Rube turned back to the car, as if he needed his briefcase and documents to support their assertion, but they were too far to doubt themselves. They were here.

"He is not here," she said. Mad nearly shouted an obscenity. Rich people, leisurely people with no real responsibilities or schedule infuriated her. They were here for their father and now this woman was toying with them. The only way it would have been more infuriating was if she was smoking a cigarette in one of those fancy holders or if she was petting a hairless cat.

"But you know our dad?" Tom asked, undeterred.

"Yes, I know your father. But he's not here and this is not his address."

"Did he leave you?" Tom asked.

"No," the woman replied, though she allowed the slightest smile. "He did not."

"Oh, wow, did you leave him?" Tom asked.

"I have an address for you and that's where you'll find him. I believe this is an important thing that you're doing and regardless of what anyone else may think, you should meet your father and be able to talk to him."

Another quest. Mad wanted to scream. Always another quest, some other thing that they had to accomplish, some mountain to traverse or some insane billionaire heiress to humor. The further you get into the quest, no matter how long it continues, you can't leave it. You're too far into it.

The woman had a piece of paper and held it out to Rube, who walked over to take it. "Thank you," he said.

"It's a very vast property," she warned them.

"Bigger than this?" Pep wondered.

"In terms of acreage, yes," the woman said.

"Well, we've taken up enough of your time," Mad said. "Thank you for the address and sorry to bother you."

"We didn't even get to see the inside of the house," Tom whispered to her. "I would like to check out the interiors for my film."

"We have to find Dad, okay?" Mad replied, and Tom reluctantly agreed. They all got back into the HHR and turned it around to head down the driveway. The woman waved.

"She didn't even tell us her name," Pep said.

"Was that Dad's new wife?" Rube wondered.

"Ex-wife?" Mad offered.

"I think we need to pretend like this didn't happen," Rube said. "At least until we find Dad."

It was quiet for a moment while the gate opened up again for them. They passed through and then they drove to the first parking lot they could find, which took fifteen minutes, in order to look at the address and compare it to their road maps. "It's in Woodside," Mad said. She was trying to figure out the map, but the address seemed to be swallowed up by empty space, acres and acres and acres of nothing. "I think dad might be hiding in the wilderness, like a survivalist or something."

"I didn't want to say it earlier, but I think he's started a cult," Rube replied.

"I think he's maybe a monk, you know?" Pep offered. "He's atoning for his sins by living in a cave and praying with squirrels."

Tom looked up at them from his notebook. "I think he probably just got married again and he has another kid."

"Jeez, Tom," Pep said. "That was brutal."

"Okay, we can get there. It's far, but not that far," Mad told them. It was hard to summon the terror they had just felt, because they started to wonder if they'd ever actually find their father. If they had to go into Canada, Mad would lose her mind. This had to be it. It had to end at some point. That's how life worked, right?

After a half hour of driving, they turned onto a road that was winding, one-way, and steeply rising. It would be so disappointing to slide off the side of a mountain and die just minutes before they reunited with their long-lost rake of a father. It would be so goddamn embarrassing. If they had died when the PT Cruiser malfunctioned and sent them hurtling toward a terrible reckoning in the vast plains of the southwestern United States, that was one thing. It was an unfortunate outcome to a quest, which is by nature fraught with peril. But if the Chevy HHR flipped end over end down a winding mountain road and their father, pushing a baby stroller, happened upon their mangled bodies the next day, well, that felt mythic. And myths were either really cool or really embarrassing, and Mad knew which way the balance would tilt for her.

They leveled out, the road still so narrow, and Mad wondered if it was a good or bad thing that not a single car had come from the opposite direction. The road forked and they observed a rotting wooden sign that simply said DARDANELLE RANCH, with

additional blocks of less-weathered wood signifying house numbers attached to the sign but without much in the way of direction. "Two-two-seven-eight!" Mad called out, pointing to one of
the numbered signs. "That's where that weird rich lady said Dad
is living."

"So we're doing this," Rube said. "We're going to see Dad,
right?"

Mad wondered what would happen if Tom simply stepped
out of the car and started walking in the opposite direction. If
Mad suddenly revealed that she did not actually want to see their
father. She knew Rube was only trying to prolong the inevitable
and also give weight to this moment, but she wanted him to drive.
They were no longer on a road that offered the distinct possibility
of death, and she wanted to go, to get on with it.

"Let's go," the rest of them said, willing themselves to be
ready for what came next.

THE DAY BEFORE, WHEN SHE REALIZED HOW CLOSE THEY WERE TO THIS
moment, she had taken Rube aside, away from Pep and Tom, and
asked him if he was okay. He looked confused and she reminded
him that he had recently admitted under great duress that he had
been planning to murder their father. And that his siblings would
serve as possible suspects to aid in evading arrest. How could that
impulse be gone? Once someone puts murder on the table, you
cannot pretend that murder wasn't an option.

Rube said, "I wish I'd never revealed that to you and Pep."

"Pep and I also wish that you'd kept it to yourself."

"The thing is, the more of you that I met, and the closer I got
to the reality of what is going to happen, I realized it was such a
terrible thing. It would ruin me. My life would end. And if you
were to witness it, your lives would end. I can't kill someone in

front of Tom. He's a child. It was just a bad idea and I ran with it because I honestly didn't know how to write any other ending. I thought it had to go that way, and now, because of you, I feel like maybe there's a better way to end it."

"Well, okay. You're being kind of fanciful about it, and I'm just worried because it felt like a very real intent to murder our dad."

"I'm not going to do it," Rube replied, trying to keep his voice down. "I promise you, Mad."

And she believed him. He had come up with the idea when he had been an only child. But they had each other now.

THEY DROVE DOWN A DIRT ROAD, MARVELING AT HOW THE DENSE WOODS periodically gave way to expansive views of hills, with sheds and barns and what looked like a fairly huge horse stable seemingly built into the landscape, the sky blue and cool and cloudless. Though they hadn't seen another vehicle or human being during the drive on this road, Mad was more confused by the lack of animals. There were no steer, no horses, not even a chicken waddling across the road. For such a huge tract of land, it seemed foreboding that nothing animated it, only Mad and her siblings in this dinky little car.

Finally, after about five miles, they reached a clearing, and the road was now paved, and they saw a sign that read HIDDEN DRIVE AHEAD, and then a series of driveways, each numbered, including one that was marked 2278, which she pointed out to Rube, who turned onto it. They drove and Mad realized that she was having trouble breathing, like it was taking effort to pull air into her lungs, and her chest was tight. She remembered feeling like this at the end of Pep's game, and she tried to suck in air without anyone noticing. Of course, everyone else in the car noticed. Rube turned to look at her. "You okay?" he asked, and she nodded. She looked in the rearview to see that Pep was also staring at her. Tom had focused the camera on her, which made her chest tighten even more. If this was a movie, she realized that she was the innocent young soldier who gets killed immediately.

"I'm having a little trouble breathing," she said. "And swallowing, too, actually."

"You might be having a heart attack," Tom offered from behind the camera.

"It's an anxiety attack," Rube said. "I get them all the time. Do you feel like you might be dying, but it's low level and you don't want to acknowledge that possibility because it will make you look weak and crazy and so that makes it even worse?"

Mad took another shallow breath. "It does."

"That's an anxiety attack," he said. "Which is perfectly normal."

"Why aren't you having one?" she asked, and he replied, "Because I'm on a lot of meds and I also took a Klonopin at the last rest stop. That's why that narrow road on the edge of the mountain didn't even faze me."

"When I get nervous," Pep offered, "like before a game? I throw up a ton and then I feel fine."

Tom admitted that he didn't get nervous or panicky.

"If we could, like, not talk about it. I just need a second, I thi—"

"We're here," Rube said, his face instantly apologetic. "We're here."

Mad looked up to see the most beautiful structure, all wood and glass, angles that could only be described as Scandinavian, absolutely pristine. It made her want to die.

"Rube!" Mad said.

He put his hand on the top of her head and instantly thought better of it, placing it instead on her shoulder, a nice, familial gesture of support. Pep leaned over from the backseat and put her hand on top of Mad's head, and then Tom did the same. And it did not feel good. It made her uncomfortable, but it also, somehow, made her want to cry. Was there ever a time in her life in all of her years on earth when this many people touched her at once, stood next to her to let her know that they loved her? No. The answer was no.

"I have never had anxiety until I met you," she said to Rube. "Thirty-two years and nothing, and now I've had two freakouts on this trip."

"That only means that you are, you know, truly living," Rube said.

"Guess I am, too," offered Pep. "I ran away from my entire team and hid by a bridge and then jumped into your car. My coach doesn't even know where I am."

"I won four thousand dollars," Tom said. "But I haven't been on the trip as long as you have."

"*We* won four thousand dollars," Rube replied. "Mad, you won a ton of money on a slot machine. Don't focus on the times you felt like you were dying, okay? That's not gonna help you. Just like Pep shouldn't focus on losing the biggest game of her entire life, right? What does that help? We're here. We're about to meet our dad. Whatever happens, it's not just going to happen to you. It's going to happen to all of us. Together."

"Do you think he's watching us from the window?" Mad asked, feeling her breathing begin to steady, not sure how to tell her siblings to remove their hands from her body.

"The whole freaking house is a window," Pep offered. "He doesn't have curtains, either. I don't see anybody."

They stepped out of the car and walked cautiously to the front steps of the deck. "I'm going to knock on the door," Rube said. "Now I feel like I'm having an anxiety attack."

"No one's in there," Pep said. "I mean, I can see inside. It looks like a freaking magazine or an ad or something. No one is in there."

"Maybe he's . . ." Mad said, trailing off. "Maybe he's incapacitated."

"Should we break in to check?" Rube asked.

Even though Mad's father had been an avowed pacifist, he'd had two shotguns on their farm. Mad wondered if Pep's version of their father owned guns, or Tom's. If they all got shot by their dad while trying to break into his cabin in order to reunite with him, they would be on every single news show in the world.

"No," Mad said, certain. "We'll just wait. We've made it this far. We'll wait until he shows up."

"I'm going to explore," Tom said, holding up the camera to take in the view.

"No, Tom, wait," Mad said. "There could be mountain lions. Predators."

"I'll go with him," Pep said.

"What if he comes back?" Rube said. "You guys will be stuck in a well, and he'll show up and I'll be all by myself."

"Well, I don't think we should split up," Mad said.

"We have my phone," Pep said, holding it up. "Oh, wait, damn, there's no reception at all out here."

"We'll all explore together," Mad finally declared. "We need to stretch our legs and it'll be less confrontational if we're not all just sitting on the deck waiting for him to come back from the general store or something." Honestly, she wanted to look around the ranch. She'd never seen this much uncultivated land in her life. It was startling and beautiful and a little scary.

"Well, what about the wagon?" Rube offered. "If he sees the car and we're not here, he'll get suspicious."

"We should cover it in tree branches and camouflage it," Tom offered.

"No, that would make him more suspicious," Mad replied. "Why don't we drive back out to the main road and then I saw a clearing where we could park and then we'll walk around. Maybe we'll even see him."

"Okay, that's good," Rube said. "I feel like the best version of our meetings was when I came to see you in Tennessee and you had time to see the car drive up from far away, you know? With Pep, we had to call, and with Tom, we had to ask his mom first. It wasn't easy to create an organic moment of communion, but if you see this vehicle in the distance, you have time to get prepared."

"Yeah, fine, sure," Mad said. "Let's all get back in the wagon," and Pep and Tom both groaned.

"You guys are overthinking this," Pep said.

"Wait," Tom said. He rolled down the window and leaned out with the camera. Pep held on to his legs without being asked, to keep him from getting tossed out of the car if they hit a bump. He tried to fix his arms as steady as possible, and then he said, "Action!" and Rube started to drive back down the road, and it was as if Mad, even though she was facing forward, could see the shot as it assembled itself, the cabin getting smaller and smaller, the sky opening up above them, this little spot in the wilderness.

Once they parked, it took a few minutes for Rube to find what he deemed a suitable walking stick, and then they were off. Mad did worry that Tom, with his T-shirt dress, might not be prepared for snakes or creatures or even just rocks if he took a tumble, but she decided against voicing this concern. He lived in a state filled with overly religious types, as he ran around in a makeshift dress until he could wear a regular dress, maybe, who knows, and she wasn't going to mess that up for him.

After thirty minutes of hiking, the group came upon a clearing atop a slight hill, but Mad let her eyes adjust and noticed that there was a tunnel built into the hill. It was bigger than a storm drain, certainly man-made, just wide enough that one person at a time could walk through it. And atop the hill was a wooden structure, what looked like a colosseum for a low-rent Renaissance festival.

"What in the world is that?" Rube asked Mad, who shrugged.

"Maybe storage for wood?" Mad offered, "or a little performance space?"

"A performance for whom?" Rube wondered? "For squirrels?"

"Let's go in," Pep said, and Tom was already walking into the tunnel.

"Wait!" Mad said. "Pep, you get in front."

"That'll mess up the shot," Tom said.

"If there's no minotaur in there that kills all of us," Mad offered, "you can go back and shoot it the way you want."

One by one, they walked into the tunnel, and Mad was shocked to find that the walls of the tunnel were warped pieces of wood, bending like the walls of a ship, but so loosely joined that dozens of rays of sunlight pierced the tunnel.

"It's like the belly of a whale," Pep said in amazement. And then she hit a section that was perfectly sealed, pitch dark, and she stopped for a second, feeling around for the way through.

When they finally emerged inside the structure, Mad noticed that the opening was a perfect triangle pointing back the way that they had come. Inside the structure, the ground was covered in sickly yellow brush and dry dirt.

"This is so weird," Pep remarked. "Like, this is exactly the place where someone like me gets sacrificed by a bunch of weirdo creeps. And I bet that, like, the virgin moonlight once every fifty years shines exactly on the opening and they bash my head in when I peek out."

"It is definitely unexplainable and ominous," Rube admitted.

"It's just a piece of art," Tom said. "It's good, too. Only one way in and one way out. You have to travel through it. Okay, Pep, go back in there and then come out of the opening with your hand over your eyes, like you just woke up from eating a poisoned apple."

Pep did as she was directed, and Tom held the camera as low to the ground as he could get. "Nice," he said, once Pep, stretching to her full height, stood inside the structure.

"Do you think that Dad made this?" Mad asked Rube, who considered it.

"I think that's very possible," he admitted. "This might be his new thing, building strange structures in unpopulated landscapes. Sure. Why not?"

The work with the wood—the bend of it so that it looked like the skeleton of a dinosaur, to make sure it was a perfectly octagonal space inside the structure—it felt to Mad like the work her father did on the farm, to be both precise and wild at the same time.

"Okay, we'd better keep hiking," Rube said. "Tom, do you wanna go first this time with your camera?"

"Yeah!" Tom said, running swiftly down the wooden stairs, disappearing into the earth. Pep followed, then Mad, and Rube took up the rear. Mad closed her eyes, tried to make her way through the tunnel by touch, the soft scraping sound of her feet on the slightly damp earth, the way slats of light played upon her eyelids. When she finally made it to the opening, she walked out into the wilderness again and opened her eyes, only to see Pep and Tom standing stock-still, Tom's camera held limp at his side. She looked up, and she saw their father.

His hair was shockingly white and came down to his shoulders, and he had a beard, his face tan and weathered, but it was unmistakably him. He was wearing a pair of cargo shorts and a ratty blue T-shirt.

"Kids?" their dad said.

"Dad," Tom said.

"It's us," Pep admitted.

Rube touched Mad's shoulder, holding her back. And then Mad noticed the backpack their father was wearing, the pack sitting high above his shoulders. And inside the pack was a toddler, a little boy, who was regarding them with utter indifference. Their brother, she imagined. They were together at last, for the first time.

"Hello, kids," their father said.

Mad took a breath and realized how easily her lungs pulled air into her chest. She was ready for this. She would not mess it up. She had found her father. He wouldn't get away from her again, no matter how hard he tried.

CHAPTER NINE

You found me," their father said. "All of you."

"We did," Rube said, stepping forward. "It was not easy. You didn't make it easy."

"How did you find me?" their father asked. "Did you all work together . . . how did you . . . ? I'm confused."

"Some rich lady gave us your address," Tom said. "She lived in a mansion. She knew you."

Their father nodded, as if this made perfect sense.

"Yes, but that was just today. I hired a private investigator after . . . after Mom died. She tracked you down, all the places you'd been. And she helped me find my brothers and sisters, who, incidentally, I had no idea even existed."

"I'm sorry about your mother, Rube," he began, but Rube cut him off.

"I don't want to talk about that. Why did you leave me? Why did you leave Mad? And Pep? And Tom?" He gestured to his siblings. "Why did you never come back to us? Or tell us where you were?"

Their father seemed to genuinely consider these questions as if he'd never once imagined he would be asked them. Like he had just been picked out of a studio audience to play a quiz show that he'd never seen before. Or maybe he was weighing how badly the answers would make all of them cry so damn much.

"Could we not do this here?" their father asked.

"Here, like, this weird sacrificial structure? Or here, like, this day and time?" Rube asked.

"Could we just go back to my place and sit down? I can make coffee. We have a lot to talk about."

"Rube," Mad said. "We need to talk to him. Let's go back. We all have things we want to say."

"Does your house have enough chairs?" Rube asked. "Do you entertain?"

"There's enough room for us to talk," he said. The little boy hovering over their father in his backpack made noises of irritation, rocking as if their father was a horse and he was spurring him forward. "C'mon, let's walk." And though it pained them to allow it, they let their father lead them back to his house, each one of them following behind, the sound of birds echoing through the trees.

BACK AT THE CABIN, AFTER QUITE POSSIBLY THE MOST AWKWARD AND SI-lent family hike in human history, their father carefully shed his backpack and removed the little boy, who Mad still believed might not actually be their sibling. Seeing her father now, recognizing his age, made her hope that he was not still making children that he would subsequently leave. Even as they traveled closer and closer to him, even as she learned about the versions of him after he left her, she wasn't prepared for the realization that her dad was freaking seventy years old. He was an old man. And here he was, delicately removing the cute little hiking boots of a toddler who she was not convinced could actually walk.

"What's his name?" Pep asked, looking at the boy.

"Rooster," their father replied, and the boy smiled at the sound of his own name. "Say hi, Rooster," their father said, and Rooster said, not quite verbal, "Ha."

"How old?" Mad asked.

"Rooster is two years old," their father answered.

"He's your kid?" Pep asked, and their father, after a second of hesitation, merely nodded.

"Rooster is kind of a cool name," Tom said, who was blinking back tears. Mad wondered what it was like for Tom, still a child, to see how easily his father had moved on, had started over. It was still so fresh. He was still expecting their father to come back to him. And now, here was this little kid. It was not the toddler's fault, but Mad kind of blamed him.

"What's his real name?" Rube asked. "I'm assuming Rooster is his nickname."

"It is," their father said. He looked uncomfortable. "His name is . . . it's Reuben."

Rube's face revealed his confusion. "What?"

"I'm sorry. Yes, his name is Reuben. It's a good name."

"It's my name!" Reuben said. "It's the name you gave me."

"But we call him Rooster," their father lamely offered.

"You're reusing names?" Pep asked. "There are, like, a million names in the world. You've used"—she took a second to be sure of the number—"Four of them and now you're plagiarizing the names of your other children?"

Mad wasn't sure what she wanted this reunion to be like, but she realized now that, if someone didn't get control of the situation, it was going to be a lot of this dynamic, their father trying to explain himself, poorly, and the kids rotating in and out to make him aware of how much he'd messed them up. She wanted to step in, to try and find a way to have a real conversation, to start from the beginning, but she realized that their father had escalated the emotional stakes with this naming mistake. He'd gone and put the end back at the beginning, and now they were stuck in a loop.

"Reuben was my uncle's middle name," their father finally

said. "I didn't have a father. He left before I was even born. I never met him. My mom's brother helped take care of me. For a while. Then he died when I was seven."

"I never knew that," Rube said. "You never told me."

"I don't like to talk about my past," their father said.

Mad wasn't sure if this was a joke, but it actually made Rube bark with laughter. Their father looked sheepish. "Sorry," their father said. "I know this is really fraught."

"It's fine. I'm not going to make you change the kid's name," Rube replied, gesturing toward the little boy. "Rooster, Rube, Reuben, whatever. It's just, god, this is all starting out so badly. I think it was coming out of that weird tunnel and finding you. I wasn't ready."

"Well, also," their father continued, "I . . . nothing."

"No, what?" Rube asked.

"I failed you. I failed all of you, obviously. I wanted to try again, and somehow I thought that if I named him Reuben, it might be nice to finally be reminded of you and that life instead of trying to always forget about it."

"The way you could have been reminded of me and that life was just to call me and let me know that you weren't dead or in the Witness Protection Program and maybe just have come to see me anytime in the thirty-some-odd years since you left."

"Yes, obviously, but—"

"And you called our moms," Mad added. "You called them but not us."

"I shouldn't have done that."

"No! You should have! You should have just called us, too," Pep said. "Just say, 'hey, here I am. Maybe we can meet up at the zoo sometime and hang out.'"

"Look, Rooster needs his lunch. Do you want anything to eat?

He has to eat and then he needs a nap. Maybe after his nap we can restart."

"*Are* you hungry, Rooster?" Tom asked the boy with great suspicion, but the toddler nodded emphatically.

"Ya," he replied.

Their father walked over to Rooster and picked him up, grimacing a little from the effort, and then held the boy on his hip as he awkwardly shuffled past Pep and into the kitchen. Mad wondered if they should go outside, sit in the car until lunch was over, and then knock on the door as if none of this had happened. But then Pep whispered to her, "I'm kind of hungry, actually." And then Tom walked over to her, as if she was somehow the envoy for the Republic of Abandoned Children, and said, "I don't want to just sit here and watch that baby eat. Can we eat, too?"

And then, noticing that they were all talking, Rube huddled up with them. "This baby is the worst!" he whispered.

"Our brother," Mad reminded him, and Rube made an expression of exasperation.

"He's not really our brother until Dad leaves him and starts a new family."

"We're hungry," Pep told him.

"Are you guys hungry?" their father called out.

"Yes," Pep and Tom replied at the exact same time.

"I've got the staples," their father offered. "Some good sourdough and cheese and pickles and some mortadella. I've got eggs, too. Some arugula for a salad."

"You could make those shirred eggs that you made for me and my mom," Mad whispered to Rube.

"Absolutely not," Rube said.

"It worked on me," Mad said. "They were so good. It kind of convinced me to come on this trip."

"Well, I'm not trying to impress our father," Rube replied. "He needs to impress me."

"What is the kid gonna eat?" Pep asked their dad. "Like, what does he like?"

"Grilled cheese," their father said.

"I'll have that," Pep said, and then Tom said, "Me, too!"

"Rube? Mad?" their father asked.

"If everyone is going to have grilled cheese," Mad said, "I'll eat one, too." It would be too weird to watch everyone else eat while she stood over them.

Rube then said, "What kind of salad would be possible?"

"There's some good options. Come look," their father said, and Rube paused.

"I'll just have a grilled cheese, too."

"That's, let's see, one-two-three-four-five-six grilled cheese sandwiches. This cast-iron skillet is going to be working overtime. Let me just use the restroom real quick, wash my face and hands from that hike, and then I'll get started." He put Rooster down on the floor and then sideways-stepped through the crowd of his children. He smiled at them and then closed the door to the bathroom. Mad heard the lock click on the door.

"So you like grilled cheese sandwiches?" Pep asked Rooster, who only stared at her. Tom lifted his camera and observed the boy through his viewfinder before letting the camera fall limply at his side.

"I don't like this," Tom said. "I thought he'd be happier to see me."

"I think he is," Mad told the boy. "I think he's less excited, you know, to see me and Rube and Pep, because we're adults and he doesn't know us as well anymore. I bet if it was just you, he'd be different."

"Maybe you guys should take Rooster for a hike, then,"

Tom offered, "and then when you come back, things won't be as weird."

Just then, they heard a slamming sound from the bathroom.

"Jesus, did Dad just fall in there?" Pep said, rushing over to the door. "Hey, are you okay in there?"

"Yes, it's fine. I dropped a big bottle of moisturizer on the dang floor. Hold on."

Without thinking, Mad ran out of the cabin, down the stairs of the porch, and around the back to find her father, staring out the open window of the bathroom.

"Dad," she said. "Please."

"This goddamn window," he replied. "I haven't opened it since last summer. The wood warped or something."

"Go back into the kitchen," Mad said. "Go make grilled cheese sandwiches for your children. And then we're going to talk. And you're going to listen."

"This is difficult, Mad," he said. "It's a lot to handle, and there are things—"

"GO. MAKE. GRILLED. CHEESE. SANDWICHES. FOR. YOUR. CHILDREN," Mad repeated, and their father sheepishly closed the window.

Back in the house, Pep asked, "Did he try to climb out the bathroom window?" and Mad nodded. "Dad!" Pep said. "It's been like fifteen minutes."

"I was getting some air. I was having, for your information, a panic attack, I think. I wasn't going to jump out the window. This is my cabin. Where would I go?" Mad was about to remind him that his entire modus operandi was to leave a place where he lived and simply start over, but he started slicing the bread, buttering it, organizing all the slices of cheese. "I just wasn't expecting guests."

"We're family," Rube said, "it's different."

Mad walked over to the stove. "Here, I'll help. I'll cook them and you do the prep."

Pep offered to take Rooster back into the living room to play, to clear out the space, and Tom offered to help. "Does he have real toys?" Pep asked. "Or is it, like, corn cob dolls or something?" Their father said Rooster liked a marble run that he had built for the boy, which was near the fireplace.

Rube said he was going to sit on the porch, and then he took two steps outside and stood right in front of the doorway, staring up at the sky.

"You've got a Lodge cast-iron skillet," Mad observed. The factory that made these was less than an hour from their farm.

"Only skillet worth a damn," their father said.

"So you buy a new one each time you leave? You have to start over completely?" Mad asked.

Their father stopped slicing the bread and considered the question. "I guess so. You kind of learn to focus on the essentials, a few things you truly need. But, honestly, life has a way, whether you like it or not, of accumulating. You always end up with more than you need."

"But not everything," Mad offered.

"Right. Not everything," their father replied, shaking his head.

As she toasted the bread, the cheese beginning to soften, she asked him, "Do you remember me?"

"I do," he answered. "I really do. Not everything. Probably not as much as I'd like. I'm old. But I do remember you."

"Back then," she said. "You remember me from back then."

"Yes," he said, "of course I do."

"Do you know me now?" she asked.

"What do you mean?"

"Do you know what I'm doing? Have you checked up on me?"

Her father paused. She knew what the answer was. She didn't

let him answer. "I run the farm," she told him. "Me and Mom. It's successful. It's a big deal. We've been in magazines."

"I'm not surprised," he said. "That's great."

She plated three of the sandwiches and started toasting the last three. She felt so embarrassed, how badly she wanted him to know that she was okay, that she'd been okay without him, and she didn't know why she couldn't say that he had made her life so much less than it should have been. She didn't know why it was so hard to look at him, nearly a stranger and yet so familiar to her that it made her want to cry, and just say, "You shouldn't have left us. And if you were going to leave us, you shouldn't have left us like that. And you should have written me a single letter in all these years to say that you missed me, and that you loved me, and that, even though you weren't a part of my life anymore, you hoped that someday you could be again."

And then she realized that, actually, she had just said all this. Out loud. To her father. In that moment, he was only her father, not everyone's but just hers.

"I know, Mad," he finally said. "I know."

"You are seventy years old, Dad," she said. "You would have died without ever knowing who I was if we hadn't found you."

"I know," he said again. "Don't let those sandwiches burn, Mad." She looked down at the skillet and flipped them.

"Grilled cheese sandwiches are ready," their father called out, and he turned away from her to set the table. She looked at the cast iron, the soft bubbling of the remaining butter turning brown. She thought about what it would feel like to place her open palm on the skillet. She remembered old comic strips where angry wives would hit their drunk husbands with a frying pan, but she knew they couldn't have been a cast-iron skillet because this thing was heavy as hell. Her father was safe, and she would keep herself safe. She turned off the stove and walked over to the table, where her siblings looked at the five seats, the exact number necessary for them to share a meal. Their father placed Rooster in the high chair and occupied the seat next to him, already slicing the sandwich into triangles. Rube sat farthest from their father, and Pep and Mad took up spots beside their brother. Tom tentatively sat next to their father, who then turned to him. "You want me to cut up your sandwich?" he asked, and Tom hesitated.

"I guess so," Tom replied, and his father sliced the sandwich into perfect sections. This was something that Mad had to remember, which was difficult. Their father had never been a bad parent. He had always been attentive, loving, and patient. He had only become a bad parent when he disappeared, when he ceased to be a part of their life. Still, it was strange for Mad to watch this man, so many years beyond the man who had been her father, attending to his kids.

Pep took a bite of the sandwich. "These are good," she said.

"Your sister made them," their father replied.

"I think you're just starving," Mad allowed, and Pep nodded as if this was also true.

Mad imagined that, in some other reality, this would have been a regular occurrence, the sharing of holidays, the summer vacations where all the half siblings made their way to wherever their father was now residing, sitting at the table and eating as a family. This was just how children of divorce lived, maybe, but it wouldn't quite be the same. Children of divorce, upon arriving at their dad's place, didn't have to learn what name he was now going by, what identity he had fashioned out of thin air. It wouldn't hold together. Their father had made it too hard to imagine a normal interaction with him. And so Mad just ate her sandwich, which was good, expertly made.

"Where is Rooster's mom?" Rube asked. "Was that woman we met at the mansion his mother?"

"No. It's a bit complicated. But Rooster's mother is around. She actually owns all this, the ranch. Her family. She and her two sisters, one of whom you met, I guess, kind of equally share custody of Rooster."

"What's her name?" Pep asked.

Their father sighed. "Lucky," he finally said.

"Rooster's mom is named Lucky?" Rube asked. "Is that a nickname?"

"It's complicated," he replied. "Lucky changed her name. All the sisters did."

"Okay," Rube said. "I'm just going to ask. Dad, are you the leader of a cult?"

Their father laughed. "Are you serious?"

"That is kind of the vibe that you're giving off," Pep interjected. "The whole place, honestly."

"No. You couldn't be further from the truth."

"Wait," Rube asked, "What is your name? Here, I mean. What name do you go by?"

"Charles," the father replied, and Rube tilted his head as if he'd misheard.

"Your name was Charles with us," Rube said, and their father nodded.

"I got tired," their father replied.

"It's not the name of a cult leader," Pep offered.

"I'm a groundskeeper," their father said. "I'm kind of the caretaker of this whole property."

"And then you married a woman named Lucky and you two had a baby."

"No, not exactly."

"Did you marry all three of the sisters?" Rube asked.

"I'm not married to Lucky or Haze or Moon," their father replied. "And I'm not in a romantic relationship with any of them. I'm not sure this is productive."

"Their names are Lucky and Haze and Moon?" Rube asked.

"Yes."

"Those sound like the names of horses, Dad," Rube replied.

"It's complicated."

"They must just be the richest women on earth to have names like that," Pep said. "Am I right? We saw the mansion. Was that Haze or Moon?"

"Moon. And they are very wealthy, yes," their father allowed. "They're of the Chelmsford family."

"They own the Golden State Warriors?" Pep asked. "And they're, like, pharmaceutical billionaires."

"I think the Warriors are owned by their uncle, but, yes, that's the family."

"And so Rooster just kind of happened?" Rube asked.

"Listen, maybe let me get Rooster settled for his nap, and then . . . well, how long are you planning on staying? Is this just an afternoon visit?"

Mad considered the logistics of this for the first time. She had imagined that they would confront their father, and either he would say something heartfelt and apologetic and they would instantly leave or he would refuse to acknowledge his actions and they would beat him up and then instantly leave. Either way, she had never imagined staying with her dad. But she hadn't yet thought about booking a hotel room in the area. Maybe they could sleep in that strange outdoor art colosseum they'd found earlier.

"Do you have some kind of pressing engagement that requires your attention?" Rube asked.

"Rube, please," their father asked.

"Can we spend the night here?" Tom finally asked.

"Oh, now, Tom, I don't know if that's such—" Mad said, but then Pep said, "I feel like we should stay a little longer. I haven't even had a chance to talk to Dad."

"A sleepover!" Tom said.

"Why don't I put Rooster down for a nap and the four of you can discuss your plans. I'm not going to tell you what to do."

"That's good," Rube replied.

"But if you're planning on staying here for longer than today, let me know so we can make arrangements for you. Does Trista know that Tom is here? How did you meet up? Okay, never mind. I guess maybe we can talk more. Maybe you should stay a little longer."

"We'll talk it over," Rube said.

"C'mon, son," their father said to Rooster, who lifted up his arms to be carried away to his nap. As their father walked toward the bedroom, the little boy watched his siblings with curiosity.

As soon as they were out of earshot, the siblings hashed out a plan. It was determined that there were simply too many questions that each child would want to ask their father, and a lot of them would overlap. They would force their father to explain himself, in chronological order, and then, if that satisfied their general need for answers, they would have individual time with their father, where he would have to answer specific questions about the years where he was with each child.

"And I need him to help me finish my movie," Tom said.

"Okay, well, you can use your individual time with Dad to do that, for sure," Rube allowed.

Their father returned from the bedroom. "He's a good sleeper," he offered. "Rooster."

"Were we not good sleepers?" Pep asked.

"No, all of you were good sleepers, honestly," he allowed.

"Are you a good sleeper?" Pep asked him.

"No. I am not a good sleeper," their father answered.

"We have questions," Rube interjected.

"Yes, I know."

"About what you did."

"Of course."

"And why you did it."

"Yes."

"And why you kept doing it."

"Yes, Rube, of course."

"So tell us."

Their father looked around at them, and then smoothed out the wrinkles in his cargo shorts. Mad noticed that his legs were hairless. "Do you guys want coffee or tea?" he asked.

"Dad, please," Rube continued.

"Okay, okay. I kind of wondered if one of you would find me. I expected it, honestly. Pep, I thought for sure that your mom would have a team of people tracking me."

"She gave up quickly," Pep said.

"Okay, well, I always figured something like this might happen. Not all of you at once. But even though I guess I knew I might have to explain myself, I never knew what I would say. There's no good way to explain it. Or I don't know myself."

"That's a terrible start," Rube said.

"Well, goddamnit, it's true, Rube. I hate that I did what I did. I don't know why I did it. I wish I hadn't. Maybe I should have stayed in Boston and just lived my life. But I didn't. At that time, I didn't think I could."

"That's fine," Rube said. "You didn't have to stay. But why did you just disappear? And why did you make up a new version of yourself? Why did you go to Tennessee and become a farmer? Or how did you even fool people into thinking you were a basketball coach? Or a filmmaker? How did you do any of this?"

Their father took a deep breath. "I wasn't happy, Rube. It wasn't you or your mom. It wasn't even the situation. But I realized that I hadn't accomplished much. I wrote those books, and it was exciting, and I thought I'd become, you know, Raymond Chandler or something, and I'd be this big deal. But no one cared. And I thought, okay, I tried something and it didn't work and now I'm stuck. And it made me feel so trapped. And it made me—and I'm sorry to say this—but it made me angry. And then I started to imagine myself in a new way. I've always had this mind where I fixate on things and just kind of have an ability to pick up information and figure things out. And I don't even remember why, but I got interested in organic farming and I started to think about a simpler life, and I read up on agriculture and it was exciting. I had this little life that I was living in my head while I was living my real life with you and your mother. And, eventually, that imaginary life was more important to me."

"You could have taken us with you," Rube said.

"Do you think your mom would have shoveled manure and driven a combine? I couldn't imagine how I'd even convince her to come. And again, I felt trapped. And this was all maybe a year or so before I actually left. But I just started to consider what that new life might be in reality. And that made me happy. It made me, for the first time in a few years, happy and attentive to you and your mom, and I just had this feeling that soon I would leave. I don't really remember, Rube. I'm sorry. I don't think about this very much. But I just left. I got on a bus, and I had packed a few things, and I left. And as I passed through all these states that I'd never seen before, the farther I got from you and your mom, the easier it was for me to believe that I was this other person. And then I *was* this other person."

"And you met my mom?" Mad asked.

"That wasn't the plan. I hope you believe this, but it wasn't that I set out to just start new families everywhere I went. But I wanted to be a farmer. And your mom's family had left her this amazing farm, but it was in trouble. She was falling into debt. I had picked up some work on a neighboring farm, I'm sure your mom told you, and she liked me. I had a chance to put my ideas about organic farming to practical use. And it seemed strange to not return her affections just because I had this other family back in Boston."

"That's like the textbook definition of infidelity," Pep offered, but their father, as if he couldn't stop himself, just kept talking.

"Because I didn't think I was the same person. And to even think about that person, who had kind of failed, was too difficult. And so I just stopped thinking about him. And I always just threw myself into the work of doing this new thing. And I did work hard. That farm completely changed once me and your mom took over. It was a big deal and it took so much time and effort. And I loved your mom. And I also loved your mom, Rube. It wasn't that. But it felt like, okay, I had messed up before, but this was working. I was making this life and we had you, Mad, and I thought, okay, this time I've got it right."

"But you didn't get it right?" Mad asked, feeling the pain that she realized Rube was feeling, that Pep would be feeling, that Tom would be feeling, that they all had to share.

"I guess not. Time passed, and I stopped feeling fulfilled by it. And I started trying to find some way to stay, to be in this life that I'd made. And, because I'd done what I'd done to Rube's mom, I was afraid of doing it again. So I started thinking about basketball, which was a sport that I didn't know all that much about, and it felt like a good way to keep my mind occupied. And I should have known what my brain does, but I thought it was a way to anchor me, but I started to realize that it wouldn't be that difficult to use these principles of basketball and actually be pretty good at coaching. I could see how it worked. I've always had a mind that could take all these complicated elements and streamline them and figure them out. And I thought of how interesting it would be to just try another life. And I tried hard, Mad. I hope you believe me, but I guess you don't have any reason to believe me, but I tried to stay."

"But you did leave," Mad allowed.

"Yes, and I understood, as I was leaving and heading out farther west, that this was probably actually not going to be the last time I did it. I kind of admitted that maybe I was mentally ill and it was something that I was going to keep doing. No matter what I did, I could never become the person that I wanted to be. And I just shut off the part of my brain that thought about you and your mom and Rube and his mom and I just reset."

"I'm sorry," Pep offered, "because it means I would never have been born, but I kind of wish if you were going to keep doing it that you didn't get married and have another kid."

"I don't wish that," their father said to her. "God, I don't wish that."

"That would have been the responsible thing to do, Dad. It was the worst day of my life when you left," she told him.

"Mine, too," Rube said. Mad nodded. Even Tom was nodding.

"I'm sorry," their father answered.

"You just kept making new families," Pep said, "and leaving them."

"I did. I just didn't think about it. I can't explain it. I wasn't the same person. I really wasn't."

"You barely changed your name, Dad," Mad said. "You went from Charles to Chuck to Chip to Carl. That's not a new person."

"It's not like changing your name to Lucky or Moon or Haze," Rube said. "That's a radically new identity."

"I'm not a psychologist," their father admitted. "I don't pretend to understand. Maybe I was trying not to lose myself entirely. I don't know. Honestly, I haven't thought about it. I know that may seem cruel—"

"It absolutely does, Dad," Pep interjected.

"Yes, okay, but I don't have an easy answer for you. I'm never going to satisfy you because there's no good reason for a man to leave his family over and over and never see them again. I was just so ashamed that I had to forget you. I just tried to keep moving forward and do my best in that new life."

"You were . . ." Tom started, but he couldn't finish. They waited for him to figure it out. "You were a good dad."

Pep said, "I hate it, but you were. You were a really good dad."

Mad and Rube looked at each other at that moment. They were too far from their time with him to believe this was true. But they wouldn't correct their siblings.

"I don't deserve that," their father said. "But thank you."

"And then you left us," Pep said, "and ended up in Utah."

"And I thought maybe that was the end. I was getting older. At that point, I don't think I even had any real belief that I could find an identity that would sustain me. I knew I wasn't going to become a celebrated filmmaker or anything. But Trista was vulnerable, had run into some difficulties, and it was hard not to step in. At the very least, though, I thought maybe I could stay this time." Their father looked at Tom, as if measuring what he knew and didn't know. "It didn't work out."

"And now you have another kid," Rube said. "And you named him Reuben. And you are somehow connected to three heiresses named Lucky and Moon and Haze, and you live on this huge ranch."

"I ended up here, and I got work on the ranch and I met Lucky. She and her sisters had just inherited this property from their father after he died. And they wanted to turn it into an artist colony, an amazing kind of enclave for creative people. And they saw that I had an ability to work with the land, and I had made art before, and I didn't even have an identity worked out. I just needed work, something to help me make peace with where I was in my life, and I just started using the pieces of my past."

"And it seems like they know about you," Mad offered.

"They do," their father admitted. "I told them. Honestly, I think they kind of found it fascinating. They're . . . quite interesting ladies. All of your moms are interesting ladies. I was lucky to meet women—"

"Please," Pep said. "Don't do that."

"Okay, sorry. Yes. But they said I could live here. I would be the caretaker and help them remake this place into their vision. And I've been building all these cabins where the artists will each stay and taking care of the land, and putting in some agricultural work to make it a little more vibrant and there are so many acres and I guess art doesn't need all of it. And that's what I've been doing."

"Did you make that structure we went into?" Mad asked.

"I did," their father admitted. "It took so long. I don't think I'm cut out for that kind of art, honestly, but the sisters wanted to have some existing art pieces for the colony before it got started. So I gave it my best shot."

"And you have Rooster."

"I do. It's . . . it's complicated."

"Stop saying that," Rube replied. "Your entire life is complicated. Rooster is not some weird outlier in the narrative of your life. Just tell us."

"The sisters wanted an heir, wanted a child. I know that sounds weird, but they wanted to share their lives with someone and provide them with the same opportunities that they had. I think they believe it's a responsibility for people with such privilege. But they weren't in relationships and weren't interested in them. And so they asked if . . . this is all very . . . well, I donated something and they used it to then make Rooster. And he's Lucky's child, entirely. I'm not on the birth certificate. I have no legal claim on him. That was the deal. But I am his father. I take care of him."

"They let you live here in exchange for providing them with an heir?" Mad asked.

"Well, yeah, I guess so. I have Rooster and he lives here with me. He knows that I'm his father. And Lucky spends at least two weeks out of the month here with Rooster. So he has a mom and dad. And his two aunts are here a lot, as well."

"So, if you leave, it's not as big of a deal," Rube said.

"I'm not leaving. I'm done with all that."

"How do you know?" Rube asked.

"I just do," their father replied, not meeting their gaze. "This is it."

"Where are Lucky and Haze and Moon?" Pep asked.

"Hmm, well, Lucky is at a gallery opening in San Francisco because she's interested in the artist being one of the first fellows for the colony. And Haze is in Vancouver on a yoga retreat. And Moon, who you already met, is working on a book, so she's at the mansion back in the city proper."

Mad wondered, if they had come on a week when their father wasn't watching Rooster, if he would have told them any of this, if he would have excised this new child and the sister heiresses from his narrative. She imagined that he would, how quickly he would shed people to create an identity that fit his needs. It was hard for her to hate him, even though he had hurt them all in such profound ways that were nearly impossible to explain to another person. Even now, she watched him trying to compartmentalize his brain and his memories in such a way that he could keep all of them distinctly separate, even as they sat around him as a unified front of resentment.

"We have all done pretty amazing things without you," Rube said. "Do you know that?"

"I haven't had the bandwidth to keep up with all of you," their father explained. "I am not surprised, as I told Mad. You were all quite impressive and talented when you were children."

"Rube is a famous writer," Pep offered. "He's had his book made into a movie."

"Wait, you wrote novels?" their father asked.

"You haven't read them?" Rube asked, disappointed.

"I didn't know about them," their father admitted.

"Mysteries," Rube said. "Detective novels."

"Oh, like I did."

"And Mad runs an organic farm and has been in magazines and is kind of a big deal with people who, like, care about farming."

"She told me," their father allowed.

Mad stepped in: "And Pep is an All-Big-Twelve guard for the Oklahoma Sooners. She was the Gatorade High School Player of the Year for the whole state."

"Of course," their father said. "Did you win state?"

"I did. For Howe."

Their father's eyes widened. "Not Pocola?"

"Nope," she said, defiant, satisfied. "Howe."

"Well done," he said.

"And," Rube continued, "Tom is a low-budget independent filmmaker."

"I'm so proud of you, Tom."

"I'm still working on our movie."

"Oh, of course. That's very good."

"I'll tell you more about it when we get time alone," Tom added. Their father looked up at the rest of them. "So you're staying the night?"

"At least," Rube said. "We have more we want to say. We feel like we should each have some time with you one-on-one."

"Well, I have Rooster for the whole week," their father said, but Pep cut in: "I think we can babysit him. He's our brother, kind of."

"Okay, I'm not going to stop you. I don't know what else I can do, don't think I can give you everything you might want, but you can stay. There's actually another cabin pretty nearby that's furnished. You can stay there."

"Can I stay here tonight?" Tom asked. "With you and Rooster?"

"Are you sure?" their father asked, again looking to the other siblings. Mad nodded her approval, and so he agreed.

"I have work I need to get done," their father said. "It's a lot of acreage, and I'm the only one out here. It's not a ton of work, but it has to be done."

"Dad," Pep said, "I really, really, really hope you aren't going to run away."

"I'm not," he protested. "I told you. I'm done. I can't do anything else. I'm tired. I'm here. You can stay as long as you need, but I'm not leaving."

"Maybe I'll come with you?" Pep offered. "That can be my time to talk. You can show me around."

"Can the rest of you watch Rooster?" their father asked.

"Will he not be worried if you're not here?" Mad asked, hoping the answer was that the toddler would be terrified to be left with them and would need to be in the company of their father at all times. But their father smiled.

"He's pretty easygoing. He won't mind."

"Okay," Rube said, who then looked at Pep. "Are you okay on your own? I can come with you or—"

"It's fine," Pep said. "Unless you want to go first. You're the firstborn and all."

"Not yet," Rube admitted. "You go ahead."

And so Mad watched as their father, visibly grateful for the chance to get out of the cabin, walked alongside his third child to an all-terrain vehicle and then traveled down the dirt road, leaving the rest of them behind. It was oddly satisfying, in a dreamlike way, to watch their father leave with one of them along for the ride.

FORTY MINUTES LATER, THEY HEARD ROOSTER CRYING FROM THE BEDROOM, a guttural, irritated moaning, and all three of the remaining siblings looked with great alarm at each other. Rube clearly did not want to handle the child, as if touching a kid who was meant to be your replacement would mean you would instantly vaporize. Mad knew, because she was the only girl in the room, and because she was the only other adult, that she should go attend to the toddler, but she also wondered if maybe Tom might benefit from spending time with his younger sibling, that it might actually be a gift to Tom to form a bond with this little boy. But Tom looked at Mad and shook his head, and so Mad muttered an obscenity to herself and stood up to somehow calm Rooster.

When she walked into the bedroom, Rooster was standing up in his crib, his mouth firmly attached to the railing, still making that weird moaning sound, like the entire crib was a musical instrument that he was playing.

"Hey, Rooster," Mad said to the toddler, who stopped making the sound, which was a huge relief to Mad, and observed her. "Did you sleep okay?" The toddler said nothing. "How do you get out of there? Are you able to climb out on your own?" Still nothing from Rooster. "Here is the thing, Rooster. I have actually never held a human child in my entire life. I've held baby calves and chicks and lambs and kids—I mean, baby goats—and, god, so many animal babies. But no one has ever handed me their child and asked me to hold them."

Rooster seemed entirely uninterested in her confession. He merely held up his arms, his face filled with exasperation.

"I'm going to lift you up, okay? I'll put my arms, I'll put them here and then here," she said, placing her hands under his armpits, feeling the weight of him, which felt both too heavy and too light at the same time, and then she lifted him out of the crib. And where should she put him? Could she drop him onto their father's bed and he would then bounce into whatever thing he would do next? Or set him gently on the floor? But then he'd be on the floor, under her feet. What could she do? She was starting to feel this low-level anxiety rising in her. Without any other ideas, she simply held on to him. And Rooster allowed it. And she kind of jostled him up and down, softly, like, "hey, let's test the limits of gravity together." And then she felt dampness, the need for a diaper change.

"Rube?" she called out.

"Is everything okay in there?" Rube called out from the living room.

"Rooster needs to be changed."

"Do you know where the diapers are?" he asked.

"Rube! Get in here," she said.

He walked into the room. "Oh, there are the diapers right there," he said, gesturing to a changing station.

Mad handed him Rooster before Rube could refuse. And then Rooster, in Rube's unsure grip, yawned so wide that it looked like he was eating the universe, and then rubbed his eyes and nestled his face into Rube's clavicle. Rube took a deep breath. He pulled the little boy into his embrace. Both of them allowed the other. Mad backed away slowly.

"I'll change him," Rube said.

"Have you ever done it before?" she asked.

"Nope," he said. "But go on. I'll figure it out."

When she went back into the living room, Tom had his video camera trained on her. "Should I go in there?" he asked, but Mad shook her head.

"I wish Dad would get back here," Tom said. "He's been gone a long time."

"Pep will make sure he comes back."

"This is a neat place," Tom observed.

"It's interesting. Pretty different from your house, right?"

"Do you think Dad would let me live here with him?" he asked her, and the desperation on his face was unlike anything Mad had witnessed with her younger brother, who seemed so impassive.

"I don't know, Tom. I think that's pretty complicated, and your mom would not have let us take you if she thought you weren't coming back."

"Just part time, then?" he asked. "Like a regular divorce?"

"Maybe," Mad said, and instantly regretted it. She had the distinct feeling that none of them would ever see their father again after they left the ranch. But what good would it do to say this to Tom? After their father had left with Pep, Tom had called his mother on Rube's cell phone, the reception barely allowing them to communicate, and told her that they'd found their father. Rube then talked to Trista for a few minutes, explaining the situation. Mad still couldn't quite believe that this woman had allowed them to take her child into the wilderness to track down their delinquent father, but what did she know? She had not spoken to her own mother since Oklahoma. She should call her. But she couldn't do it yet. She didn't want anyone else to be a part of this moment, even her own mom.

Rube walked into the room, holding Rooster, who pointed to

the marble run, and Rube walked over to the contraption. "He's a good kid," Rube informed them.

"Did you think he was a bad kid?" Tom asked.

"Yes," Rube admitted.

"It's never the kid's fault," Tom said.

"Of course not," Rube replied, looking intently at Rooster as the little boy grasped a handful of marbles, offering them to his oldest brother.

"Can I film you?" Tom asked. "The light is nice."

"Sure, why not?" Rube replied, smiling at Rooster before taking one of the marbles and sending it on its way. Rooster placed another marble, and just as the first had settled itself at the end, no longer moving, the new marble softly clinked against it. Rube put another marble, and Rooster placed one right after. It was hypnotic, the sound of the marble, compelled by gravity, so inevitable, following the same path, each time, *clink-clink-clink*, until every marble rested at the end.

PEP AND THEIR FATHER RETURNED, BOTH OF THEM SWEATING, THEIR FACES tinged with dust. Mad could instantly see that Pep had been crying, her eyes red, but it seemed to have passed. She was calm now, the slightest smile, as if to prove to Mad and Rube that she was okay.

"He had me do actual work," Pep told them. "I hauled stuff."

"It's easier with someone else," their father admitted, and Mad wished he'd think about that statement a little more, but he was already heading to the sink for a glass of water.

"You should have gone with him first," Pep said to Mad. "You work outside. With your hands."

"You're in way better shape than me," Mad offered, but Pep shook her head.

"I don't like the outdoors, honestly. It's too big."

"Are you okay?" Mad whispered to her sister.

"Not really," Pep admitted. "I don't know what I expected. It's just hard. There's not enough time. It's weird, but I didn't want to make him too sad. And, honestly, he's not the person I remember. I think it's just been too long."

"You'll be okay," Mad told her. She hugged her sister, didn't think about it, and Pep actually accepted it.

"I know. I will. Thank you."

THEIR FATHER RETURNED TO THEM, HOLDING A GLASS OF WATER FOR PEP, who accepted it. "If you're staying for dinner, we need to get some food."

"We're staying for dinner," Tom replied.

"I can go get some food. It's a bit of a drive," their father offered.

"We can just have sandwiches again," Mad said.

"Most of the bread is gone now," their father told them. "I don't keep much food on hand. Rooster eats mush and I eat rice and beans mostly. I can run into town."

"Go with him," Rube said to Mad, who looked to her brother to make sure it was okay. He nodded. "I'll stay here with Rooster," he said.

"Can you handle it?" she asked her father. "Do you need some time to yourself?"

"No, let's do it," he said. She could hear what he meant, that he wanted to get it over with, but maybe that was her own anxiety.

"Okay, let's go," she told him, and they walked out of the cabin. He had a truck, and he held open the passenger door for her. It gave her a slight flash of her childhood, of climbing into the truck, sitting in the middle seat between her father and mother, on their way to the market.

When they were both in the truck, he started it up and said, "Feels like I'm running a gauntlet here." Mad felt a slight tinge of anger wash over the warm feeling of that old memory.

"Didn't have to be," Mad told him.

"I guess you're right," he said, and off they went.

IN THE SILENCE OF THE RIDE, BOTH OF THEM UNSURE OF HOW TO START, MAD talked about one of the few areas of interest that she knew they shared. Or that they had once shared. Her father might not care now, but she realized that *she* cared, and so she told him about corn. Mad had been cultivating a species of corn that was called Tennessee Red Cob.

"It's got this rich red germ," she told him. "Mostly I was doing it because an older guy I knew at a seed legacy project gave me some to try, and it was good for our specific region. There wasn't much call for it in the county, but I always kept some to make cornmeal and it made good polenta, honestly. It tastes like the fanciest version of Cream of Wheat. And so I started talking to some restaurants and then I worked with a local mill with an actual waterwheel that powers the mill."

"I'd like to see it," her father offered. "It was harder to do heirloom stuff back then, or maybe farmers weren't as keen on sharing or searching it out."

"Well, it's not really viable for most farms," she told him.

"We never cared much about that," her father said.

"Yeah, we still don't," Mad said, and she almost laughed, the way the *we* bent and shifted, but she let it go.

"Maybe we should have polenta tonight," he offered.

"Tom can stir it," Mad said.

"Okay, we'll do polenta and I'll get some chard. You grow chard?"

"Nope," she said. "Is it in season?"

"In California it is," he said. "And we'll get some pork sausages. There's a place that sells Cambridge sausages and they're amazing."

"I thought you mostly eat beans and rice," she said.

"It's a special occasion," he replied.

"Okay, so we have the menu set," she said. "How much farther into town?"

"Fifteen minutes at least," he said, "in this thing."

"Oh," she said. She had hoped maybe the food talk would last the entire drive.

"Are you married?" he suddenly asked.

"No!" she almost shouted. "I mean—what?—no, I'm not married."

"Are you dating someone?" he asked.

"No time," she replied. She never had to explain herself back on the farm. And now, all these family members, all this time on the road, she had to keep explaining that there was no time because of the farm, but she had been away from the farm for a while now. It made her mad, to have her very nice and solid excuses start to wobble under repetition and self-scrutiny. This was what other people did to you, she decided. They made you question the things you'd always taken as fact.

"There's time," he said, like some wise old man, which, Mad allowed, maybe he was, but she still didn't want to hear it.

"You left us," she said, "and so to keep the farm going, I couldn't leave."

"You could have," he said.

"No," she said. "I couldn't. People can, yeah. I couldn't."

"Because of me?"

"Kind of?" she allowed. "Does that make you sad? I'm not trying to be mean, but, yeah, because of you. You left and I never saw you again. I had to help Mom run the farm. And then it became mine, mostly, the running of it. And it just seemed like a relationship wasn't worth it, because if it didn't work out, what would I have?"

"I'm sorry."

"It is what it is. I know it's not your fault that I've never been in a relationship, that I'm this weird, lonely farmer, but it is kind of your fault."

"This is . . ." He paused. "I guess this is why I never tried to stay in touch with you kids."

"Mom finally told me you sometimes called her. You never once asked to talk to me? That hurt me almost as much as you disappearing. If I'd just heard your voice once since you left, maybe this wouldn't be so hard."

"I regret that the most. I know I couldn't have stayed, but I could have reached out. I won't forgive myself. But I thought that if I just forgot about you, ignored the fact that you were growing up that entire time, I could imagine a life where you were happy and fine and didn't miss me at all."

"I *am* happy," she said. "I'm fine. I mostly don't miss you."

"Okay, fair enough. I just mean that you seem lonely."

"I AM LONELY!" she shouted, finally giving up on politeness, of protecting him from her anger and confusion. "You left and never came back and I thought maybe you were dead, like you'd jumped into a lake with your pockets filled with rocks. I thought an alien had abducted you. I thought you were mad at me. You messed me up."

"Maybe I'd have messed you up if I'd stayed."

"Probably! You probably would have because you have this thing inside of you that makes you live outside of your own life and never fully be present, I guess. And that probably would have made me messed up in some other way, but that would be normal.

I could talk to other people and say, 'My dad is a good guy, but he's a little sad because his life didn't work out, and sometimes that sadness makes my life difficult,' and they would say, 'Same here,' and I'd just move on. But you disappeared, and how could I talk about that with people I'd just met? I had to erase you from my mind so as not to think that I'd failed you in some way. I kept the farm going. It's better than anything you did with it! It's famous! John T. Edge mentioned me in a book! I've never yelled this much in my life!"

"I'm so sorry, Mad," he said. "I cannot do anything about it."

"And the farm is still there. It's not going anywhere because I kept it going. And if some miracle happens and I have kids, they'll have the farm. I'm not letting the farm go, because it's the place I know. It's good, you know, to have roots."

"Of course I know that," he said. "And it's why I'm so deficient. I don't have that. I'm glad you have the farm. I was just hoping you had someone to talk to."

"Well, I don't."

"I understand. I wanted to live that life, honestly. I wanted to be self-contained. I was so obsessed with what was in my head, what I wanted to accomplish. But it was so complicated in my brain. Every time I started over, I'd get to work on the life I was making and then I needed someone to talk to, to share things, and I'd meet someone and it would begin again. I needed people after all, I guess."

"Well, I don't." She was so tired suddenly. It was quiet for a few minutes.

"You have siblings now," he offered.

"Dad, please. I might never see them again after this. I might not want to."

"I was so terrified of all of you, how much I'd hurt you. But this is good. I'm glad you found me."

"Even though you thought we might kill you."

"In my dreams, yes."

"I'm not going to kill you," she said.

"We're here, by the way," he said, turning into the parking lot of a little market. Mad rested her head against the dash of the truck.

"Oh, god. I cannot believe we are going to walk into this grocery store and buy food and, like, drive home and cook it and then sit at a table and have a family dinner."

"It is not how I thought my day would go," her father replied. Neither one of them would get out of the truck.

"Well, I have had days and days and days to prepare for seeing you and I still didn't think this is how it would go, either."

"What's the alternative?" her father said. "You found me. We can try to be a family of some sort."

"I guess there's not many options," she admitted.

"It's either this or all of you kill me," their father said, and it made her laugh. It made him laugh. She looked at her father, who was so old. He was too old to be her father. Maybe the key was to truly believe that her father had been abducted by aliens and, by some strange miracle, here he was again. Maybe the only way to keep living was to willingly forget large parts of the narrative of your life and then just live with what was left. She hated that idea. But it was so quiet in the truck, the silence turning even more awkward.

"Let's go buy some chard," she finally said, and he nodded.

RUBE AND ROOSTER WERE PLAYING OUTSIDE AS THE TRUCK PULLED UP TO the cabin, and the little boy waddled over to his father. Rube looked sheepish, his shirt untucked and his hair sweaty, dirt on the knees of his khakis. There was a red kickball at his feet.

"We got food," their father said to Rooster, who grabbed his father's hand and then gestured to Rube.

"He loves that ball," the father said.

"It's a very *Little House on the Prairie* kind of existence," Rube replied.

"Where are Tom and Pep?" Mad asked him, and when he replied that they were at the weird structure in the woods, Mad volunteered to get them, handing the bag of groceries to Rube. Rooster waddled back to Rube and picked up the ball, gesturing for Rube to play, so their father took the groceries and went into the cabin.

"Okay," Rube said to the boy. "I guess . . . you want to keep rolling this ball back and forth?" Mad started to run a little bit to make sure she didn't get pulled into the game.

"YOU'RE BACK," PEP SAID, REGARDING HER WITH SUSPICION AS MAD ENTERED the inside of the strange fortress. The sensation of coming out of the tunnel, the expansiveness of the open air juxtaposed with the wooden walls, made her feel like she was either coming out of or falling into a dream. Mad could only nod. Tom was pacing around, holding his hands to frame a camera shot in the way that Mad had seen movie directors do in old cartoons.

"How did it go?" Pep asked.

"I don't know, honestly," Mad said. "I don't know what I expected. We just kind of talked."

"Don't tell me what you talked about," Pep suddenly said. "I don't want to know, because if he said the same thing to you that he said to me, it will make me feel bad, like he was refining his speech to us."

"He was mostly feeling out whether or not we were going to kill him," Mad said.

"Yeah, he definitely was wondering about that," Pep replied.

"But don't tell me how he apologized or if he apologized or if, when you said his apology was bad, what he then said to try and explain why the apology was bad. I don't want to know."

"Agreed," Mad said.

"You aren't crying," Pep observed.

"Well, we had a long drive back here," Mad offered. "So maybe I had time to compose myself."

"I guess so," Pep said.

"And, Pep, honestly? It's been a long time since I've seen him. He doesn't even look like my dad. I think maybe for me and Rube, it might be a different sensation than it is for you and Tom."

"Rube might be the most effed up about it. Maybe you're just different."

"Maybe I'm in the sweet spot," Mad allowed. "Like, I'm not close enough to being left that I still feel like he could be my dad, but I'm not so far away from it that I feel like my whole life is explained by him."

"Or you are repressing the emotions so hard, and it'll come out some other time and you'll have to check into a hospital."

"I yelled at him!" Mad said, defending herself.

"Oh, yeah, me, too," Pep offered.

"You yelled at him?" Tom said. They realized he was standing right next to them.

"Yeah," Pep said.

"Not me," Tom said. "I mean, unless it's for the movie."

"Of course not," Mad offered. "I don't want you to feel like you have to yell at him."

"He did have another kid, though. I don't like that," Tom admitted, staring at the opening of the tunnel.

"Welcome to the club," Pep said, and Tom actually laughed, as if the sharpness of Pep's comment had jarred him loose from the uncertainty of the situation and reminded him that he was a part of their weird little family. He pulled on the hem of his shirt and then picked up his camera. Pep descended into the tunnel, Tom went next, and Mad, waiting a few seconds to ready herself, followed.

"TELL US WHAT YOU REMEMBER ABOUT US," RUBE SAID TO THEIR FATHER AT dinner, their plates heaped with polenta and sliced sausages and electrically bright chard.

"What do you mean?" their father replied, looking slowly around the table, as if trying to simply remember their names.

"You always were obsessed with home movies. You filmed all of us. You kept some of them, right?"

"Home movies? You saw them?"

"I had them," Tom told him. "You left them behind. I showed Rube and Mad and Pep. I thought they were short films."

"I knew I'd forgotten them," their father said, "but I couldn't go back. Once I realized, it was too late. It's not even that I watched them. But, yes, I did keep them."

"Something in you wanted to hold on to your kids, even if you tried to forget later," Rube continued. "So talk about a single memory you have of each one of us. Not important. You haven't seen us in years, decades for some of us. So here we are. What do you remember?"

"Oh, goodness, okay." Their father took a sip of water, considered the question, and then took a bite of sausage. "I feel like I'm auditioning for something."

"Nope, you're our dad," Pep said. "You got it already."

"Who do I start with?"

"Me," Tom offered. "It should be easiest, since it wasn't that long ago."

Their father looked at Tom, nodding.

"Don't try too hard," Rube said. "Just the first thing that pops into your head."

"Okay, okay, Rube. It's a lot of pressure. So, for Tom, I remember we were at a parade, maybe the Fourth of July? We were set up along the street, and people were throwing fistfuls of candy into the crowd from the floats. Oh, it *was* Fourth of July, because there were these women dressed up like the Statue of Liberty and the music was 'Born in the USA,' but edited so it was just that refrain, over and over."

"I don't know if I remember that. I remember parades, though."

"Well, you were pretty little. But they threw candy and there was this one piece, butterscotch hard candy, and it came skittering right at your little feet. And it wasn't in a wrapper and it was just there on the hot asphalt. And before I could stop you, you picked it up and ate it, just crunching so hard with your baby teeth, so I wouldn't try to get it back."

"I do remember that!" Tom said.

"Yes, and then you saw that I was worried about it, and so you found a piece of candy from another float and unwrapped it and threw it on the ground, and I picked it up and ate it, and that made you happy."

"So we'd both get sick," Tom replied. "You said Mom wouldn't be as mad."

"Do me next," Pep said, "but not about basketball. I remember all that probably better than you do. Something else."

"I remember the Oklahoma/Arkansas State Fair? They still have it?"

"Of course they do. I won the junior division Rabbit Skill-A-Thon when I was ten. Thirty bucks."

"You raced rabbits?" Tom asked her.

"No," she replied. "You did these stations where you had to

answer questions and determine the breed and the ear carriage and the faults. It's Midwest stuff, don't worry about it."

"We were there at the rides in the amusement park and you'd eaten all this cotton candy and corn dogs and popcorn and so we said you couldn't do the roller coaster or spinning things for thirty minutes. So you went into this ball pit, and you were playing in there. And I was supposed to be watching you. And I was! But it's kind of a blur of activity. Anyways, after a while, I realized that I couldn't see you. So I thought you'd left."

"Oh, my god," Pep said, nodding. "I'd forgotten this."

"You were so little. And I looked around and you weren't anywhere. And I was calling for you. And I talked to the guy running the ball pit, but he was high as a kite and so bored. And I was pretty upset because your mom was going to kill me. And then I could barely hear your voice, so squeaky, in the ball pit. So I jumped in and kind of waded around, sweeping my hands around, until I found you. You had fallen backward into the balls, and then got covered over and I guess you were so full of junk food that you couldn't get back up."

"I used to have nightmares about that," Pep said.

"And when I got you, you said to never tell your mom, because you were so embarrassed."

"I never told her," Pep said.

"Well, neither did I," their father replied.

"Do Mad next!" Tom yelled.

"Oh, god, give me a second," their father said, taking a deep breath. "This is like opening Al Capone's vault," he told them. "It's not easy."

"There wasn't anything in Al Capone's vault," Mad said.

"I'm not good with similes," he said, and Mad replied, "You were a writer."

"Not a good one," he admitted. "And not with you." It took

her breath away a bit, to realize that he still kept the versions of himself separate, that the father with her had been a farmer of few words, whereas the father with Rube was a writer.

"Okay, do you remember when I won that barbecue competition? At that water park in Nashville?"

"I was telling Rube about this," Mad said, shocked to feel the echoes of her memories actually rebounding off of another person. It was so rare for the signal of her own life to reach a receiver.

"Oh, yes, I won a huge trophy, with the gold pig on top of it. And you were fascinated with it. I think you used it for a lot of make believe, like you won a beauty contest and you'd have this princess dress on and you'd be holding the pig trophy and waving to the audience."

"I don't remember that," she said.

"But the thing I remember is that sometimes you didn't like to get up in the morning. It was a bit of a chore getting you to wake up, and we had early, early mornings on the farm. And so, if I ever came into your room to wake you and you were already up, I would run out of the room and get the trophy and bring it into your bedroom and cheer and give it to you, like you'd won a big competition."

"Oh, yes, yes. I do remember that."

"And I think that's why you became an early riser over time. Because you had this sensation that waking up, another day, was an achievement."

"Well, thanks."

"Do Rube!" Tom said.

It was strange, how their father had to stare at Pep, Rube, and Mad for a moment, as if his eyes had to refocus, to see them as they had been as children, because he didn't quite recognize them. He couldn't place them in the life he currently lived and so it took a moment to shuffle things around. But then he nodded.

"We found this game at a garage sale. Escalado. It was a horse-racing game, with these lead ponies with jockeys on them, and you put them on this board and turned a little crank or something, and the vibrations made the horses move toward the finish line. It was kind of jittery and unpredictable, and we'd pick our horses and cheer for them to win. And your friends loved it, and you started having races where kids bet a dime or something and then the winner would get the pile of coins. And you kids got so loud and animated, and you were screaming at these horses. Rube, you always picked the same horse. I don't remember the color of the horse."

"I don't, either," Rube replied, smiling.

"Anyway, one of the kids had this dad who owned two or three grocery stores and they were pretty rich and I think he thought you were trying to scam them out of their fortune, because he called me and said that you were running an illegal gambling operation and that he was going to talk to a friend of his in the city government."

"That was Jimmy Asta! His dad did that? I didn't know any of this."

"Well, it's not something you tell your kid, I guess. He said I needed to return the money, something ridiculous like forty cents, and that the kid was not allowed over to our apartment again."

"Wow."

"And I wrote him into one of the books, but I called him Tony Astor, who was this shop owner who ran over a gangster's poodle and then got killed in retaliation."

Rube was nodding, remembering the moment in the book.

"Was that good?" their father asked, and Rube said that it was.

Rooster got fidgety and their father pulled him onto his knee, bouncing him gently.

"If you'd stayed with us," Pep finally said, "there would be so many of these memories that you'd remember."

"If he'd stayed with us," Rube said, "he'd only have memories of me."

"If he'd just stayed longer with us each time," Mad offered. "Waited until we were in college."

"I don't know if I'd even be born yet, then," Tom said, a little indignant. "You'd all have more time with him and I wouldn't exist."

"There was no good way to do it," their father admitted. "I messed up every single time."

"They were good memories, though," Mad said, trying to make all of them feel better.

"They were," their father said. He looked so tired now, so old. After Rube had appeared at the farm and told her about their father, the people he'd left behind, the changing identities, she'd thought of him as selfish, narcissistic. But the way he talked about his obsessions, the lengths he went to in order to escape himself, she realized he had a mental illness. It had diminished him. She felt sorry for him, for maybe the first time since he'd disappeared.

It was quiet for a moment. They were done with dinner. It was hard to think of what to do next. If they had that horse-racing game, maybe they could have done that. But their father didn't take it with him when he left. It was stuck there, in Boston, in that memory. And Mad sat there with this sadness. But, strangely, she also felt content. If this was all there was, only these few memories, it was more than what she had before.

"Rooster needs a bath," their father finally told them. During the course of the storytelling, Rooster had rubbed a ton of polenta into his hair. If the siblings had ever raised children or had been a part of their younger siblings' lives, they would have noticed how quiet and amenable this toddler had been during long stretches of storytelling, all of them strangers in his house, and they would have known how rare it was for a toddler to not be the center of attention. If a toddler is quiet, they are rubbing polenta into their hair, and Mad filed this away for the future.

Rube and Mad gathered up the plates and silverware, while Pep and Tom slouched over to the sofa to avoid dealing with the plates and silverware. But Mad called to them, like she was their mother, and told them to come help clean up, and Pep and Tom both rolled their eyes but followed after their siblings. Tom scraped the dishes, then handed them to Rube, who washed the dishes, who handed them to Pep, who dried the dishes, who handed them to Mad, who put the dishes away. Mad turned toward their father and noticed that he was watching them. She wondered what he was thinking, this little team, so efficient, that he had put together. Maybe he was feeling the shame that he'd never let them know about each other before now, how much they could have done if they had each other. Or maybe he was thinking that Mad was putting the dishes in the wrong place and how he'd have to fix it later. Who knew? Who knew what her father was thinking, but at least now the mystery had a physical presence to hold that uncertainty. She nodded to him, and he nodded back. That was all family had to be, at the most basic level, someone seeing you, even if you didn't know what they saw.

PEP AND MAD MADE UP THE BED IN THE OTHER CABIN. IT WAS STRANGE HOW each sibling had grown up an only child and yet here they were, sharing rooms, sleeping in the same beds, navigating the space another body took up. Maybe, she reasoned, it wasn't as strange to Pep, who lived an athlete's life, locker rooms and showers and team buses and dorms and hotel rooms. Mad, on the other hand, could not remember the last time, before this strange journey began, when she had spent more than four hours in the same room with someone. But that was part of the pleasure of the trip, how much of a dream it felt like, how you knew it was temporary, perhaps not even real, and so you and your younger sister put fresh sheets on a bed that, in a few hours, you would both be sleeping in.

Tom was getting to spend the night sleeping in the cabin with their father and Rooster, and he would have the morning to continue working on their film. Rube was playing Solitaire on his computer, waiting for this evening, when he and their father would meet on the porch of the cabin and have a drink and talk, and Rube would get to ask all of his questions in the moonlight while Pep and Mad tried not to spy on them.

There was a TV, but it only had four channels, though one of them would be playing the NCAA basketball tournament. "Do you want to watch a game?" Mad asked her sister, who shook her head.

"I don't even know who is left," she admitted. "I know my mom wanted to tell me, and I've been getting a ton of emails and calls from my teammates, but I'm not checking them." Mad hadn't considered this. She and Rube had phones that basically were to be used only when they drove their PT Cruiser off the highway in some nameless town in the Southwest. But Pep, she had an actual social life. She had friends. She had a phone that, under normal circumstances, she would be using to talk to people that wanted to talk to her. She did not want to think about Tom, who maybe even had pen pals in other countries, children who were also low-budget independent filmmakers. She could not blame her loneliness entirely on her father disappearing, on the farm that he had left her, the genetics he had passed on. Some of it, maybe a lot of it, was just that she was a weird person.

"Do you think we'll leave tomorrow?" Pep asked her. Mad had honestly not fully understood the timeline of things, where they went from here. She did not look forward to the drive back across the country to Tennessee, all those miles in reverse, without the manic energy of seeking vengeance upon the father who abandoned you. That's the thing with quests, she realized. You had to get back to where you started. And then you had to keep living. The danger of a quest, of getting eaten by a dragon or stabbed by an orc, was tolerable because you at least wouldn't have to ride a Greyhound back home, weighed down with all the emotional trauma of what you'd done.

"I don't know," Mad admitted. "Maybe? I definitely don't want to meet Lucky and her sisters."

"The 'Horse Sisters' are what I'm calling them," Pep told her. "And, you know, I kind of need to get back to school. I have to graduate."

"Oh yeah. You have school."

"And you have . . . chickens? You have chickens that are laying tons of eggs, right?"

"We could fly back home," Mad said. "We could fly out of San Francisco and we wouldn't have to drive that whole way back."

"I don't have an ID!" Pep told her.

"Oh, maybe you could still fly," Mad offered, but she had no idea. She wasn't a seasoned traveler, rarely even got on a plane. But even living on a farm in the middle of nowhere, the airline industry had done a good job of making her aware of the fact that you had to have proof of your existence to board an airplane.

"You're an All-American women's college basketball star. They might recognize you."

Pep stared at her. "That is not going to get me on a plane, Mad."

"Can your mom mail it to you?"

"I don't want to ask my mom to mail my photo ID to this place, in care of the Horse Sisters. It would be a nightmare."

"Oh, wait! We have Tom, too. We can't take some kid who doesn't have our last name and no identification on a flight."

"I'm not sure Tom will even let us take him home. He kind of hates his mom's new boyfriend. I think this was his great escape."

"I guess we'll have to drive."

"We're stuck in that supersize PT Cruiser for all of eternity."

"We will get back," Mad assured her. "We'll find our way back home."

"Do you think we'll see each other again?"

Mad felt shocked by the question. She had been living in the present, the absurd present that required her to block out the rest of her life. But now she had to imagine a future where her siblings existed but they weren't in some car, being conveyed to their father. But, yes, she wanted to see them again. Maybe she only ever wanted to see them and no one else. She was too nervous to answer, afraid that Pep would be embarrassed by her need.

"What do you think?" she asked Pep.

"Yes," Pep said, not looking at Mad, though the statement was firm.

"Me, too," Mad said. "I hope so."

"You can come to my graduation," Pep offered.

"You can . . . come to the farm."

"If Atlanta drafts me," Pep offered, "I'd be pretty close to you."

"Is there a team in Boston or Utah?" Mad asked, and Pep shook her head. "Not one in San Francisco, either. Los Angeles, though."

"Dad could get season tickets."

"I don't think Dad is ever going to leave this place," Pep said. She was quiet for a moment. "And I probably won't play in the WNBA. I'll probably be in Russia or Spain or, like, Turkey. If I even keep playing."

"You'll keep playing," Mad assured her.

"Well, someday I won't."

"You can come work on the farm with me when you retire."

"I actually will, Mad. I would do it. For you."

Mad so badly wanted to hug her sister, but she was not the kind of person who hugged people. And Pep, she was certain, was not the kind of person who received hugs from people. But she still said, "Can I hug you?"

Pep nodded. "Yeah, sure." She hugged her sister.

"It's weird to ask, but I'm also glad you asked," Pep said.

Their father, his absence, had shaped her life in ways both visible and invisible. He had left all of them. But he had helped make them. He had given them to each other. They were so unique, so strange, and they would now know each other for the rest of their lives, beyond their father, long after their father. It was, Mad realized, a gift she had never expected. She was a gift to someone else. She had never felt like that before in her entire life. Not once. She hugged her sister again. In this strange world, who else did they have?

MAD AWOKE TO RUBE STANDING OVER THE BED. "ARE YOU AWAKE?" RUBE asked them. Mad struggled to acclimatize herself to her reality. It was now a constant necessity since she'd embarked on this quest, to take a few seconds to realize, *oh, these are my siblings,* and *oh, this is a tiny cabin in the woods of Northern California,* and *oh, I have left my farm and my mom and have found my delinquent father* and *oh, thank god, I am wearing clothes,* and *oh, thank god, I am not spooning with my newly discovered sister and now best friend,* and *oh, this guy weirdly standing over me is my brother, and he probably has something devastating to tell me that will upend my sense of self.*

"Yes," Mad finally said.

"Good," Rube said. Mad looked over at Pep, who could sleep through anything. Mad calculated the amount of time since Pep had played basketball, had run sprints, had exercised at all. Why was her sister still sleeping this much?

Rube pointed to the copy of his third novel that was lying open on her chest. "My book put you to sleep?" he asked.

She and Pep had both finished his second book, which they liked even more than the first, and had bought this one in Utah. She had been reading it aloud to her sister that night before they fell asleep.

"Rube, what time is it?"

"Late," he said. "I need to talk to you."

"Do you need me to get up? Do I have to go somewhere? Is this a secret?"

"Just, god, Mad, just scooch over a little and let me sit down. I need to tell you something."

"Let me wake up Pep," Mad said, trying to delay the inevitable weirdness.

She shook Pep until her sister groaned. "Are we leaving?" Pep asked. "What's happening?"

"Rube needs to tell us something," Mad told her, and Pep groaned again, then awkwardly sat up, trying and failing to focus on Rube in the dark. Mad reached for the lamp and saw that Rube, of course, had been crying.

"Was it bad?" Mad asked.

Rube sat down. "Yeah, of course. I pretty much just talked uninterrupted for about thirty minutes, and I kind of alternated between trying to tell him that he ruined my life but then also trying to tell him that I am doing great and am very successful and he missed out on so many great things about me and my development. Sometimes I got mixed up and said that good things about me were bad things and vice versa. I'm never going to get what I wanted. He knows he did something that hurt us. But I don't think it's possible to make him understand what he did exactly."

"What about his own dad? His uncle?" Mad asked. "He understands absence."

"He doesn't have a memory of his dad before he left them. And both of them died. They weren't somewhere in the larger world, still living. I don't think he understands how we feel, and I don't know how to make him understand. And he's so old now. It feels like he's a different person."

"Well, duh," Pep said. "That's his thing."

"No, I just mean it's hard to summon the anger I felt toward the father who left me and my mom when I look at him now. I just wish I'd found him sooner."

"But what happened? Why are you waking us up?" Pep asked.

Rube took a breath. "He's sick."

Both sisters sat up straight. "What the hell, Rube?" Pep shouted, "What are you talking about?"

"Why didn't he tell us?" Mad asked.

"So after I did that monologue that I've basically spent my entire life preparing to deliver, he looked at me and ruefully shook his head and apologized and then just said, 'I'm dying, Rube,' and I felt like a jerk."

"Oh, god," Mad replied.

"It's early stages," Rube continued. "He found out after Rooster was born. It's like Parkinson's, but it's not exactly that. And he kept saying that it's not genetic, or it's not proven to be genetic, because I think he was worried I'd be mad if I got it later in life."

"Oh, god," Pep said.

"I mean, whether he left us or not, my genes are partly his. That's science. Can't get mad about that. He apologized for getting sick more than he did for leaving us."

"What's happening, though?" Mad asked. "He didn't seem sick."

"It's early, like I said. It could be a year or two before it gets worse. It could be sooner. It could be ten years. But it's muscular and his brain. He'll get unsteady, have trouble walking and also breathing, maybe issues with his heart rate. It's basically anything that your body does without having to think about it."

"And he's just out here in the woods by himself?" Pep asked, angry. "Taking care of a baby?"

"Well, he's got Lucky. And Moon. And Haze."

"The Horse Sisters," Pep said.

"Ooh, that is good. But, yeah, he's got all their money. Medical care won't be a problem. It's not immediate. He's not going to die tomorrow. Honestly, I think he said it like that to deflect my intense emotional outburst. You saw him. I think he's okay at the moment."

"But sooner rather than later," Pep said, and Mad wanted to mention that their father was old. He was an old man. He had lived multiple lives, too, which she felt added even more years to his timeline. He was not going to live forever. But it still hurt to know that it was even more likely that if they'd waited, if Rube had not searched for all of them, they'd have never found him. Or each other.

"He doesn't want us to tell Tom," he told them. "Not yet."

"I feel like I want to tell Tom," Pep said. "He's our brother. He should know, right? I'm kind of mad he didn't tell me. Or Mad."

"I think we should let him tell who he wants to tell. I think he knew I'd tell you guys."

The three of them sat in the bed, imagining their own futures, where their lives would touch up against the death of their father, the time that would come after. And Mad thought of Tom, in the cabin with his father and Rooster, still so young, who thought he'd finally gotten his father back.

"I need to tell you something," Mad then said. "Tom? His mom took me aside before we left."

"You were convincing her to let us take Tom," Rube said.

"Kind of? Not really. She was convincing me. But the point is, she told me something and swore me to secrecy."

"That's not good," Pep said. "She barely knew you. You didn't know her."

"Dad isn't actually Tom's father."

"What?" her siblings both asked.

"Yeah, she got pregnant by some famous Utah news anchor, and he wanted her to get rid of the baby, and so Dad stepped in and raised Tom as his son."

"That's so insane," Pep said. "Is this what aging did to him? He swooped in after leaving me and took somebody else's kid? That's so strange."

"But Tom doesn't know. No one knows but us."

"This is the second secret we're keeping from Tom," Pep said. "That's so messed up. He's going to be so angry."

"Not with us," Rube said. "Why with us?"

"I haven't had brothers and sisters long, but you should tell your brother . . . well, okay, now I guess it's more complicated."

"Right," Mad said. "He's eleven. I'm not going to tell him. I'm not sure anyone was ever going to tell him. But now, with Dad back in the picture and his mom letting him spend time here, maybe he'll find out."

"He's still our brother," Rube said. "That doesn't matter. He's one of us. He got left behind. And then he came with us. He's our family."

"Of course," Mad said. "Of course he is. But I wanted you to know. So much has been going on, it was hard to remember all the secrets we had uncovered and who knew them."

"Maybe his mom will tell him when we all take him back to Utah," Pep said.

It was quiet for a moment, and Mad considered that conversation, how Tom had even more he had to learn than the rest of them. But maybe he also had more time to live with it and figure it out. Maybe none of them were ruined. That was what she wanted to believe.

"I'm staying," Rube finally said.

"Here?" Pep asked. "In the bed?"

"With Dad," Rube replied. "I'm going to stay here."

"Why?" Mad asked. "Do you feel like you have to stay here? Because he's sick?"

"I don't have anything else, really. My mom died, Mad."

"You have us," Mad told him.

"Pep has to go back to Oklahoma or she won't graduate. She's going to be a basketball player. You have the farm and the . . . chickens? All those chickens." Mad did not like how much her siblings thought her life was entirely devoted to a bunch of chickens, no matter how true it might be.

"So you'll stay here?" Pep asked.

"I want to be with him a little longer," he told them. "I don't have a real job. I write detective novels. I can do that here. I could help Dad with getting the artist colony set up. I could help with Rooster. I could just be around him. I want to know what it's like, and maybe if I'm here for long enough, he'll slip up and reveal something important."

"Okay," Mad said. She didn't feel betrayed that Rube wanted to stay. But she also knew she could not manage it, had no desire to prolong the trip. This trip was the thing that would push her into the next part of her life. It was *not* the next part of her life.

"And . . . never mind," Rube said. They pressed him and he kept going. "It's just, after all this time when he was out of my life, and I had no idea where he was, and he had forgotten us . . . if my presence occasionally makes him have to remember what he did, if I sometimes make him feel regret, I wouldn't mind it."

It was better than killing him, Mad decided. If this was what Rube needed, he could have it. She wouldn't stop him.

"When should me and Mad and Tom leave?" Pep then asked.

"Whenever you want," Rube replied. "Whenever you need to."

"We probably need to get Tom back to his mother," Mad admitted.

"You guys could come back this summer."

"The WNBA season goes all summer," Pep informed them. "If I even get drafted. Euroleague is the fall, though."

"It's always busy," Mad said. "There's no slow season in farming. But okay."

"You're staying," Pep said to her brother, as if convincing herself that this was true. Rube nodded.

"The HHR is in both of our names," he reminded Mad, "so you won't have any problem getting it back to Tennessee."

"It's late," Mad told them. "I need to sleep. It's two in the morning. This is a lot."

"It's been a lot for a while," Pep admitted.

"Maybe I should have waited for the morning," Rube said, but Mad simply touched his shoulder because she could not handle him spinning himself into another monologue. "We'll see you in the morning," she said.

"Good night, Mad," Rube said.

"Good night, Rube," Mad replied.

He stood up.

"Good night, Pep," he said.

"Yeah, good night, Rube."

He walked out of the room, shutting the door behind him. It was quiet for a moment.

"Good night, Mad," Pep then said, and Mad was grateful to hear her voice.

"Good night, Pep." Mad lay there, eyes closed, the silence so lovely, just her and her sister breathing almost in unison, the most hypnotic sound in the world. And then she was asleep.

CHAPTER TEN

Their father had made pancakes for Tom and Rooster. When the other siblings arrived at the cabin, Tom was helping cut the pancakes into little pieces for his new brother, feeding him with a fork. Rooster, to his credit, was amenable to anything. Maybe having four parents and being the heir to a vast fortune and living on a plot of land the size of a small country meant you accepted most things because you never lacked for anything. Four siblings? The more the merrier. Rooster held up the soggiest piece of a pancake, his hands sticky with syrup, and offered it to Mad. She could not have refused an offering more quickly, but then she recanted, leaned forward, and Rooster placed the bite of pancake in her mouth. After the instantaneous sensation of revulsion, a child's hand in her mouth, passed, she watched her little brother observing her, smiling. She chewed the pancake. It was so sweet. She loved it.

"Very good," she said, smiling, and Rooster cackled.

She had thought about Rooster that morning. Of course, he was their brother, another sibling, but he had not been left. She would not wish that on a toddler, and it's not like any of them had known their father would abandon them at some point. And then she realized that even if their father wouldn't leave him for another family, he *would* die. Rooster would lose his father, though perhaps it would be more certain, a finality none of them had received. But when their father was gone, left this world for whatever was next, Mad would hold on to Rooster. That's when he would need all of them.

"Hey," Tom said.

"Did you have a good night?" Mad asked him, and he nodded.

"We worked on the film," he said, "this morning."

"Oh, is it finished?" Rube asked.

"Oh, no, not at all," Tom said. "It'll take a lot longer to finish it. And, you know, I have to edit it. Score it. Add the credits. Design the poster."

It made sense to Mad. Why would Tom ever finish the movie if it meant he could stay close to their father?

"And I talked to my mom last night," Tom continued. "And she talked to Dad. For a little while. It was a little weird, but I think they're going to let me come back when school's out and stay here for the summer. I told her I needed it for my film."

Rube looked to his father. "And you worked it out? Tom can stay?"

Their father, who was putting more pancakes onto a platter, looked over at them and nodded. "I guess I'll need to work out the logistics and talk to Lucky, but it's fine."

Mad thought about their father's health, what Rube had told them last night. He looked fine, but what she'd previously chalked up to simple age, the shock of seeing him after so many years, did suggest a slowing down. Maybe it was just his own body failing him that forced his mind, always churning, to finally accept the fact that he couldn't start over again. Maybe reconciliation was just about exhaustion.

There was no good way to bring up his health problems now. Maybe she'd never have to bring it up. But if Rube and Tom were already planning an extended relationship with their father, perhaps she needed to think about it, too. It was too much, at the moment. She would eat the pancakes, go home, and then she'd figure out what to do. She'd never wanted a relationship with her father. She'd wanted answers. But now she realized the answers were so vague that there was no real way to understand what had happened. Maybe if she saw him again, later, it would help.

"We're going to leave after breakfast," Mad informed Tom, who instantly regarded her with suspicion.

"Already?" he asked. "We just got here. That was a long time to spend in the wagon just to turn right back around."

"You have school. Pep has school. I have work. You'll be back pretty soon."

"What about Rube?"

"He's going to stick around and sort things out," Pep offered.

"I'll just stay with him," Tom explained to them, as if he'd solved a problem that they had been incapable of figuring out.

"Tom," Pep said, leaning closer to him. "We have to go."

Tom looked down at his plate of pancakes. "I feel like I might never see him again," he finally said. "It's not fair."

"He can stay," their father said, walking over to the table with more pancakes. "If his mom lets him, he can stay a little longer."

Tom looked up at his father, nearly crying. "She will say it's okay, I promise."

"But you'll have to go home eventually," Pep informed him.

Rube looked at his dad and then back at Tom. "I'll bring you back to Salt Lake City when it's time," he said. "Is that good?"

Tom nodded, and Mad was about to mention that it was more than twelve hours back to Tom's house, but it wouldn't be her problem. Rube seemed to have accepted that driving thousands of miles was just his life now.

"Wait, so just me and Mad are leaving? The rest of the family is staying here?" Pep asked.

"You can stay," Tom said.

"We can't!" Pep said. "I just thought we'd all leave together."

"You can come back," their father said. "Anytime."

"Okay," Pep said, not quite satisfied. "I guess so."

"Wait," Rube interjected, "I'm so confused. Who is staying here and who is leaving?"

"Rube!" Pep said. "Mad and I are leaving. And you and Tom and Rooster are staying."

Tom said: "And Dad is staying."

"Okay, that's settled," Mad said. "Let's just eat pancakes." She wasn't used to all this conversation in the morning. She wasn't used to waking up without a specific set of tasks. Even away from the farm, this quest, every morning she knew what she was doing. She was gathering up heretofore unknown siblings. She was driving through empty highways of the western United States. She was searching for her missing father. What was there now? Home, she supposed. She was going home.

SHE HATED TO LEAVE RUBE BEHIND, BUT SHE COULDN'T STAY. HE SAT ON THE bed as she packed her bag, both of them finding it hard to talk.

"Are you sure you want to do this?" Mad finally asked him.

"Yes," he said. "Not forever, but for right now."

"We went so long without knowing the other existed. And then we were together for such an intense time. And now I won't see you again for a while."

"We can talk. We can email."

"I feel like Dorothy in *The Wizard of Oz*."

"I think all of us feel like Dorothy in *The Wizard of Oz*."

"Well, for me, you're kind of the Scarecrow."

"Oh, okay, yes. I mean, in my mind, I'm Dorothy, and you're the Scarecrow."

"And Dad's the Wizard," Mad realized.

"Oh, and you're going back to your farm," Rube said. "Yeah, I think you are Dorothy."

"Who would the Witch be?"

"I think it's best not to think of it as a direct one-to-one relationship."

"The PT Cruiser was the tornado."

"Wait, what the hell. Were Dorothy's parents dead?" Rube suddenly asked.

"Oh, yeah, she was living with her aunt and uncle. Yeah, they were probably dead."

"Or disappeared. They ran off to become basketball coaches."

"I never read the book," Mad admitted.

"I'm going to miss you so much, Mad."

Mad observed her brother, who was smiling but also about to cry. It was how she would best remember him, always on the verge of these competing emotions. "I'm going to miss you, too. If it wasn't for you, none of this would have happened."

"Well, no, if it wasn't for *you*, none of this would have happened. If you hadn't come with me, it would have been so much worse. I definitely would have done something stupid and ruined everything. You made this happen. I'll always be grateful that you did this with me. You didn't have to."

"Come see me, please," she said.

"I will," he told her. "I'll keep you updated, too. Who knows what else might happen?"

"I do want to know about the Horse Sisters. Keep Tom safe, okay? Help him."

"I will. I'll do my best."

"Okay."

"Can I say that I love you?"

"Yes, of course. You already have."

"Can I hug you?"

"Yes, sure."

He stood up and they hugged. She held on to him. "You're my sister," he told her.

"We're family," she said. "You'll always have me. Anything else that happens, you'll always have me. And Pep. And Tom. You have us now, okay?"

"Okay."

"Truly. If Dad leaves again. If something happens between you. You will always have us. You're not alone."

"Okay."

He hefted her bag and they walked back to their father's cabin, where Pep was waiting with Tom. It was so strange, this feeling of leaving. She worried that the moment she was no longer tethered to Rube, both of them would be ruined, something bad would happen. But she trusted that it would work out. He had found her once. If anything happened, she'd find him. They were not lost to each other.

HER FATHER TOLD HER NOT TO BE A STRANGER. THERE WAS NO PLATITUDE that worked, nothing that a father could say to the child he had abandoned that didn't cause a twinge of psychological pain. And yet they had to exist within these phrases because they didn't really know each other. And probably never would. They would say "have a safe trip" and "keep in touch" and "give my regards to your mother" and "take care of yourself" and after they had exhausted them, there was nothing else to do but leave, to separate. She did not hug her father, and he, to his credit, did not try. Maybe she had wanted that when the trip started, that kind of intimacy, to be held by the person who made her, but she didn't actually want it. She nodded, and he returned the nod, and it was enough, the acknowledgment: I know that you exist and you know that I exist. How sad that a father and daughter might come to this, but for Mad, after so many years of nothing, it was enough.

Tom felt no sense of finality. He was so young. For him, the story had only just begun, and he had no concerns that this was the end of anything. Although, she reminded herself, he had already been left behind once without any sense of why. He had been scarred like them. The difference was the distance between being lost and being found. "Thank you for playing the slot machine for me in Nevada," he finally said. "When you did what I asked and it worked out, I knew we would be okay."

"'Bye, Tom," she said.

"'Bye, Mad."

SHE AND PEP GOT INTO THE CHEVROLET HHR AND THEIR FAMILY WAVED goodbye. Tom, of course, filmed it, their wagon driving down this road, leaving them behind. This was the way a normal family worked, she reminded herself. It came together and broke apart over and over again, all the amorphous ways it accommodated expansion and contraction. But they were not a normal family, and so it felt like an ending. It wasn't long before they couldn't see their siblings, their father. It was only Pep and Mad now.

"I'm hungry," Pep announced. "We should get some snacks."

AND EVEN THOUGH THE QUEST HAD FELT LIKE A DREAM, IT NOW SEEMED SO concrete and tangible, all of them in the car, the accumulation of experience. It was the most solid thing that had ever happened to Mad. The return to her old life, this is what now felt like a dream.

And that was the sensation for those days, a sense that she was in between experiences, and this feeling continued across the interstates as they headed east. It continued in Oklahoma, when Mad pulled the HHR up to Pep's dorm and Pep walked back onto the campus of her university, so emphatically returned to her life. It continued as Mad drove across the Mississippi, as she stopped in diners and coffee shops, everything so quiet.

It continued for the rest of the trip, even as she drove down the dirt road that led to her farm, the place she had always lived. It continued as she turned off the car and sat there, in the driver's seat, this little bubble of time where nothing was real and nothing mattered. And it continued when she stepped out of the car and walked along the familiar paths of the farm. And maybe it would never end, this feeling. But she was home now. She had come back. It was so strange, how time gets away from us. She could live in this moment forever, maybe, but then she walked to the chickens, shuffling along the fields, and she saw her mother. And she decided that she would enter back into her life.

She closed her eyes and she centered herself. She was Madeline Hill. She was the sister of Reuben Hill and Pepper Hill and Theron Goudy and Reuben Chelmsford. She was the daughter of Rachel Daggett. She was the daughter of Charles Hill. These things anchored her to the earth and she could feel her body take up space in this world, insisting upon itself. She listened to the sounds of the farm, and when she opened her eyes, she knew where she was. She was home.

ACKNOWLEDGMENTS

Thanks to the following:

Julie Barer at the Book Group, always and forever the most amazing agent and my friend and family beyond the books.

Helen Atsma at Ecco for working with me every step of the way on this novel and figuring out how to get me to the end.

Sonya Cheuse, Meghan Deans, Miriam Parker, Allison Saltzman, and everyone at Ecco, who have supported me and made each book something I could be proud of.

Jason Richman at United Talent Agency.

Ann Patchett, my favorite writer and person.

The University of the South and the English and Creative Writing Department.

My family: Kelly and Debbie Wilson; Kristen, Wes, and Kellan Huffman; Mary Couch; Meredith, Warren, Laura, Morgan, and Philip James; and the Wilson, Fuselier, and Baltz families.

My friends: Will Albaugh, Bryan Ashby, Brian Baltz, Aaron Burch, Lucy Corin, Lee Conell, Lily Davenport, Marcy Dermansky, Isabel Galbraith, Meredith Jade Garrett, Brandon Gilliam, Aymeric and Sandy Glacet, Elizabeth and John Grammer, Jason Griffey, Brandon Iracks-Edeline, Kate Jayroe, Gwen Kirby, Shelley MacLauren, Kelly Malone, Katie McGhee, Mary Miller, Matt O'Keefe, Cecily Parks, Anthony Petrochko, Misha Rai, Betsy Sandlin, Matt Schrader, Heidi Siegrist, Christian Skotte, Leah Stewart,

David and Heidi Syler, Jeff Thompson, Rufi Thorpe, Lauryl Tucker, Zack Wagman, Elyzabeth Gregory Wilder, and, with all my gratitude for her friendship, Caki Wilkinson.

And, as always, with all my love: Leigh Anne, Griff, and Patch. The family I wished for and somehow found.